A COURTSHIP IN CATANIA

A NOVEL IN THREE PARTS

THE GRAND TOURS OF THE ARISTOCRACY
BOOK 1

LINDA RAE SANDE

Twisted Teacup
PUBLISHING

ALSO BY LINDA RAE SANDE

The Daughters of the Aristocracy

The Kiss of a Viscount

The Grace of a Duke

The Seduction of an Earl

The Sons of the Aristocracy

Tuesday Nights

The Widowed Countess

My Fair Groom

The Sisters of the Aristocracy

The Story of a Baron

The Passion of a Marquess

The Desire of a Lady

The Brothers of the Aristocracy

The Love of a Rake

The Caress of a Commander

The Epiphany of an Explorer

The Widows of the Aristocracy

The Gossip of an Earl

The Enigma of a Widow

The Secrets of a Viscount

The Widowers of the Aristocracy

The Dream of a Duchess

The Vision of a Viscountess

The Conundrum of a Clerk

The Charity of a Viscount

The Cousins of the Aristocracy

The Promise of a Gentleman

The Pride of a Gentleman

The Holidays of the Aristocracy

The Christmas of a Countess

The Knot of a Knight

The Holiday of a Marquess

The Snow Angel of a Duke

The Ivy of an Earl

The Heirs of the Aristocracy

The Angel of an Astronomer

The Puzzle of a Bastard

The Choice of a Cavalier

The Bargain of a Baroness

The Jewel of an Earl's Heir

The Vixen of a Viscount

The Honor of an Heir

The Rose of a Sultan's Son

The Ladies of the Aristocracy

The Lady of a Grump

The Lady of a Sultan

The Pursuit of a Duchess

The Lords of the Aristocracy

The Abduction of an Earl

Beyond the Aristocracy

The Pleasure of a Pirate

The Making of a Mistress

The Bride of a Baronet

The Caton of a Captain

Puss and Pots

The Betrothal of a Baron

Masquerade Meow

The Soho Club Collection

The Grand Tours of the Aristocracy

A Courtship in Catania

An Affaire in Athens

A Lover in Luxor

A Rogue in Rome

Revenge of the Wallflowers
The Wager of a Wallflower

Stella of Akrotiri
Origins

Deminon

Diana

The Lyon's Den (Dragonblade Publishing)
The Courage of a Lyon

The Lady of a Lyon

The Loyalty of a Lyon

Note: Translations of select titles are available in German, Italian, Spanish and Portuguese.

PART I
A COURTSHIP BEGINS

CHAPTER 1
AN ENGLISHMAN
IN CATANIA

*E*arly January 1833, Catania, Kingdom of the Two *Sicilies*

Lifting his face to the bright Sicilian sun, Donald Slater closed his eyes and took a deep breath. He was sure he had never experienced such a glorious day in England, especially not during the month of January. Although most in the city of Catania wore some sort of overcoat when they went out—they no doubt thought the weather on the cool side—Donald had elected to take his exploratory walk without wearing his greatcoat.

The owner of his lodgings in Via Garibaldi, Signore Pietro Caravallo, was used to hosting young men on their Grand Tours. He had drawn a crude map of the city, explaining how Donald could simply use Mount Aetna as his guide. The imposing volcano, which loomed to the north, wasn't spouting any steam as it had been doing the day before. The continuous white puffs had been a reminder the volcano wasn't extinct, and Donald wondered how anyone could live in its shadow without the constant worry of it erupting.

The evidence of earlier eruptions could be found everywhere, for everything in Catania seemed to be made of lava. Since an earthquake in 1693 had leveled most of the buildings in the city, the current architecture was mostly Baroque, its lava base covered in plaster and painted in colorful shades befitting the Mediterranean island's setting. Streets were constructed of large lava bricks, their rectangular shapes fitted tightly together and the result far smoother than their cobblestone counterparts in England. Scattered about the pavements were tiny black particles, evidence that steam wasn't the only thing Aetna spewed out of its peak.

Near the city's center, Donald consulted his map and realized he had already come to the green space his host had explained belonged to Ignazio Paternò Castello, prince of Biscari. "You can go there," Pietro had explained. "Get lost in the labyrinth. He will not mind."

Donald wasn't sure why his host had recommended he visit the prince's property. Garden mazes were quite common in England—his aunt Hannah had even had one planted behind Gisborn Hall, despite his uncle Henry's protests that it took away part of a field he once used for farming. Uncle Henry, Earl of Gisborn, wouldn't have denied his countess anything, though, and his four sons teased him about it mercilessly.

Just you wait, he had warned them. *When you marry the love of your life, you'll do anything to keep her happy.*

Nathaniel, the oldest, was apparently learning that

particular lesson first hand. He had married a young woman from Oxford the year before, and now that she was due to give birth at any moment, Nathan admitted he was at her beck and call.

As Donald made his way in the direction of the prince's labyrinth, grinning at the reminder of how the Earl and Countess of Gisborn now found excuses to get lost in the tall maze, his attention was suddenly captured by a young woman. She was exiting the labyrinth on the arm of a much older man.

Had anyone happened to notice Donald, they would have seen his mouth open in awe, for she was the most beautiful young woman he had seen in his entire life.

Wearing a stunning silk de Naples gown in deep red and a headdress that appeared as if it was from the Middle Ages, she looked as if she might be the queen of Sicily.

A thought that she might become the queen of his heart didn't register with Donald at that moment. Nor did his father's warning about falling in love.

Will Slater, Earl of Bellingham, a former commander in the British Navy, and heir to the Devonville marquessate, had warned him that some woman somewhere would one day take hold of his heart in her small hand and squeeze it until it hurt. Bat it about as if it was her favorite plaything. Kiss it until it was healed and then do it all over again. *And you'll love every minute of it, because that ache in your chest will remind you that you're alive. That you have someone to live for.*

Despite the fact that his father's words had probably

been said about Donald's mother didn't make them any easier to hear at the time. After a warning like that, Donald had long ago decided he would guard his heart. Spend his days looking after a stable of horses for Uncle Henry, and spend his nights writing.

What better topic to write about than a young man's Grand Tour?

So when his father suggested he travel to the Mediterranean when he completed his studies at Oxford, Donald had jumped at the chance.

A Grand Tour. The trip of a lifetime. The opportunity to see first-hand the places he had learned about in school. Walk in the footsteps of famous philosophers and rulers. Gaze upon Greek temples and Roman ruins. Marvel at pyramids. Breathe the same air as those who had lived centuries ago.

He was also discovering the places of the past had a present populated by peoples both modern and old-fashioned.

The Italian aristocracy might best fall into the latter category. Although he had met a number of their members during his tour, Donald had never seen a more beautiful young woman. The fact that she was clinging to the arm of a much older man at first annoyed him.

The hint of jealousy had Donald experiencing surprise.

When she acknowledged his existence with a nod of her head, Donald quickly removed his top hat and bowed deeply. When she offered her hand—ungloved— he bestowed a kiss on the back of it rather than simply brushing his lips over her soft knuckles. Her fingers, long and lean, ended in fingernails of perfect ovals. They bent slightly to grip his hand, as if she didn't want him to let go.

That simple touch had him mesmerized. Her reaction—he was sure a frisson had passed through and up her arm—caused her to inhale softly. She dipped a curtsy and let go of the older man's arm to introduce herself.

"*Sono la Signora Nicoletta D'Avalos, e questo è mio padre, il Conte Enrico D'Avalos,*" she said as her head angled toward the man. *I am Lady Nicoletta D'Avalos, and this is my father, Conte Enrico D'Avalos.*

Donald understood her Italian well enough to feel a wave of relief. The older gentleman, her father, was an aristocrat, although Donald also knew they no longer held much in the way of power in the Bourbon-controlled country. But why had she been the one to make the introduction rather than her father?

He knew she understood his response when he said, "Donald Slater. *Sono lieto di fare la tua conoscenza.*"

I am pleased to make your acquaintance.

What she did next had Donald blinking in alarm. She waved off her father and took his arm as if they were long lost friends.

"*Mi porterai in cima, no? La vista è magnifica,*" she said as if she was used to giving orders.

You will take me to the top. The view is magnificent.

Donald looked to the Conte D'Avalos for permission, but the man had already sauntered off with another, even older aristocrat, their heads bent in quiet conversation.

"*Sì*," he murmured, stunned he had been singled out for her attentions. He led them in the direction she indicated.

"*Non ti ho visto prima qui*," she said as they made their way to the highest point of the beautifully kept gardens.

I have not seen you here before.

"*Sono appena arrivato, da Syracusa*," Donald replied.

I've only just arrived. From Syracuse.

"*Ma tu non sei di lì, sicuramente*," she countered.

But you are not from there, surely.

He grinned. "*Io sono dall'Inghilterra.*"

I am from England. "Oxfordshire."

Her face lit up as if a thousand candles had been set aflame around her. The sun was no doubt the culprit, but Donald didn't consider it the source of her glowing complexion.

"Then you must allow me to practice my English," she stated, a smile lighting her face even more than the sun was doing.

Something deep in Donald's chest seemed to contract. As a result, he struggled to breathe, and not only because they had been climbing stairs that took them to the highest part of the prince's property. "You know how to speak English?" he asked in surprise.

"I am still learning," she replied, holding up a hand to shield her eyes from the afternoon sun. Her headdress did nothing to protect her face from the bright rays, but perhaps her olive-toned complexion didn't require it. "Will you correct me when I misspeak?"

Donald nodded. "If you wish." They turned around, and he inhaled softly. From the top of the labyrinth, located in the middle of the city of Catania, he had an unfettered view of Mount Aetna to the north. All around him, the Baroque buildings, many in need of a new coat of plaster, housed the diverse population of Catania in their upper stories, while shops and offices occupied their ground level. To the east was the Mediterranean, it's water a shade of blue he had never seen before.

"It is *bellisimo*, is it not?" Nicoletta asked, her attention on him rather than on the view.

Donald turned to regard her with a grin. "Not as beautiful as you, but... *sí*." The words were out of his mouth before he could censor them, and he could feel the flush of red creep up his neck to color his cheeks. As a sandy-blonde-haired, blue-eyed Englishman, he feared she would note his embarrassment and tease him.

But she didn't.

In fact, she tittered as a blush of peach colored her cheeks. "So bold," she remarked, her ornately painted fan fluttering open. She fanned her face a few times.

Donald's eyes rounded. Perhaps he had been too daring with his comment. "I merely spoke the truth," he replied, deciding it best he simply own the comment. It was a compliment, after all, and if the young lady didn't take it as such, then she was the one in error.

"Am I beautiful enough for you to... consider... accepting an invitation to a ball?" she asked in her heavily-accented English. Her occasional pauses indicated she was struggling to remember the correct words.

"Of course," he replied. "But your beauty would not be a requirement for me to attend a ball," he added. "I do like to dance."

This bit of news seemed to have Nicoletta D'Avalos even more intrigued. "You do?"

He nodded, hoping she didn't expect him to give her a demonstration right then and there. Despite the richness of the prince's gardens, there was no music by which to dance.

"Then you must attend our ball. Tomorrow night at House D'Avalos," she insisted. "It is not far from here. Your driver will know it," she added, obviously unaware that he had walked to the prince's property from his lodgings near the center of the city.

He nodded. "What time are your guests arriving?"

"You must not come before eight o'clock in the evening," she replied. "But not after ten o'clock, or I shall not have any dances left on my card."

He grinned at hearing her edict. Apparently balls in Sicily were much the same as they were in England. "May I reserve a waltz with you now?" he asked, deciding it couldn't hurt to ask.

Her eyes rounded. "You *are* bold, Signore Slater," she accused, although from the way she grinned at him, Donald knew she didn't mind one bit.

"Something tells me you would not wish me to be otherwise."

She dipped her head, her headdress bobbing with her move. "Do you find me so?"

Donald chuckled softly. "I admit I was surprised by your introduction. Is it usual for young ladies to give their names to strangers so readily?"

Nicoletta turned to face the Mediterranean as she audibly sighed. "It is true we have not met before, but you are hardly a stranger."

"What's this?" he asked, his gaze going from the blue waters to regard her with suspicion.

She lifted a shoulder in a shrug. "My aunt received word of your arrival to Sicily several months ago. We have been hoping you would include Catania in your itinerary."

About to ask the identity of her aunt—he was sure he hadn't met her during his travels—Donald was prevented from doing so when a shout sounded from down below.

Scanning the grounds, he discovered Conte Enrico D'Avalos waving at them.

"Oh, I must go," Nicoletta said on a sigh.

"I'll escort you down, my lady," Donald said, offering his arm.

"And you will come to the ball?"

He nodded. "Are you quite sure it's acceptable that I do so? I shouldn't wish to show up uninvited."

"*I* am inviting you. If I did not, I would suffer a scolding from Armenia. She is anxious to meet you," she explained.

"Armenia... she is your aunt?" he asked, not recognizing the name.

"Indeed," Nicoletta replied as they made their way to where her father waited next to a town coach. "May we drop you at your lodgings?"

Not ready to return to his rooms, Donald shook his head. "I have more to see, my lady, but I thank you for the offer." He took her hand to his lips and kissed her knuckles. "I will see you tomorrow evening. Before nine o'clock, I expect."

"Do not keep me waiting," she ordered before allowing a groom to help her into the town coach. Her father had already stepped into the equipage, acknowledging Donald with a nod before he did so.

Donald couldn't help the chuckle that erupted. "Yes, my lady," he replied at the same moment the groom shut the door.

Stepping back, he watched as the servant hopped up and onto the back of the coach, hanging on with one hand as the horses were set into motion.

Lifting a gloved hand to wave, Donald watched the coach until it merged into the traffic of the busy street. He was fairly certain Nicoletta was spying on him from a window, so he made sure to remain in place until the coach was no longer visible.

"Bossy little thing, she is," he murmured before he made his way in the opposite direction. "Bossy but damned beautiful."

CHAPTER 2
A SICILIAN LADY
PREVARICATES

moment later, inside the D'Avalos town coach
When the young Englishman was no longer visible from the town coach window, Nicoletta settled back into the deep blue velvet squabs and turned her attention to her father. "It *is* him, Father," she said in the southern Italian language most aristocrats used. "The one Armenia spoke of," she added happily. "I invited him to the ball."

The conte turned his gaze on his daughter and arched a graying brow. "You like him," he said, not making it a question.

She inhaled to answer in the affirmative, but quickly reconsidered. "Does it matter?" she countered, quickly sobering. "You have already decided who I must marry, have you not?"

Enrico D'Avalos regarded his daughter for a moment before saying, "Perhaps. Or perhaps I am merely waiting for a better offer for you."

Nicoletta's eyes rounded. "Offer?" she repeated.

Briefly closing his eyes—he did that frequently these days in an effort block out the image of a daughter who looked too much like her late mother did when she was Nicoletta's age—Enrico sighed. "I believe you are old enough to learn the truth of the matter," he said in a low voice, barely audible over the sound of the coach wheels on the street.

Stiffening in the squabs, Nicoletta repeated, "The truth?"

"There is little in the way of money left in the coffers," he blurted. "Whomever I marry you to must offer a generous sum for the honor of marrying you."

Her brows furrowing in confusion, Nicoletta scoffed. "Aren't *you* supposed to pay a dowry to whomever I marry?"

His shrug was all she needed to see to know that the conte didn't believe the usual rules applied to him.

They rarely did.

For her entire life, Nicoletta had watched the members of the aristocracy carry on lives far different from the commoners who made up the general population of the Mediterranean's largest island. Their entertainments and lifestyles were always at odds with the much poorer people. Their sense of entitlement sometimes had her bristling. Why should some be allowed such extravagance while others suffered in poverty?

Money seemed to have little to do with it, especially if what her father said was true. He expected her future husband to provide him with a dowry rather than the other way around!

"How much?" she asked meekly, well aware that whatever sum he quoted would be a general assessment of her worth to him.

"We will not talk of money on this day," Enrico stated, his tone suggesting they end the conversation. "It is more important you know to do your duty when you are married."

Duty.

Nicoletta didn't bother to ask what *that* might be. Her duty as an aristocrat's wife had been made clear the entire time she had been growing up in House D'Avalos —she was to run an aristocrat's household and give birth to an heir and a spare. Any baby girls would be merely tolerated.

When the coach turned a sharp corner, she knew they were close to the house. "The man you were speaking with today—"

"Ricardo Malgeri. He is the Marchese Montblanc."

Although she hadn't recognized the older aristocrat— he was said to favor living in his castle on the southwest side of Mount Aetna during the warmer months— Nicoletta had guessed it might be him given his expensive suit and fine leather boots. "Did you invite him to the ball?"

Enrico's manner changed as he straightened in the squabs. "I did, of course."

"His presence will be most welcomed, I should think."

"I am counting on it," her father said. "Although he has a fine villa here in town, he is rarely in residence. It shall be our honor to host him."

Nicoletta nodded, glad when the town coach came to a halt in the courtyard at House D'Avalos and she was able to escape her father's presence.

For if she had spent even one more moment with him, she had feared her father was going to tell her she was to marry the ancient marchese.

CHAPTER 3
A BALL IN CATANIA

he following evening

Dressed in his black satin pantaloons, black shirt, red waistcoat, and black silk cravat, Donald approached the top of the marble stairs leading down to the D'Avalos ballroom and paused. He was suddenly glad he had chosen a red satin waistcoat over the silver one, its embroidered birds tumbling about in gold metallic thread, for he would otherwise disappear in the garish colors on display below.

Sicilian aristocrats were obviously popinjays.

Never before had Donald known a grown man to pair an apple green satin topcoat and breeches with an amethyst waistcoat. Or a high-born woman to wear a high-collared gown that completely hid her shoulders and arms but left her pert, round breasts on full display.

Perhaps she had taken a cue from a former French queen.

He watched as a footman carried glasses of fizzy

Prosecco on a silver tray held aloft as he weaved his way between undulating silks and satins. The strains of music from a quintet were occasionally interrupted by deep laughter and high-pitched tittering. Scents of sweet perfumes and sandalwood and amber colognes wafted past his nostrils. Hundreds of glittering candles in the three massive chandeliers drenched the ball goers in a golden wash.

That light was about to highlight him, for the butler cleared his throat and announced, "*Il signore Donald Slater of Oxfordshire.*"

Donald had to suppress a smirk. What would these aristocrats think if they learned he was an earl's bastard?

His gaze swept over the ballroom, his search for Nicoletta interrupted by an older gentleman who stopped him at the bottom of the stairs. Donald immediately recognized him. "Conte D'Avalos," he said as he bowed. "*È così bello rivederti.*"

So good to see you again.

"My daughter was most anxious to learn if you had arrived," D'Avalos replied in English, his assessing gaze sweeping down and back up to regard Donald with an arched brow. "She said you are from Oxford."

Donald quickly corrected the conte. "Oxford*shire*, my lord. About twenty miles from the city of Oxford. I attended university there, of course."

"Your father is...?"

Dipping his head, Donald realized the man was probably more than simply curious. Apparently Nicoletta had told him everything she had learned about him the day before. He hadn't offered any information about his family, but then, she hadn't asked. "William Slater, Earl of Bellingham and heir to the Devonville marquessate, my lord," he stated with a nod.

"Ah, I *knew* it," D'Avalos replied, one of his fingers stabbing the air. His grin displayed white teeth obviously bestowed by the dental gods. "You look like an English aristocrat," he accused. "You are on your Grand Tour, are you not?"

"Yes, my lord," Donald replied at the same moment Nicoletta appeared at his elbow and placed her arm on it.

"*Lascialo stare, padre,*" she said before directing her smile on Donald.

Leave him be, Father.

Donald immediately took her hand to his lips. "Good evening, my lady," he said as he bowed.

"I feared you would not come," Nicoletta replied, pulling him from the bottom of the stairs. Donald directed a quick look of apology to her father and allowed the young woman to drag him toward the part of the ballroom where no couples stood. The quintet began playing music he had never heard before, but from the tempo, he understood they were to waltz.

"I would have sent my regrets if I could not come," he said in response to her comment.

"You were about to lose this waltz to the Marchese Montblanc. He has been most attentive this evening," she said, lifting one white-gloved hand to his shoulder and placing the other in his right hand.

"I have not had the pleasure of meeting the

marchese," he said as he led them in the first steps of the waltz. Despite his day spent touring the market and the area down by the harbor, he hadn't introduced himself to anyone but a tailor to whom he had paid a call to acquire the black cravat he wore.

"He was with my father in the prince's gardens yesterday," Nicoletta replied, her dancing skills good enough to overcome Donald's occasional bobble. "We haven't been formally introduced, though."

"You are not friends with his daughter?"

Nicoletta's brows furrowed. "He has no children. I do not believe he has ever taken a wife. Or... if he has, he must be a widower."

Donald took a quick glance around the ballroom, partly to determine if he was going in the right direction and partly to discover if he could locate the older aristocrat. He didn't see anyone he recognized, though. "He must have an heir," he commented. "Or are they not as necessary for Italian aristocrats as they are for their English counterparts?"

Giving him a scolding glance, Nicoletta withheld her response until after they had completed an intricate turn. When she faced him again, she said, "They are. The better question would be if Italian aristocrats are necessary."

Stunned the young woman would put voice to such a comment, Donald nearly lost his place in the dance. "Are they?"

She managed a shrug. "I rather doubt they will be within my lifetime." When she noted his look of shock, she added, "There are too many machinations occurring in the Kingdom of the Two Sicilies," she murmured. "Too many who are not happy with the current situation. I may look like a spoiled chit, but I listen, and I read," she added.

Donald regarded his dance partner in a new light. It was true he had thought her a spoiled aristocrat's daughter, what with the way she had ordered him about the day before. Now he found his opinion vastly different. "I'm not sure if I should scold you or kiss you," he said, a smirk lighting his face.

"Why does it have to be one or the other?"

Blinking, Donald nearly stopped in his tracks, which would have sent the circle of dancers colliding with one another. "Are you flirting with me?" he asked in awe.

For a moment, Nicoletta displayed a look of worry. Then she seemed to sort what he asked, and her face brightened. "And if I am?"

The strains of the waltz settled into silence, and the two came to a slow halt as they stared at one another. Helping himself to two glasses of Prosecco from a passing footman, Donald handed one to Nicoletta and then offered his arm. "Is there a garden where we might cool off?"

"The courtyard," she replied, leading him in the direction of large doors that had been opened to the dimly lit middle of the villa. He gulped a lungful of chilly air as they stepped outside.

"Would you like my coat?" he asked as he set his glass on a pillar and moved to take off his topcoat.

"I am quite warm," she replied, flipping open her fan and waving it lazily in front of her face.

"You dance beautifully."

"As do you, when you're not distracted," she countered with a grin. She took a sip of the bubbly and watched with widened eyes as Donald nearly drained his glass in a single gulp.

"I haven't been to a ball this large in my entire life," Donald said. Even the ball his grandmother had hosted on the occasion of his grandfather's seventieth birthday —only a few days before Donald had departed for Europe—couldn't boast the same attendance, although Cherice had mentioned she was rather judicious with her invitations. *Mostly family and friends*, she had said when his father had commented on the smaller crowd. *I didn't want a crush.*

"Then you must not live in London," Nicoletta commented. "I hear all the balls are very... crushing."

Donald chuckled. "They are a crush, yes," he agreed with a grin, amused at her unintended misuse of the word. She had a point, though. London balls could be crushing. "And no, my home is most of a day's drive from the capital," he added, remembering her other comment.

"Will you go there for Parliament?"

Impressed she knew about England's government, he shook his head. "My grandfather, the marquess, is still alive. My father will take his seat in Parliament when he inherits, and given he is a hale and hearty man, he may outlive me," Donald said, neatly sidestepping the issue of inheritance.

"So you will be an aristocrat at leisure always," Nicoletta commented.

"Hardly," he replied with a chuckle. "I actually see to the stables of my uncle's earldom."

"A groom?" she questioned in confusion.

He displayed a grimace. "You could call it that."

"You... you *work*?" she pressed, her dark brows furrowed in disbelief. "Perform labor?"

He nodded. "I do. I have helped on my uncle's farm since I was old enough to walk, as has my younger brother and my cousins," he explained.

"And your uncle? He is an earl... a count?" she asked, struggling with the English equivalent.

"He is. The Earl of Gisborn. My aunt Hannah—my father's sister—is his countess."

"Does she work also?"

Inhaling to respond, Donald paused. He had been about to say 'no,' but then remembered that Hannah saw to the earldom's books. She oversaw the staff for the house. She tended the citrus trees in the greenhouses. "In a manner of speaking, she does," he finally said. "It's a large farm, and there is always something that must be done. Ledgers, for example. Do you see to your father's books?"

Nicoletta shook her head. "I know my... my numbers. Arithmetic," she stammered. "But I do not believe my father would ever allow me to keep even the household ledgers. We've a housekeeper for that, and he has a... a—"

"Man of business?"

"A *secretary* for his business dealings," she finished, obviously proud she remembered the English word.

"Ah, very good," Donald replied. He glanced towards the ballroom, wondering if her presence had been missed. "How long are we allowed to stay out here?"

Nicoletta angled her head to one side. "The next dance on my card is for the one after this," she replied.

"So.... am I allowed to kiss you? Or will I find myself at the business end of a sword if I—?"

His words were cut off when she suddenly stood on tiptoes and took his lips with her own. The kiss was awkward and quick, mostly because she couldn't keep her balance.

Donald blinked as he stared down at her. "You minx," he accused, a grin finally lighting his face.

Her eyes rounded. "What is a minx?"

He chuckled before he placed his hands on the sides of her shoulders, bent his head, and took her lips with his. He dared not linger, but he wanted desperately to continue what she had started. Besides her willingness, he was able to learn what pleased her as she did the same with him.

He was about to move his tongue farther into her mouth when the noise from the ballroom suddenly increased—the doors had no doubt been opened. Sure they would be caught, Donald quickly ended the kiss with a whispered apology. *"Mia signora, devo insistere perché entriamo, per non prendere un brivido."*

My lady, I must insist we go inside, lest you catch a chill.

Nicoletta gave him a quelling glance. "Coward," she whispered, before she turned on a heel and headed toward the ballroom.

The couple they passed on the way paid them no mind, their voices indicating they were in the middle of a rather heated argument.

Donald hoped he and Nicoletta never sounded like them as he offered his arm and they entered the ballroom.

"How long will you stay in Catania?" Nicoletta asked as they wove their way between clusters of attendees engaged in conversation.

"I haven't yet decided," Donald replied. "I want to be sure to have enough time in Taormina before I head to Messina. From there, I'll board a ship bound to Valencia and then another to England."

She whirled to face him, her eyes wide. "You have only just arrived," she complained.

He dipped his head. "In Catania. But I've been on Sicily for nearly four months," he explained. "Before that, I was on the mainland, and in Greece before that," he added. "When I left England, I thought I would only be gone a year."

"Can you stay longer? I insist you do so."

From the manner in which she made her comment, Donald found he didn't want to disappoint her. She apparently liked him. Her willingness to be the one to initiate their first kiss was a testament to her regard for him. "I can stay longer," he said, smirking when he saw what appeared to be a look of relief cross her face.

"Good. Then you can escort me," she replied.

"Escort you?" he repeated. "To where?"

She gave him a look of disbelief. "Everywhere, of course," raising a nearly- bare shoulder to emphasize her comment.

When the music started up for the next dance, an older gentleman appeared next to her and said something Donald couldn't make out. Realizing he was to be her dance partner and had come to claim her, Donald gave a short bow and stepped back as the two joined a number of couples in what appeared to be a cotillion.

Satisfied to simply watch from where he stood, Donald wasn't aware of Conte D'Avalos stepping next to his right side until the aristocrat said, "Has she requested you escort her about town on the morrow?"

Giving a start, Donald stared at D'Avalos a moment before he nodded. "She has, my lord. Am I even allowed such an honor?" he asked.

The older man chuckled before he took a sip of his drink. "Ah, young man, you are not only allowed, but now you are *expected* to do so. No later than eleven o'clock in the morning. If you'd like, I can have my carriage collect you from your lodgings."

Stunned Nicoletta's father seemed to be encouraging his interest in her, Donald felt a thrill. "Oh, that won't be necessary, my lord," he replied. "My rooms are not far from here. But where exactly will I be escorting Lady Nicoletta?"

Rolling his eyes, D'Avalos said, "Anywhere she wishes to go."

"*Anywhere*, sir?" He couldn't help the note of incredulousness from sounding in his voice.

"Stay within the city," D'Avalos ordered. "She'll mostly wish to shop, and she'll want your opinion on everything before she buys it."

Donald angled his head to one side. "And what shall my opinion be?" His mother and aunt had taught all the boys in the family that a woman's request for input wasn't to be taken lightly. But they had also implored them to use reason. *You won't want your wife-to-be looking ridiculous,* Hannah had warned.

"She won't abide ambivalence, young man. Be truthful. But do be kind. I shouldn't want my Nikky crying and demanding your head be removed from your body when she is returned here in time for dinner."

Chuckling, more to lighten the mood than because he found the man's words amusing, Donald said, "Of course, sir, and I do appreciate your concern for my head." He paused a moment. "Is she truly allowed to buy whatever she wants?" he asked, hoping he wouldn't have to be the one to tell the young woman 'no' should she want something particularly expensive.

Laughing in his deep, rich baritone, D'Avalos shrugged. "I indulge her, I know. But it is my right while she resides in my villa. Soon she will marry, and then she will be some other man's spoiled woman." He leaned in closer. "Her mother died several years ago, so I allow her to spend what my countess would have spent on clothes and such," he explained.

"That's very generous of you, my lord."

D'Avalos seemed impressed by Donald's assessment. "Have you an allowance, Signore Slater?"

Shocked that the conte would bring up the topic—it wasn't polite to speak of money in England—Donald raised a shoulder. "I do."

"Are you a gambler?"

Donald shook his head. "I am not."

D'Avalos seemed surprised by his answer. "No cards?"

Once again shaking his head, Donald said, "I occasionally play a hand or two with my cousins, although our bets are made with sixpence coins. I would rather spend my blunt on travel and a good pair of boots."

"And when must you return to England?" The conte waved to a footman, who rushed over with a tray of drinks. Taking two glasses, D'Avalos handed one to Donald.

"Thank you, sir. I have enough funds to last another two or three months, if I am judicious in how I spend it," Donald explained, before he took a sip of the bubbling wine.

"Then do watch how you spend it. Nikky will have you robbed blind if you do her bidding," the conte warned, one of his dark brows arching in warning.

"Of course, sir."

"There is a matron of some importance who is without a dance partner," D'Avalos said as he nodded toward an older woman who stood holding a glass of Prosecco. She was watching the proceedings with the manner of a bored aristocrat. "Perhaps you could favor her for the rest of this set?"

Donald's eyes rounded a fraction before he understood the conte's request. "Of course, sir." He bowed to D'Avalos and sauntered toward the matron.

Dressed in a dark red velvet gown, the black-haired beauty might have been forty or fifty or even sixty, but what Donald immediately noticed was that she looked familiar.

He bowed before her and reached for her hand. *"Posso avere questo ballo, mia signora?"*

May I have this dance, my lady?

The woman straightened and regarded him a moment with a look of surprise. Then her gaze darted to D'Avalos. "Did my brother send you?" she asked in heavily-accented English.

Donald glanced at the conte before turning his attention back on the woman. "If Conte D'Avalos is your brother, then yes, he did ask if I might be willing to dance. I am," he replied.

She held out her gloved right hand, and Donald was about to bring it to his lips when she grasped his hand and shook it. "Armenia Nicoletta Adeline Victoria D'Avalos," she said, giving him a nod.

Blinking at the odd introduction, Donald said, "Donald William Henry Slater, my lady, at your service."

Armenia beamed in delight. "By the gods, but you look just like your father did at your age."

Donald blinked again. "My lady?"

Placing her hand on his arm, Armenia led them around the perimeter of the ballroom. "My older sister is Adeline, Marchioness of Morganfield," she said, watching carefully for his reaction.

She wasn't disappointed.

"I *knew* you looked familiar," he said as a smile had a dimple appearing in his lower left cheek. "You're obviously the younger one, though," he quickly added, remembering what his mother had said he should say in such circumstances.

Armenia tittered. "Your mother has obviously trained you well," she said with a grin. "However, I do not believe I have had the pleasure?"

Donald shook his head. "Barbara, Countess of Bellingham. Her father was the late Maxwell Higgins, Earl of Greenley," he explained. "And she is rarely in London."

Angling her head to one side, Armenia said, "Are *you* much in the capital?"

He shook his head. "I have remained in Oxfordshire most of my life," he said. "But I have been to my grandfather's house on several occasions, and to a few *ton* balls. Which is how I met your sister. I attended Oxford with her grandson David," he added.

"Ah, I've not seen him since he was a small boy," she

said, a wistful sigh following the claim. "But I expect he will pay a call whilst he is on his Grand Tour in the next year or so. Tell me, Signore Slater, how long have you known Nikky?"

Donald found the change in subject odd given she seemed anxious to hear more about the people they knew in common. "I only met her yesterday. At the Prince of Biscari's gardens," he said.

Rolling her eyes, Armenia scoffed. "Let me guess. She ordered you about, and you did her bidding."

Chuckling, Donald felt heat climb his neck and color his cheeks. It didn't help that the temperature in the ballroom had risen several degrees since his arrival. "Something like that," he admitted.

"Has my brother asked that you escort her on the morrow?"

"He has, my lady."

"Which you no doubt find odd," she guessed.

"Trusting me after barely meeting me has given me pause," he admitted. "Should I be worried?"

At his query, Armenia slowed her steps and pulled him closer to the wall. "If you are to be a willing pawn in whatever game he is playing, then you needn't worry. He obviously trusts that you won't kidnap Nikky," she said in a quiet voice. "But if I know my brother, he has plans, and you may be part of them without even knowing it," she warned.

Donald dared a glance in the direction of the conte, his brows furrowing when he noticed the man was speaking with the same older gentleman he'd been in conversation with the day before at the labyrinth. "I can hardly imagine why," he finally said. "Unless he expects I'll offer for her hand, and I hardly think that's likely given my situation." He meant the words for two reasons—he was due to return to England in a couple of months, and his status as a bastard hardly made him husband material for the daughter of a conte.

He watched as Enrico D'Avalos presented the older aristocrat to Nicoletta. After she curtsied, Donald leaned his head closer to Armenia. "Who is he?"

"The Marchese Montblanc. Rich as Croesus and still without a wife," she whispered.

For a moment, Donald wondered if the woman had at one time been a contender for the role of the Marchesa Montblanc. He noted how she stared at her brother once the conte had stepped away from his daughter and the music resumed for the next dance. "He will not expect you to offer for her hand," she murmured, her elegant brow still furrowed. "But do be careful what you promise my niece," she added. "She can be a flirt when it suits her, and I don't wish you to leave Catania with your heart broken."

His gaze going to where Nicoletta was dancing with the older aristocrat, Donald nodded his understanding. "I won't be here long enough to form an attachment," he said. "But I do appreciate the warning, my lady."

• • •

When Donald finally left House D'Avalos at almost two in the morning, his thoughts weren't on Armenia's warning but rather on Nicoletta's parting words.

"No later than eleven o'clock in the morning, but I do insist you arrive earlier so that you might attend me during my *toilette*," she said, gripping his forearm with a silk-gloved hand.

Donald wasn't sure he heard her edict clearly at first. "I'm not sure I understood what you said," he responded carefully.

She tittered. "You must arrive in time to see me safely into my bathtub. And out of it, of course."

Left speechless at the thought of attending to her during a bath—isn't that what a lady's maid was supposed to do?—Donald leaned over and kissed the back of her hand. "I will be sure to arrive on time," he promised.

"I will make it worth your time," she said, arching a dark brow suggestively.

Donald blinked, his cock threatening to come to attention. "Good night, my lady."

He took his time returning to his lodgings. Despite the chill in the air, he had trouble controlling his arousal.

Whatever did she mean when she said she would make it worth his time?

CHAPTER 4
A MARCHESE MAKES A DEAL

eanwhile, in the study of House D'Avalos Ricardo, Marchese Montblanc, settled into a chair in Enrico's study and clasped both of his hands atop his lion-headed cane. "Quite a fête you've hosted this evening," he remarked, accepting the glass of port Enrico offered.

"You honor me with your presence," the conte countered. "Did you enjoy yourself?"

The older man leaned back in his chair before nearly draining his glass. "I did. I spend so much time at my vineyards, I forget there is a different life here in the city."

Enrico took the chair adjacent to the marchese's and directed his gaze on the fire a footman had set only a few minutes before their arrival. "I will admit I felt privileged by our conversation yesterday. When I received your note to bring Nicoletta to the prince's property, I had no idea of your plans," he claimed.

The statement wasn't entirely true—he had hoped the marchese might propose an alliance to include Nicoletta's hand in marriage.

"Liar," Ricardo accused, although a grin accompanied his comment. "She is a beauty and will do nicely."

"So... you *do* wish to marry her?" Enrico asked carefully.

The marchese shrugged. "I am not getting any younger, and I fear my time may have already passed."

His serious expression had Enrico confused. "Your time, my lord?"

Ricardo inhaled. "Your daughter is beautiful. She is everything I would have wanted in a wife... thirty years ago," he said on a sigh. "I had one once. She died in the childbed, as did the babe. Now, however, I'm too damned old. I fear I may not be able to... to…" He allowed the sentence to trail off. "I have pined for no fewer than a half-dozen young ladies over the years, but none were interesting enough to have me marrying them."

About to say something, Enrico clamped his mouth shut when the marchese held up a staying hand.

"Your wife among them," Ricardo said, turning his gaze so it bored into Enrico. "I cannot tell you of my jealousy when she gave you an heir," he stated.

Enrico furrowed his brows. "I... I did not know," he murmured.

"Nicoletta looks just like her mother," Ricardo said.

"She does," Enrico agreed, although his response was guarded.

"I will not leave this earth without the assurances of an heir," the marchese went on, ignoring the conte's comment. "Which means when I marry Nicoletta, she must already be with child."

Enrico blinked in confusion. "*What?*" He nearly stood from his chair, his expression turning to one of shock.

"This boy from England... she likes him, and he's the grandson of a marquess. An appropriate match, wouldn't you say?"

Enrico struggled to respond, not sure what the marchese expected him to say. "But... my Nicoletta is a virgin—"

"I don't expect her to be one on our wedding night," Ricardo interrupted. "She must be with child."

Scoffing, Enrico stared at his guest for several seconds. "You expect Signore Slater to... to bed her?" he asked in disbelief.

The marchese nodded. "During our dance this evening, I suggested he would make a suitable husband, and that she should do what she must to see to it he favors her. To seduce him. There is no one better for her in Catania, and once he learns she is to wed me, he will leave."

Enrico stared at the marchese for a long time. "I will not allow my Nikky—"

"You will, for I will favor you with a substantial

settlement, and upon my death, you can have my damned vineyards," Ricardo stated.

Settling back into his chair as if all the air had gone out of him, Enrico considered the proposal for several seconds before he finally nodded. "Agreed. You don't think it will be suspicious when she gives birth to your heir sooner than expected?"

Ricardo shook his head. "She will spend her confinement at the castle, and no one in town shall know of the birth until the christening," he explained. When the conte didn't put voice to a reply, he added, "Have your secretary draw up the contract and let us plan for a wedding in... say two months? Three at the latest?"

Enrico nodded. "Two months," he finally agreed, the promise of gaining the Montblanc vineyards enough to overcome his initial revulsion at the arrangement.

He hoped it would be enough time for Nicoletta and the Englishman to form more than an attachment.

CHAPTER 5
ATTENDING A YOUNG LADY

The following morning

As rain threatened the island of Sicily, Donald made his way on foot to House D'Avalos. Although his trek the day before had made the old city seem charming—he thought the streets made of lava blocks and the Baroque architecture especially unique—his thoughts on the matter were changing now that he was seeing a different part of the city in the light of day.

Many of the buildings looked as if they needed a new layer of plaster. A new coat of paint. Rust stains dribbled down from where Juliet balconies were hung below tall windows. Some shutters were crooked, their attachments having come loose. *Elegant rot*, he thought as he paused to examine a villa that had probably been rather beautiful a century ago.

The morning air carried with it unpleasant odors of rotted fish and sewage. The puffs of white hovering over the top of Mount Aetna had Donald wondering if the volcano was about to blow.

He found the large wooden doors of House D'Avalos closed but not locked. Slipping into the courtyard, Donald paused to see that the decorations from the night before were still in place. In the dark, they had seemed magical, the wires and the thin strings holding them in place hidden from sight. Now they seemed like cheap ornaments.

A single horse-drawn carriage and its beast were parked in the middle of the courtyard, its driver looking as if he might have imbibed too many glasses of Prosecco the night before.

"*Buongiorno*," Donald called out.

The driver nodded in his direction but didn't say anything as Donald made his way to the doors he had entered for the ball the night before. Lifting the iron knocker, he banged it three times and stepped back to wait.

Nearly a minute passed before one of the doors opened and the butler appeared.

"*Sono qui per accompagnare Lady Nicoletta*," Donald said.

I am here to escort Lady Nicoletta.

The servant waved him into the hall. "*Devo portarti nel suo salone*," he said as he led him up the stairs to the first floor, down a corridor, and up a second flight of marble stairs.

I am to take you to her salon.

Pausing before a carved wooden door, the servant

knocked and opened it but didn't go in. Instead he waved a hand for Donald to enter.

Expecting the room to be a parlor, Donald stopped short when he was past the threshold. He would have taken a step back except the butler had already closed the door.

Upon seeing the canopied bed, ornate dressing table topped with a huge ancient mirror, and a large armoire, Donald knew he was in a bedchamber. When Nicoletta appeared from an adjacent room, he realized it was hers.

"Pardon, my lady. I..." He lifted a hand and waved backwards. "The butler brought me here," he stammered.

Dressed in a white chemise and an open dressing robe, Nicoletta regarded him with a sly grin. "That's because I told him to," she replied, moving toward him. "I wanted your company whilst I see to my *toilette*." She stood on tiptoes and kissed him on the cheek. "*Buongiorno*."

"*Buongiorno*," he replied, swallowing nervously.

She angled her head to one side, the messy bun on top threatening to tumble down. "Have you never been invited to an English girl's *toilette*?" she asked, sounding curious.

Not quite sure what she meant by the query, Donald shook his head. "Men are not allowed in lady's bedchambers," he whispered. At her upraised brow, he added, "Well, I suppose they are after they are married."

She turned and crooked a finger, intending for him to follow her. "Come. There is a chair for you in my bathing chamber."

"Wh... where is your lady's maid?" he asked nervously, finally making his way into the other room. The bathing chamber was nearly as large as her bedchamber. The tub, already filled with water, stood in the middle of the black and white marble-tiled floor. A stack of bath linens were on one chair while another, placed near the edge of the tub, was empty.

"I will ring, and she will come when I am ready to dress," Nicoletta replied as she waved to the chair.

Donald paused, not about to be seated whilst she was still standing. "Who will help you into the tub?" he asked.

She doffed her dressing gown and tossed it onto the chair with the linens. "Well, you, of course," she said as she held out a hand.

Swallowing, Donald took her hand and watched as she stepped into the tub. When she let go, he thought to turn his back—he could see her chemise was translucent where it was already wet at her knees.

Lowering herself into the water, Nicoletta sighed with pleasure and leaned back, the water barely covering her breasts. Donald could only imagine how many trips had been required by the servants to fill such a large tub.

"Will you bring me the ball of soap?" she asked, one of her arms lifted onto the edge of the copper tub. A finger pointed in the direction of a sink and a water pump.

"Of course," he replied, doing her bidding. When he turned around to give her the soap, he found he couldn't avert his eyes. Given the chemise barely hid her nakedness and the water was clear, he stared in awe.

Nicoletta angled her head to one side, well aware of his perusal. "Are English girls so very different?"

Donald blinked and quickly handed her the soap. "Uh..." he stammered. "I really couldn't say. I've never seen one in a bath before."

A teasing grin slowly formed on her face. "Have you never seen a naked woman before?" She pulled up the chemise to reveal one knee and lifted it from the tub to apply the soap.

His mouth opening and closing much like that of a fish, Donald dropped into the chair and ran a hand through his sandy blonde hair. "Uh, not exactly," he finally replied. He'd seen his younger cousin in all her glory, but she had been very young at the time. Maybe three or four. They had been swimming in the River Isis on an especially hot day.

"Statues," he announced suddenly, reminded that he had seen several marbles of naked women whilst on his few visits to the British capital. He had seen even more whilst on his tour of Greece and the few Greek city states located on Sicily.

"But you have made love to a woman."

Donald blinked and watched as she raised her other knee above the water line. He wasn't about to admit one of his goals on this trip to Europe was to finally rid himself of his virginity. He would have done it whilst at university, but none of the tavern maids seemed especially interested at the pub he frequented, and he didn't wish to spend his blunt on a prostitute.

"I am still a virgin, of course," Nicoletta said with a sigh, as if she had decided he wasn't going to answer her. "My father used to think it was my only redeeming quality."

Frowning, Donald asked, "Why do you say that?"

She shrugged and sat up straighter, which had her chest rising out of the water. Despite the chemise, her pert breasts were on full display. When Donald turned his head, she huffed. "Do you see something wrong with me?" she asked.

He shook his head. "Not at all, my lady. I was merely giving you some… privacy," he replied.

"You're embarrassed," she said, her eyes rounding in understanding. "I did not mean to embarrass you," she added, lowering her chest beneath the water.

"You're a very beautiful woman," Donald stated. "I am honored that you have invited me to your bath. That you feel comfortable enough with me that you would allow me to see you… like this." He was about to say more. Maybe mention that if she didn't finish soon, he would be tempted to take her virtue. His cock had hardened, straining the fabric of his pantaloons. The full skirt of his top coat was barely able to hide the evidence of his erection.

Nicoletta regarded him with a thoughtful expression and settled back into the water. "*Grazie*," she whispered. After a moment, she said, "I am ready to get out."

Thinking that meant he should leave the bathing

chamber—he would see far more of her than what he had already seen when she was in the tub—Donald was about to make his way to the door when she said, "You will help me dry off, I hope?"

Donald stopped in his tracks, his gaze going to the bath linens. "Uh... of course," he replied, taking the top one and unfurling it. He held it out and up in front of his line of sight.

She giggled as she wrapped the towel around her torso. Holding the linen with one hand, she held out the other and Donald grasped it as she stepped up and out of the tub.

"Oh, my. I *have* embarrassed you," she murmured, noting his reddened face. Her gaze lowered, taking in his tented pantaloons. "You are aroused," she added in awe.

Unable to deny it, Donald finally nodded. "As I said, you are a beautiful woman. Seeing you like this..." he waved a hand down her front, "is like seeing Venus in all her glory."

Nicoletta inhaled softly. She stepped forward and gripped his lapel with one hand as she lifted herself on tiptoes to kiss him.

Donald returned the kiss, and while doing so, wrapped an arm around the back of her waist to pull her against the front of his body. He could feel the dampness of her chemise through the bath linen, feel the bumps of her spine down the middle of her back. His other arm joined the first, his splayed hand covering one of the globes of her bottom to hold her even closer. He could feel his erection cradled in her soft belly, and he wished he could shed his clothes and bury himself in her body.

About to end the kiss, he heard her soft mewl of protest and simply angled his head in the other direction to continue. He had a passing thought that the entire front of his clothes would be soaking wet by the time they pulled apart, but he didn't care. She was warm and tasted of Prosecco and strawberries. She smelled of the lemony soap she had used in the bath. From the way she clung to him, he knew she would allow him to bed her.

When he finally ended the kiss, mostly because he needed to breathe, Donald dropped his forehead to hers and closed his eyes. "If only every morning could begin like this," he whispered.

She glanced up, her eyes hidden beneath the curtain of her long lashes. "You say that as if it cannot be," she replied sadly.

Donald's arms moved higher up her back to hold her shoulders. "I did not intend for it to sound like that." He kissed the top of her head as he pulled her so her cheek rested against his chest. The scent of lemons drifted past his nose again, no doubt from her hair.

"So you must come again tomorrow morning," she said brightly, pushing away from him slightly.

Letting go his hold on her, Donald watched as she dropped the bath linen over the edge of the tub, pulled her chemise over her head, and helped herself to another linen.

She didn't even bother wrapping it around her body before she made her way into her bedchamber, as if she knew full well Donald's gaze was glued to her bare backside.

"You minx," he accused as his feet finally moved from where they'd been stuck since she had risen from the water.

Venus, indeed, he thought with one last look at the tub.

He paused on the threshold and watched as she finished drying off, one of her feet lifted to the edge of the bed to display a perfectly curved calf and well-turned ankle. Her olive tinted skin glowed in the morning light, and he wondered if his kiss had helped in that regard.

Although he had imagined she would have a more girlish figure—her gowns hadn't given away what was beneath them—it was apparent she possessed a fully formed body. Besides the breasts he had already seen in the bath, her hips flared from her waist, and the opposite curve continued down her thighs.

He would have continued to stare but she turned and froze in place, as if she had just then remembered he was still in her company. "You are more beautiful than Venus," he stated. If she didn't get into some clothes, and quick, he was going to allow the goddess of love to take over and have her way with him.

Apparently, Nicoletta was waiting for him to say something, for she paused and regarded him with an expression of uncertainty. "Do you... do you wish to make love to me?"

Donald blinked. Was she asking hypothetically if he

would? Or was she asking him to make love to her right then and there?

"Now?" he countered.

Her shoulders dropped, although the action did nothing to lessen the pertness of her breasts. "Is the morning not a good time for you?"

Pushing himself off the door jamb, Donald decided there was no time like the present. He dared a quick glance at the bedchamber door and then hurried to it to drive home the bolt. He had her in one arm an instant later, his mouth finding hers as his other hand tore at his buttons and the knot of his cravat.

Nicoletta pulled away to take a quick breath. "We must be quiet," she whispered, a finger moving to her lips. Then her hands joined his in undoing the buttons of his waistcoat.

"Is there a particular way you like it?" he asked, wondering how she could still be a virgin when she behaved as if she'd had a string of lovers. She was far too comfortable in his presence for this to be the first time entertaining a man in her bedchamber.

Her eyes rounded. "Particular way?" she repeated, as if she didn't understand the English words.

"To make love? You'll have to help me, because..." He allowed the sentence to trail off, not willing to admit aloud that he hadn't done it before. At least he had read books on the topic. Studied the illustrations and admired the colored plates.

"I have not done this before," she whispered.

Donald blinked. He swallowed. His gaze darted to

the bathing chamber. "Am I truly the first man to attend you in there?"

Her bare shoulder lifted slightly. "You are," she admitted.

Donald's brows furrowed before a slight grin lifted his lips. "I am honored, my lady," he whispered.

He resumed removing his clothes, his new concern that she would find his broad shoulders and muscled body repulsive. Working the fields of his uncle's farm and spending most days seeing to the horses of the Gisborn earldom meant his physique was not the usual for an English man. From what he had witnessed of the men at the ball from the night before, Sicilian aristocrats' physiques were much like those in England.

Before he could give it another thought or to warn her, Nicoletta had his shirt pulled up and over his head, her arms stretched up as far as they would go to manage it. With her breasts pressed against his bare chest when she let go of the white linen garment, Donald was lost. Whatever happened going forward, he knew he would have no control.

CHAPTER 6
A YOUNG LADY'S SEDUCTION

From the moment she had awoken that morning, Nicoletta's thoughts had been on the words the Marchese Montblanc had said to her during their dance the night before.

You'll not find a better young man in all of Catania. He comes from a very good family. You must do what you can to see to it he marries you one day.

Although she had demurred at first—was the marchese suggesting she seduce Donald to secure an offer of marriage?—by the time the dance ended, she felt empowered. If she wanted the young Englishman to be her husband, she would have to ensure he was given every opportunity to spend time with her.

After the last of the guests had departed House D'Avalos the night before, Nicoletta spent nearly an hour in the library pouring through several books featuring color plates and illustrations of sexual congress. Although she had always known of them, it was her first time climbing the ladder to the top shelf where they'd been kept, probably in an effort to prevent her from accidentally finding them when she was younger.

Most of the illustrations had her wincing in disgust. A few had her turning the pages before she had a chance to see too much. Two had her turning the book almost upside down in an effort to determine what she was seeing. One had her staring in awe, for her entire body seemed to react with a pleasant frisson.

Could she convince Donald to do what was depicted in the drawing? Would he be familiar with the act?

Surely he had bedded a woman before. Surely he would know what to do.

She absently ran a hand over one breast, stunned to discover the nipple hard beneath her touch. Moving her hand to the other nipple, she realized it, too, was hard. The thought of him touching it had her insides reacting in ways she had never felt before. The space at the top of her thighs had grown damp, throbbing in a manner that had her wishing he was there to do whatever it was he could to relieve the ache.

She had glanced at two other books before helping herself to the one with the drawings. Making her way back to her bedchamber, she had removed her night rail, climbed onto her bed, and imagined what it would be like to have Donald see her naked.

Would he be repulsed by her breasts? They weren't as flat as the current fashions preferred.

Would he favor the shape of her hips? The curve of her calves? The turn of her ankle?

Did he find her as beautiful as the marchese claimed she was?

The thought of how the old man had stared at her—as if her ballgown didn't exist and she was naked before him—might have bothered her, but he hadn't stared at her as if he lusted for her. His gaze was one of longing, as if he wished he were years younger and she was older.

By the time she had fallen asleep, her thoughts had once again turned to Donald. When the rays of sun woke her from a stream of pleasant dreams, she knew exactly what she wanted him to do.

CHAPTER 7
SERVICING A YOUNG LADY

The moment Nicoletta turned to face the bed was when Donald knew that what she was expecting him to do and what he intended to do were entirely different.

That she would expect him to take her over the edge of the bed bothered him. Even upon witnessing the perfect shape of the globes of her bottom as she bent, upon seeing her upturned quim glistening in the morning light streaming in from the nearby window, he knew he had to redirect her expectations.

Yes, it would have been easy to simply use his hands to spread her legs apart, to slide his engorged manhood along her wet folds, grip her hips in his hands, and to finally thrust himself into her. Easy and oh, so tempting.

He didn't know why he thought it wrong. Perhaps it was the memory of seeing his father making love to his mother late one night, the window in her bedchamber left open so he was able to watch from the edge of the drapes covering his window. He had discovered soon after they had moved into Ellsworth Park that he could see her from his bedchamber, one floor above hers and in an adjacent wing.

Reminded of how his father had claimed his wife of only a few months that morning, of how he had flipped back the bed linens and crawled atop her, of how she had spread her legs in invitation as his father kissed his way down her body until his head was between her thighs, Donald knew exactly how he wished to make love for the first time with Nicoletta.

He reached out and slid his hands down the sides of her torso and hips, shocked at feeling the softness of her skin. Lowering his head, he placed a kiss at the base of her spine even as he slid one hand back up and over one of her breasts.

The way her body shuddered beneath his touch had him realizing his move was entirely unexpected. He resisted the urge to pinch her engorged nipple between his thumb and forefinger, instead allowing it to slide between the length of his fingers until he heard her whimper.

Smoothing his hand back down the front of her body, he pulled her up until her back was pressed to the front of his. He guided her, turning her around until she faced him. "Lie back, my sweet," he whispered, nudging her until her knees were forced to bend at the edge of the bed.

Her eyes wide, Nicoletta scrambled backwards until she was in the middle of the mattress. "What...?"

"Shh," he whispered, crawling onto the bed until he hovered over her. His turgid manhood seemed to understand what to do even if he wasn't exactly sure. "Spread your legs for me."

She did his bidding, and from there, Donald knew exactly what to do. As he leaned down to kiss her lips, he lowered his hips to hers. He had to break off the kiss in order to take a labored breath. The tip of his manhood had already found her entrance, the warm wetness inviting him to press further into her.

"Hurry," she breathed, lifting her hips in invitation.

He remembered the image of what his father had done. "Patience, my sweet," he murmured. He shimmied down the length of her torso, his lips trailing kisses along her lemon-scented skin until he reached the dark curls surrounding her wet folds. Not sure exactly what to do, he reached out with the tip of his tongue and flicked it across her quim.

Her entire body seemed to buck in response, her inhalation so sudden, he nearly laughed with relief. Trying again, he soon found what had her reacting.

Gripping the globes of her bottom with this hands, he pressed harder with his tongue, not allowing her to escape the ministrations of the rough-textured surface against her most private place. Her mewls and soft cries urged him on until he understood what he was touching with his tongue. He blew on the swollen bud and then captured it in a kiss, which seemed to send her into a pleasant spasm, for he could feel her body react in his hold and hear her muffled cries.

"Hurry," she said again, her voice nearly breathless.

He didn't need to be told twice. He moved up her body, once again trailing kisses until the tip of his manhood was at her entrance. A timid push followed by a more determined thrust had his manhood buried as far as possible. Her gasp and raised chest had his eyes rounding.

Could anything be more lovely than her breasts rising to meet his chest? More lovely than the way her raven hair splayed out over the white linen covering the pillow? More lovely than her kiss-reddened lips saying his name on a whisper?

"Are you all right?" he asked, not daring to move lest he hurt her.

She nodded in the pillow.

The need to retreat and thrust into her had him trying it once. The sensation he felt was so pleasurable, he did it again and again until he felt as if he was about to explode. He might have held on a moment or two longer, but her hands were sliding down his sides, her fingers finally gripping his buttocks in an effort to hold on as he increased his rhythm.

The sudden release had him ceasing his movements. Had him hovering atop her until he knew he had spilt his seed in her. All at once, any bit of energy he thought he had possessed left his body, and he slumped down. At the last moment, he knew enough to reach out with a hand to stop his downward fall onto her. He had a thought to roll off of her and onto the bed, but her arms were latched around his back, clinging to him.

He chuckled softly when he finally settled his head next to hers on the pillow. Kissing her cheek, he waited a few seconds in an effort to regain control of his breathing before attempting to speak.

"*Grazie,*" was all he could think to say.

She turned her head and regarded him with wide eyes. "For a moment, I thought you were in pain," she whispered.

He scoffed softly. "I assure you I was not." His brows furrowed. "What about you?" Lifting himself onto an elbow, he saw her wince when he pulled his shrinking manhood from her body, and with it, the rest of him.

She immediately pulled her legs together, bending her knees slightly. "It did not hurt," she murmured, although there was uncertainty in her voice.

"I don't think it's supposed to," he countered. He leaned over and kissed her lips. "It's supposed to be... pleasant," he stammered.

Grinning, she lifted his free hand to place it atop her belly, leaving one of her hands on top of it. She guided it so the flats of his fingers smoothed over the soft skin, and when he understood what she wanted him to do, he began rubbing soft circles over her heated skin.

She inhaled softly, her eyes closing. When he leaned over to nibble one of her nipples, her eyes flew open and her hands moved to hold the sides of his head. "It's time I dress," she whispered.

"I'll help you to the bath," he whispered, thinking she would wish to wash away the evidence of him from her skin.

Before she could respond, he was off the bed and moving to lift her into his arms.

"I can walk," she whispered in complaint.

"But I can carry you," he countered, dropping his lips to her forehead. He took her back to the bathing chamber and lowered her into the tepid water.

She hissed when she was settled onto the bottom of the tub. "I'd rather you didn't watch me," she murmured, her arms wrapping around her bent knees.

For a moment, Donald thought to argue with her—she had been perfectly fine with him seeing her naked in the light of day only a few minutes ago—but he thought it best to leave her to her ablutions. "I'll go get dressed," he replied. "But I'll help you out of the tub when you're done. Please don't try to step out of it by yourself. I don't want you to slip and fall."

At this, she looked up at him for the first time since he had placed her in the water. "If you can arrange my hair, I shall let go my lady's maid and hire you instead," she teased.

He chuckled. "Minx," he accused before he made his way back toward the bed to retrieve his clothes.

An entire hour passed before Nicoletta was out of the tub, dried off, gowned, and sitting at her dressing table with her lady's maid stabbing pins into her hair.

During that time, Donald waited patiently, sitting in a nearby chair while he wondered if all Italian women hosted men during their *toilette*. And if they did so, did they also make love to them?

It was certainly a wonderful way to start the day. His

body felt recharged and lethargic all at the same time. In fact, if the young lady had been so inclined, he would have gladly made love to her again.

His gaze went to the bed, where the rumpled counterpane had been straightened enough to hide their carnal activities. Only a small bloodstain showed against the white linen beneath, proof that, like him, his first was a virgin.

First and only, he thought. He had taken her virtue. As such, he was determined to marry her. It was the honorable thing to do. He liked her. Decided he would grow to feel even more affection for her once she agreed to marry him.

His thoughts went back to last evening's ball. Her father's words of warning had been said in a sort of calculated dare, as if he knew Donald could be persuaded to at least attempt a courtship with Nicoletta.

Meanwhile, her aunt's words held a different sort of warning, as if she was already convinced pursuing the conte's daughter wouldn't be in his best interest.

Given the woman's relationship to someone he knew in London, Donald thought her words about her niece were odd.

Perhaps he would discover why during their excursion.

If they ever left her bedchamber.

He was about to give in to nap when she finally announced she was ready to go.

Rising from the chair, Donald offered his arm and the two took their leave of House D'Avalos.

. . .

Although it was nearly dark when they returned, Donald would have been happy to spend even more time with the conte's daughter. From the moment they had entered the first shop, where she had looked for a pair of gloves but left with a flowered bonnet, until they departed a bookstore with a stack of novels and an illustrated map of the country, he found her enchanting. Charming. Flirty and fun. The concerns he had felt about what they had done earlier that morning had dissipated before they enjoyed a coffee and pastries near the water. By the time the sun was setting over the side of Mount Aetna, Donald had begun imagining how they might spend the rest of their lives together.

CHAPTER 8
LOVE BLOOMS IN TAORMINA

A month later

Loaded with several trunks, the D'Avalos traveling coach departed Catania on an early February morning and headed north. The clear skies and bright sun rising over the Mediterranean promised a pleasant day.

"I feel especially privileged your brother would allow me to escort you to Taormina," Donald remarked, his gaze on the scenery beyond the coach window. He knew they had to be on a road close to the water—he could make out the unique blue color on the horizon.

"I am happy you think so, since Enrico is not a very diverting traveling companion," Armenia replied, grinning. Next to her, Nicoletta dozed, the novel she had been reading threatening to fall from her gloved hands.

"Do you often go to Taormina?" he asked.

"I would *live* there if we owned the property," Armenia replied. "There is a reason the Ancient Greeks settled it. Nikky will have to take you to the theatre so you can see for yourself."

"I had planned to go on my own," Donald explained. He motioned to the journal on the seat next to him. He had been keeping copious notes in one while following instructions from another, rather dated book on the topic of Grand Tours. "But I shall enjoy it more seeing it with you two."

Armenia tittered. "There's no need to include *me* in your plans, young man. I have my own reasons for wanting to spend a few months there."

Donald gave a start, oblivious to the older woman's insinuation she would be joining a lover in the resort town. "A few months?" he repeated. Although he had given up his lodgings to come along on this trip, he had left his trunk in the care of the innkeeper in Catania, explaining he would return in a week's time.

"She's going for a few months. We're only going for a week," Nicoletta said, briefly opening her eyes to show she had been listening to their conversation. "At least, I've been told that's all the longer we can stay." Her brows danced with mischief.

"Oh," he replied, before his eyes widened. "Will someone be joining us for the return trip to Catania?" he asked. "Here in the coach? You'll require a chaperone, I should think."

Armenia dipped her head. "I hardly think that will be necessary, young man. You have proven yourself most trustworthy when it comes to my niece."

Donald couldn't help how his face reddened with her

remark. Even though he and Nicoletta had done their best to keep their burgeoning relationship from appearing more than friendly, he suspected Armenia knew it was more.

Much more.

For the past week, Donald had contemplated how he would approach the Conte D'Avalos to seek permission to marry his daughter.

Nicoletta had already pledged her love to him on more than one occasion. Since he was frequently expected to attend her morning *toilette*, they usually made love before she ever stepped into the bathtub. The idea he could do so every morning after they were wed had his cock hardening in anticipation.

He couldn't imagine falling in love with anyone else.

"I appreciate you saying so," he managed, hiding his embarrassment by using a finger to part the coach curtain. "Oh, my. Is that it?" he asked, stunned at the site of buildings set at various heights upon the side of a mountain. Traces of the triple walls once surrounding the city were still evident, although from his vantage, the entrance called the Porta Catania was hidden.

"Indeed," Armenia said. "You'll have to test Nikky. See if she can remember what everything is called."

The mention of her name had the young lady once again roused from a nap. "It's a positively gorgeous vantage," she said, straightening on the seat until she could see out the window. "Besides the Greek and Roman monuments, there are fountains and buildings of all sorts. Gardens, too."

When the coach finally halted in front of a golden yellow cube of a building, Donald had to tear his gaze from the view looking out on the Mediterranean from a higher perspective than what he had seen since his time on Greece. Never in his life had he seen such beauty, the greenery of gardens and trees spread out beneath him to where the land met the turquoise waters of the Bay of Naxos.

"We're here," Nicoletta said, grinning as the driver opened the door. She stepped out first, followed by Armenia and then Donald. His attention went up immediately, for the three-story villa, surrounded by greenery, seemed especially large and full of windows. Black wrought iron Juliet balconies popped out from in front of the white-trimmed windows on the upper stories.

"Is it staffed?" he asked, offering his arms to both women. They headed towards the stairs that led up to a front door.

"Mostly," Armenia replied. "The Conte Mancino owns it but won't be in residence until the day you are scheduled to depart. He is currently in Naples, I believe."

Donald felt his face redden when he realized she had come for a long assignation with the conte and had probably done so many times in the past. "I had hoped to thank him personally for allowing me to stay," Donald said with disappointment.

"I will be sure to tell him of your gratitude," Armenia offered as a butler opened the door.

Several footmen passed them on their way to see to

the luggage as others were assigned to escort them to their rooms.

Like the other villas he had been in on the island, he found this one similar in decor—plastered walls topped with moldings—although this one didn't include hints of a leaky roof.

"I should like to go for a walk after I refresh myself," Nicoletta said to her aunt.

"Well, be sure you go with a servant... or Mr. Slater," Armenia commented as they climbed the marble stairs. "I'm going to take a nap and have a bath."

"I shall be happy to escort you," Donald said. "I am anxious to see the gardens." He felt a pang when she directed an especially teasing grin in his direction.

"I won't keep you waiting." Led by a liveried maid, she disappeared into a guest bedchamber. The butler continued to the next door and paused as he held out his hand. "Signore Slater."

"*Grazie*," he said, nodding as he stepped into the bedchamber. From the dark colors and ebony furnishings, he knew it was intended for a male guest. Or perhaps it was the master suite—the painted ceiling and marble floors seemed far too fine for simply a guest.

"*Ti servirà un cameriere?*" the butler asked.

It took a moment for Donald to interpret the query, *Will you require a valet?* "No, *grazie*."

The butler disappeared when a footman arrived with his valise and set it on a bureau. Once he cleared the room, Donald shut the door and turned his attention to another door in the room. Curious, he moved to it and pushed down on the door handle, surprised when the soft *click* of the latch released. Peeking through the opening, he had to suppress the urge to chuckle—they had put him in a room next to Nicoletta's. She inhaled softly when she caught his reflection in a dressing table mirror and stared at him, a grin slowly appearing when she realized what he had discovered.

"*Ciao, bella,*" he said when she hurried to him. He would have welcomed her into an embrace, but she hurried past him and halted just past the threshold into his room.

"Where do you suppose Lady Armenia's room is located?" he asked in a whisper.

Nicoletta turned to regard him as her eyes darkened. "They took her to the conte's suite," she replied. "Upstairs."

Donald swallowed. Hard. He turned to stare at the bed in his suite and then at the smaller bed in hers. "This is terribly convenient," he whispered.

"Make love to me," she said.

He gave a start at hearing the plea in her voice. "Nikky," he murmured in a scold.

"Please?"

He didn't have a chance to answer, for she wrapped her arms around his shoulders and kissed him. For a moment, he thought to wriggle out of her hold—they had only just arrived—but his manhood had already reacted to her closeness, to the way she pressed her body to his. Spurred into action at feeling her purr of satisfaction, he guided her until the large bed was behind her, lifted her skirts to her hips, and pushed her back until she was seated on the edge. Even as he kept his lips locked with hers, he undid the placket of his pantaloons, his hands tangling with hers when she attempted to help. His turgid rod sprang forth, dripping with his need of her.

Bending over Nicoletta, Donald supported himself on his arms as she wrapped her legs around his thighs. The fine silk of her stockings was as smooth as her bare skin would have been, and he was forced to break off the kiss to let out a breath of awe.

He hadn't meant to enter her right away. He had thought to kneel at the edge of the bed and prepare her with his tongue and lips. Before he could do so, though, Nicoletta gripped his cock and guided it to her opening. He thrust into her as her back arched, burying himself to the hilt all at once.

Above the layers of skirts bunched up around her, the tops of her rising moons were evident. When he tugged the edge of her bodice down, he was rewarded when a swollen nipple emerged. At hearing her breathy mewl, he swept a hand over her gown's shoulders, pushing the fabric down until her other breast escaped the bodice. He suckled it for a moment before moving his attentions to the other.

He watched in wonder as her torso seemed to undulate as he surged into her over and over, her eyes closed but her face displaying an expression of happiness he had never seen before.

Suppressing the urge to groan at the pleasure he felt,

he lowered his lips to hers. He hadn't expected her to orgasm when she did, for her to break the kiss to inhale sharply and for her inner muscles to grip him so tightly, so he was unprepared for the ferocity of his own release. Not only had her arms finally moved to his back, her hands were splayed at his hips, pulling him even harder against her.

Caught in a maelstrom that was familiar but not, he gave into the pleasure and collapsed atop her.

He might have stayed where he was for an hour or more, but he felt her giggle beneath him and lifted his head in order to determine what she found so amusing.

"What is it?"

She grinned and stretched her arms out. "I do not believe I have seen you this shocked. At least not since that first morning you made love to me," she whispered.

"That's because I was shocked," he admitted. "Still am." He pulled himself from her body, struggling to remove most of his weight from her as she mewled her disappointment. She lowered her legs until they hung over the edge of the bed while he straightened and refastened his pantaloons. Pulling a handkerchief from his pocket, he offered it to her, his gaze momentarily fixed on her bare breasts. He felt the oddest sensation at the thought of a babe suckling her nipples.

Their babe.

"I do hope you don't regret it," she murmured, using the square of linen to wipe away the evidence of their coupling.

"Of course I don't," he replied, holding out a hand to help her to stand.

She shook out her skirts and put her bodice to rights, giving him a grin when his expression showed disappointment. "You can see them again later," she murmured.

He chucked softly. "Did you still wish to go for a walk?"

"Indeed," she replied, hurrying into her bedchamber to regard her reflection in the dressing table mirror. She went to a trunk and opened it to remove a bonnet.

"I don't think I've ever seen you wear a bonnet," he commented, watching her from the connecting doorway.

"That's because I prefer hats," she replied. "But this will hide my mussed coiffure." She turned, angled her head, and arched a brow.

He smiled at seeing her teasing expression. She was still flushed from their lovemaking, her olive skin glowing in the late afternoon light streaming in through the window. "You look like an English miss," he said, shutting the connecting door behind him.

Her expression faltered for a moment, and Donald noticed. "Actually, you're more lovely," he quickly added, moving to join her. He used a finger to lift her chin and dropped a kiss on first her nose and then her lips.

He didn't expect her to deepen the kiss. To wrap an arm around his shoulder and hang on so tightly.

When she finally let go, he stared down at her. "If we don't leave right now, we'll never make it out of this house."

Nicoletta nodded. "The garden isn't far," she said, taking his proffered arm before they took their leave of her bedchamber.

The butler saw to the front door as they made their exit from the house, but before he took the steps down to the street, Donald paused. "Wait one minute for me?" he said, turning to go back inside.

"Of course," she replied, her brows furrowing.

He rushed back into the house and up the stairs, his heart racing at the thought of what he was about to do.

Once back in his bedchamber, he rifled through his valise and found a small box. Removing its contents, he stuffed it into his waistcoat pocket.

By the time he had rejoined Nicoletta, she had made her way to the bottom of the stairs and was sniffing a white bloom, the flower one of several flanking the walkway.

"Is everything all right?" she asked.

"Everything is perfect," he replied, once again offering his arm as his gaze swept the horizon. Although a few trees prevented a clear view, the sun-dappled surface of the Bay of Naxos was one of the most beautiful sights he could ever remember seeing.

As they strolled, descending the hill into which the conte's house—and several others—seemed precariously perched, he realized Mount Aetna was visible to the south. A few white clouds hovered at its apex, and he once again wondered how the residents of the island could live with the constant threat of an eruption.

"It does warn us," Nicoletta said, as if she understood his unspoken concern.

"Enough so you have time to get away?"

She shrugged. "It is the same if we were in Naples," she reasoned. "Vesuvius is not far from there."

"We don't have volcanos in England," Donald commented.

"But you have rain. Floods?" she guessed.

He nodded, remembering the year the Isis overflowed its banks. Despite the irrigation system his uncle had built for the Gisborn farmlands, water had spread out and nearly reached the manor homes and greenhouses on the estate. It had taken weeks for the water to recede and the lands to dry enough to begin the spring planting.

Nicoletta indicated a dirt path that led into a green space dominated by trees and bushes. Clusters of oleanders provided color to break up the predominant green of the gardens. Once they were near the middle, the canopy of trees above blocked much of the harsh light, the shade providing a blessed coolness and a serene quiet.

"I can understand why you wished to walk here," he said, pausing to stare out at the water when there was a break in the foliage.

"It is my favorite place in all of Taormina," she whispered.

"Would it remain so if this is where I ask you to marry me?"

Nicoletta inhaled softly, her eyes rounding. "Are you?" she queried. "Asking me?"

He nodded, one hand moving to fish something from his pocket. "Nicoletta, will you do me the honor of becoming my wife?" he asked. He held up the circle of gold he had purchased in Catania, its only adornment a small red gemstone. "I must ask your father for his permission, of course, but—"

"Yes," she replied. "Yes!"

Donald slowly smiled, heartened at hearing her enthusiasm. He pulled her hand into his, tugged the glove from it, and slid the ring onto her fourth finger before bringing it to his lips to kiss her knuckles. "You have made me a very happy man," he murmured.

She stared at the ring a moment and then turned her attention to him. "You have made me very happy," she said, gripping his arms so she could stand on tiptoes to kiss him. "I can hardly wait to tell Aunt Armenia."

He took a deep breath. "I realize there is much to discuss. Where we'll live and such," he added, attempting to put the glove back on her fingers.

"In England, will we not?" she replied, taking the glove from his hand to stuff it into a pocket in her gown.

Sobering, Donald considered how to respond. He had yet to tell her he wasn't an heir to an earldom—his younger brother David would have the title given his parents hadn't been married at the time of his birth—but surely his connections would be enough for her and her father. "Of course," he replied finally. He offered his arm. "Will you show me more of this place?"

She placed her bare hand on his arm, wiggling her fingers playfully. "It will take the entire time we are here to see it all," she warned.

"Then we best not dawdle," he teased.

For the next seven days, the two spent every day exploring what had one time been an Ancient Greek resort town, Nicoletta acting as guide. Although she didn't seem to know the historical significance of some of the ruins they visited, Donald was able to discover their history from books in the conte's library, and he added the information to his own journal.

As for Armenia's reaction to their announcement, she seemed eminently pleased. "I am so happy for you both," she said, examining the ruby on Nicoletta's ring. "It is a shame I will not be in Catania when you return to tell my brother," she added.

Neither Donald or Nicoletta noticed her look of worry when they retired for their last night in the conte's villa.

They spent it making love to one another.

CHAPTER 9
A MEETING WITH A FATHER

Ten days later, Catania

The rain-slick lava blocks making up the thin streets of Catania didn't slow Donald's hurried steps as he made his way to House D'Avalos. He had decided today would be the day he would ask the conte for his daughter's hand in marriage.

Upon their return from Taormina, they had discovered the conte gone, a servant informing them he would return in a few days. An invitation to a ball hosted by Ricardo Malgeri, Marchese Montblanc, was waiting for Donald at his lodgings, and he thought it best he secure permission to marry Nicoletta. Perhaps their betrothal could be announced at the marchese's ball later that evening.

When he arrived at House D'Avalos, he was surprised to see a traveling coach in the courtyard. He recognized the crest on the door—the House of Mancino.

Had Armenia already returned?

From what she had told them when they had traveled to Taormina—she expected to stay for three months—he wondered if something had happened to shorten her trip.

"Is Conte D'Avalos in residence?" he asked when the butler appeared at the door.

"He has returned, but I don't know if he is taking callers," the servant said, stepping aside to allow him entrance.

"I can wait," Donald said, prepared to do so in a parlor. "Is Lady Armenia already back in residence?"

"She is. She arrived late last night," the butler replied, leading him up the steps. "I did not ask about her travels as she seemed… preoccupied."

From the servant's expression and arched brow, Donald had the distinct impression something was wrong. A moment later, raised voices—those of Armenia and her brother—sounded from above when the butler opened the door to the first-floor parlor.

Donald stiffened. "Perhaps… I should call again later," he murmured.

"Lady Nicoletta is expecting you."

Heartened to hear it, Donald nodded and made his way to a chair. "I will wait."

When the butler exited, he left the door open. Donald could clearly hear Armenia scolding her brother. From the words he could make out between her sobs and angry curses, he realized she had indeed returned to Catania earlier than she planned.

"I had no choice," he heard the conte yell. "The coffers were empty."

The sound of crashing pottery punctuated Armenia's response as did a slamming door.

Thinking to simply return the following day, Donald was about to rise to make his way out of the parlor when the conte suddenly appeared.

"Lord D'Avalos. So good of you to see me," Donald said, quickly coming to his feet to bow.

Enrico nodded. "I did not intend for you to return Nikky to an empty house. I was called away to Roma the day after your departure and only returned last night."

A trip that had happened that quickly was no doubt due to an emergency. It would have taken over two days by ship. "I hope all is well in Rome?" Donald replied, returning to his chair when the conte took a seat in the adjacent chair.

"It is now," the conte said. "I have rid myself of a costly property in exchange for a generous price."

"Ah," Donald replied. "Then congratulations are in order."

"*Grazie.*" The conte poured a heavy dollop of vermouth into a tumbler and offered it to Donald. "I am surprised you have paid a call on me and not on Nikky," he said.

Surprised to be offered a drink so early in the day, Donald gingerly took the glass and waited until the conte had poured one for himself. "I wished to speak with you about Lady Nicoletta," he replied.

"Oh?"

"I wish to ask your permission to marry her," he said.

The conte didn't show any surprise at hearing the words. "I am aware you already proposed to her," he said before taking a sip of his drink.

Donald winced. "I did. In the gardens in Taormina," he admitted. "I am quite in love with her, my lord, and I believe she loves me."

"Oh, she does. Or, at least, she thinks she does," Enrico replied.

Hearing the challenge in the man's voice, Donald stiffened. "She does, my lord."

"Tell me, Mr. Slater. Does she know that you are not the heir to the Devonville marquessate?"

Donald straightened in his chair, immediately realizing the conte had learned he was a bastard. Had Armenia told him? "If she knows, it is not because I have mentioned it," he admitted. "My brother has that honor."

"Your *younger* brother," D'Avalos stated.

"Yes," Donald acknowledged. "My father was a commander in the British Navy when I was born and did not marry my mother until he completed his service to Crown and country."

"So you admit you are a bastard?"

He nodded. "I do. I have never denied it. But I can assure you, your daughter will never be in want of anything. She will be most welcome in England—"

"You planned to take her to England?" D'Avalos asked in disbelief.

Noting the past tense version of the word, Donald

stiffened. "If she wishes it," he replied, wincing when he realized the conte had already made up his mind about him.

Or had he?

"I will think on your question and make my decision soon," Enrico said before draining his drink. "In the meantime, have you planned to attend Montblanc's ball this evening? His villa in Via Dei Crociferi is not one to be missed," he added, referring to a street featuring some of the most beautiful homes in all of Catania.

Donald nodded. "I did receive an invitation. I had hoped for a dance or two with Lady Nicoletta."

"Very good. We will see you there."

Realizing he was being dismissed, Donald stood and bowed to the conte. "Until then, my lord."

While Donald took his leave of House D'Avalos, he was unaware he was being watched.

CHAPTER 10
SECRETS UNRAVEL

*M*eanwhile, *outside the parlor*
Nicoletta hurried to the end of the corridor and out of sight from the parlor doors when she realized Donald's meeting with her father had ended.

She had been surprised when he didn't ask to see her when he had arrived the hour before. She knew he had come to the house. Knew his plan to ask her father for her hand in marriage.

Had something gone wrong? Had her father denied him?

Once Donald had taken his leave of House D'Avalos, she rushed to a window overlooking the courtyard and watched him as he made his way to the iron gate. Not once did he look back.

When she turned, she gave a start when she discovered her father standing not far behind her. "Father," she said. "Did he ask permission to marry me?"

"He did," he acknowledged.

Nicoletta blinked when he didn't say more. "What did you say to him?"

Enrico merely shrugged. "I told him I would consider his request. He will be at the ball this evening. I shall give him my answer then."

Exhaling the breath she had been holding, Nicoletta nodded her understanding. "Thank you, Father. I do love him," she admitted, hoping to reinforce what Donald had told him in their meeting. "And he loves me."

Chuckling softly, Enrico said, "Ah, young love. I remember it well." He sobered. "See to it your hair is styled appropriately for the Montblanc ball, and do wear your very best gown."

Nicoletta's eyes rounded. "Of course, Father," she said, her heart racing at the thought that this would be the night her betrothal was announced. Everyone in the aristocracy would be present for the marchese's ball. He rarely entertained, but when he did, Montblanc spared no expense. There would a quintet playing the dancing music and a midnight supper, the food the finest in all of Catania.

She bobbed a curtsy and hurried off to her room to summon her lady's maid.

She couldn't help but feel giddy.

*E**arlier that morning, while Donald was being led to the parlor*
Armenia regarded her brother with narrowed eyes,

her hands on her hips and her bearing suggesting the conte was in for a scolding.

"How could you?" she asked in a low voice. "Did you think I would not discover what you've done? That Mancino would not tell me what he knew?"

Enrico audibly sighed and waved her into the parlor. "I wondered why you came home early," he said.

"I have ended the *affaire*," she said. "He has too many lovers in Naples. Younger lovers," she said, struggling to keep anger from sounding in her voice. She had known her liaisons with Conte Mancino in Taormina would someday end. She hadn't expected it to be so soon, though. The conte had been her lover for over a decade. "Besides, I wish to attend Montblanc's ball this evening." She inhaled and held the breath a moment, as if preparing for a battle. "Why did you sell the villa in Roma?"

Enrico made his displeasure with her evident. "I had to do it," he said, his voice tinged with anger. "I had no funds. No way to pay the bills," he added. "Would you rather live in the streets?"

"But why the villa in Roma? You could have sold *this*..." she said with contempt, spreading her arms to indicate House D'Avalos. "Roma is our *home*. Our heritage," she went on, tears streaming down her face.

Falling into the nearest chair, Enrico huffed. "There is no money here, Armenia. No one wants a two-hundred-and-fifty-year-old villa in the heart of Catania," he argued. "But in Roma..." He rubbed his thumb and forefinger together. "I have funds again. Money to last the rest of my life."

Her arms hugging her body, Armenia settled onto the velvet settee. "You're a bastard," she spat out. "You should have talked with me about it."

Enrico chuckled, his laugh sounding maniacal. "As it turns out, *I* am not the bastard."

Armenia stiffened. "What are you saying?" she asked, her gaze going to the worn Turkish carpet in an effort to control her anger.

"When I was in Roma, I found a copy of the English book about their noble families," he said. "I looked up Donald Slater and the Devonville marquessate."

Swallowing hard, his sister finally looked up. "Oh? And what did you discover?"

"What I think you knew all along," he accused. "That Mr. Slater is nothing more than a *mister*," he spat out. "And will never be a marquess. The boy is a *bastard*."

Determined she not cower in his presence, Armenia lifted her chin. "His father has always acknowledged him as his own," she countered. "You cannot hold those circumstances against him. He is a good man. He loves Nicoletta, and she loves him," she went on.

Enrico waved a hand dismissively. "Love, love," he chided. "My Nikky will not be marrying him," he stated.

Armenia's eyes rounded. "You won't," she said under her breath.

He gave a start. "I won't *what*?"

"Marry her to another."

"I will," he stated. "She is to marry Montblanc. No

later than the first day of spring," he claimed. "The betrothal will be announced this evening."

Knowing her anger might have her evicted from House D'Avalos, Armenia stood and was about to march out of the parlor when she paused. "Does *she* know that?"

Her brother lifted a shoulder in a careless shrug. "She will when she hears of it this evening."

For a moment, Armenia thought of what she could do for the young couple. Wondered if she could sneak Nicoletta out of the house and arrange for her and Donald to escape Catania. Put them on a ship headed north.

Practicality gave her pause, though. Where would they go? What would life be like for a couple on the run from an arranged marriage to a powerful marchese?

Could Donald even support a wife? If he could pay for Nicoletta's passage to England, what sort of life would she have there? Would his family accept her? Would they have a villa of their own? Servants?

Or would she be forced to live the life of a commoner?

Frustration had her fuming in silence before she finally let out a howl. Grabbing the nearest ceramic vase, she hurled it at her brother. He easily ducked the flying pot, but it impacted the edge of the fireplace and shattered. "You *bastard!*" she cried out.

The rest of Armenia's curses for her brother went unheard until she reached her bedchamber, at which point she let out another howl of desperation and sank onto her bed as the tears once again fell.

CHAPTER 11
A FAREWELL

The next day

Gray skies and an incessant drizzle only worsened Donald Slater's already poor mood. The thought that England at this time of the year would be the same or worse—it would be cold as well as rainy—didn't help his demeanor.

Only two months ago, he had decided his tour of the island of Sicily would be complete in a few days, and he had been looking forward to boarding a ship bound for England. Today, he stood beneath the archway leading into the courtyard of the House D'Avalos wishing he could stay in Catania for the rest of his life.

He probably could, except he would have to convince his father to continue funding his Grand Tour beyond the agreed-upon two years.

For the rest of this life, though?

Donald knew it would be impossible. Even if he

could find work as a clerk, he lacked command of the written version of Latin the Sicilians had adopted. Lacked a suitable character. Who would vouch for him?

Despite his despair, he chuckled. He could read and write Latin. He could read and write Greek. He had mastered his native language of English thanks to a diligent tutor and the instructors at Albion and Oxford. Never had he thought he might wish to live and work in the Kingdom of the Two Sicilies.

All because of her.

He almost regretted the day he had met Lady Nicoletta D'Avalos.

Almost.

She certainly had become the queen of his heart.

The queen or the devil.

At the moment, he wasn't quite sure which one she was. She had been that convincing and that frustrating. Because of what he'd learned the night before, he wasn't sure whether to be angry, relieved, or feel sorry for her.

He certainly felt pity although he was fairly sure he was feeling it on his own behalf.

*D*onald emerged from his reverie when the door to House D'Avalos suddenly swung open to reveal a breathless servant.

"*Buon pomeriggio.* Apologies, sir. Please come in from the rain." The butler waved an arm as he spoke, his head dipping as Donald handed him a calling card.

Closing his umbrella and doffing his top hat upon entry into the villa, Donald took a quick glance around. Although he had been to the house many times during the past two months—for the ball to which Nicoletta had invited him and for the many forays for which her father insisted he escort her—the courtyard beyond was no longer richly decorated, nor were any lanterns lit given the rain that continued to pour down.

"Is Lady Nicoletta in residence?" he asked, realizing the butler had spoken his greeting in English.

"She is expecting you, *signore*. I will take you to her," the servant replied.

The comment had Donald giving a start. He hadn't mentioned intending to pay a call when he had left the Montblanc ball the evening prior, but he felt a moment of elation at learning she expected him.

What did she think of what was about to happen to her? From her expression during the announcement of her betrothal—to the Marchese Montblanc—she had appeared as if she might faint.

Did the spoiled daughter of a Sicilian conte expect her English suitor to rescue her from her fate in the middle of a downpour?

Donald winced at his uncharitable thoughts of the young lady. He loved her. He wanted to marry her. She had said she wanted to marry him.

Surely none of this was her fault.

Donald followed the butler up the flight of black marble stairs and down the wide corridor to her small salon. Although he had at one time expected a lady's maid or other servant to act as a chaperone when he was in residence, he knew from his first time alone with Nicoletta that there would not be a servant present. Rather than allow him to go to her and extend his greetings, she rose from an ornate velvet settee and rushed into his arms, nearly knocking him from his feet.

"I feared I would never see you again," she murmured, her words muffled in the fabric of his top coat. The ring he had given her in the gardens in Taormina was still on her finger, the only piece of jewelry she was wearing on this day.

His heart clenching at hearing the relief in her voice, Donald felt his resolve weaken. He had come to say his farewell. To inform her his Grand Tour had come to an end. To gain her permission to write to her upon his return to England.

Instead, he wanted to strip her bare. Make love to her in one of the nearby guest bedchambers—there must have been twenty of them in the house—and pledge his undying love and devotion.

Ask her to elope.

And he would have if not for what he had learned the night before.

"I could not leave Catania without seeing you," he said as he cupped one of her cheeks with his hand. He wanted desperately to kiss her. To slide his lips over her berry-colored lips and down her cheeks and along her swan-like neck to her shoulder and down her arm to the hand that bore his betrothal ring.

The ring he had given her. Before he knew.

If he hadn't spent the blunt on it, he would have enough funds to spend another two months on the Continent.

His father had warned him, of course. Warned him that when he did find a woman he thought he loved, he would do foolish things. Say foolish things.

Be foolish.

I speak from experience, of course.

When Donald had pressed his father for more information, Will Slater had simply chuckled and reminded him it was why he had ended up choosing Lady Barbara Higgins—Donald's mother—as his bride.

Donald lifted Nicoletta's hand and rubbed his thumb over the small ruby, reminded of how difficult it had been to choose which gemstone to have the goldsmith place in the simple solitaire setting. "Thank you for wearing it today," he said.

"I will wear it always," she countered, her lips parting to say more before they began trembling. "So you *are* leaving?"

He closed his eyes and nodded. "I cannot stay. Not when I know what's about to happen," he replied. He could give her the other reason why he now knew they could never marry, but *he* didn't want to be the reason for their parting.

"Father likes you very much," she blurted.

Donald jerked his head straight up and wondered why she would say such a thing. "Apparently not enough," he said. "Your aunt has been especially good, though. It has been a pleasure to know her." Never had he known aristocrats to be so welcoming, especially toward a young man who could have easily put a chink in their plans for the only daughter of the conte. Yet Conte D'Avalos had not once denied Donald entrance to his home nor told Nicoletta she could not see him.

Certainly the conte knew of their *affaire*? Or at least had guessed they had become intimate over the course of the two months they had spent attending the same events. The afternoon liaisons spent at the ancient Roman theatre, where she had taught him how to kiss her the way she liked it. The carriage rides to the prince's grounds, where they would hide in foliage surrounding the labyrinth. She would guide his hand to her breast and then lift her skirt so that same hand could slide up her thigh and cup her mound. Rub her womanhood until her breaths ceased and she buried her head into his chest lest her cries of ecstasy be heard by anyone but him.

Until he had bedded her their first full day together, Donald was sure she had been with another man. How else did she know what to do if she hadn't already done it before? So he had been shocked to discover he was her first.

I have watched others make love, she had said, her eyes twinkling in delight when they had sipped limoncello next to a public garden.

Donald would happily marry her if he could. Although they had both been exhausted from the long coach ride from Taormina, they had been filled with excitement over the possibilities of their future together.

Until they learned they would not.

Could not.

I cannot give her in marriage twice, Conte D'Avalos said sadly, only an hour into the ball the evening before. *She is already betrothed.* At seeing Donald's look of shock, the conte had shrugged and added, *Worry not for her future, Signore Slater, for her husband-to-be is quite wealthy. If you would like, I could arrange a position in his household on your behalf.*

Perhaps the conte didn't care what his daughter did before marriage—or after. With her future secure, Donald supposed there was no reason for the man to care.

"Father says if you need the means to stay in Catania, he can arrange a position for you," Nicoletta said, tears blurring her eyes.

Donald gave a start. He had never once mentioned his depleted funds, nor implied he would stay if he had a position in Catania. "That's very kind of him—"

"He feels guilty," she blurted. "As he should." This last came out tinged with anger, as if she had realized her father had used her as a pawn. Used Donald as a pawn. A tear escaped the corner of her eye and rolled down her cheek.

Dipping his head, Donald didn't dare agree. Her father had no doubt made the arrangements for her betrothal long before Donald had met her. Perhaps when she was still in leading strings. That her future husband was old enough to be her father—maybe even her grandfather—was beside the point. The man was apparently in possession of a huge fortune, but he lacked an heir.

Had Nicoletta known she was betrothed when Donald had met her that first day at the maze, though? Had she latched onto him—given him her virtue—as a means of experiencing a relationship with a man closer to her own age knowing she would be stuck married to an older man for the rest of his life?

The thought had crossed Donald's mind more than once the night before. Still numb from his meeting with her father—he should have known the conte would discover his situation—Donald decided the conte would never have agreed to marry off his daughter to a bastard, even if Donald was the son of an heir to a marquessate.

Perhaps her betrothal to another was a blessing.

"I didn't know," she blurted.

He furrowed his brows. "Didn't know?" he repeated.

"I didn't know Father had already made arrangements with the marchese" she whispered. "Lord Montblanc is a widower, but he doesn't yet have an heir." Her words were broken up by quiet sobs. "They think I should be happy to be his marchesa. I only have to give him an heir, but... I don't care if I have a title. A coronet. It means nothing to me," she said as she struggled to take a breath.

Furrowing his brows, he realized she was telling the truth. "Nevertheless, you must abide his decision," he whispered. He kissed her forehead as he squeezed his eyes shut. "As must I."

Despite his father's warning, he'd had no idea how

much this would hurt. How much his chest would ache at the thought of never seeing her again.

"Where will you go?" she asked, tears streaming down her cheeks. "What will you do?"

Donald gave a start. "I'm going home," he replied simply, lifting a shoulder to emphasize the simple response. His gaze darted to the salon's only window. Beyond the glass, Mount Aetna was hidden by low clouds. He wondered if it was spouting steam as it had done so nearly every day he was in Catania, or if the incessant rain had drowned it.

What would he have done if he had never met Nicoletta D'Avalos?

He blinked. Unlike all the other places he had visited over the past two years, he had barely documented his time in Catania. Time with Nicoletta had filled his waking hours. She had consumed his thoughts. Except for their time in Taormina, she had kept him from his intended purpose.

A moment of clarity had him narrowing his eyes. He had spent two years exploring the lands he had studied at university. Spent several days at each location taking notes and drawing pictures of Greek and Roman ruins. Spent more time than he cared to remember negotiating travel and arranging lodging.

Surely someone else could benefit from his notes. From his experiences.

Suddenly the idea of taking a position in Oxford as a clerk or secretary held little appeal. Writing a book on his travels, however, seemed a logical next step in his life.

He could compile all his notes, improve his drawings, and find a publisher.

"I'm going to write a book. A travel guide," he stated, as much to himself as to Nicoletta. "For those who wish to go on their Grand Tour."

Her eyes rounded. "Oh," she murmured, sniffling softly.

For the first time, Donald noticed her tears, and he suddenly scoffed. "Apologies," he whispered, pulling a handkerchief from his pocket. He dabbed her cheeks with it.

Before she had claimed she didn't know about her betrothal, he had wondered if her tears were real. Thought perhaps she was putting on a show for his benefit. Now he saw her pain was real, and he chided himself that he would think she had merely used him. Kept him close until such time as she was forced to marry an older man.

She did have feelings for him, though. Her tears were real. Trembles wracked her entire body.

"He's an old man," Nicoletta whispered. "Armenia says I should not despair. That I will soon be a widow. Then I will be free to marry whom I please."

Donald once again furrowed his brows. "Oh?" After he had heard her father's words the night before, he hadn't considered there might be a future for the two of them.

When he didn't offer more in the way of a response, Nicoletta stood on tiptoes and kissed him on the corner of his mouth. "Will you wait for me?"

For a moment, Donald thought his heart might explode. The way it tightened and thumped had him lifting a fist to his chest to press it hard against his ribs. Deciding it was a sign—he really did love her—he nodded despite what it would mean for his immediate future. Did he really wish to relive the pain he would feel knowing she was with another man? Every day until the Marchese Montblanc died?

Would he have anything to live for if he *didn't* wait for her?

"Ten years," he whispered. "I'll wait ten years. No more."

Nicoletta embraced him, her grip around his shoulders forcing him to bend down slightly. "It will be less than that," she murmured. "I promise."

Donald scoffed softly. "How can you say for certain?" Montblanc was old, but he might live far longer than ten years.

"Because I cannot abide the thought of being with him any longer than that," she replied, angling her head back so she could make eye contact with him. "I'll run away if I must," she claimed.

"Nikky," he scolded softly.

"I love *you*," she whispered. "I don't care if you're a bastard or—"

"Who told you?" he interrupted, stepping back to regard her with furrowed brows. Although he had been tempted to explain his situation, he had never done so, deciding it would never matter.

She inhaled softly. "Armenia. She... she has a book

about the English peerage. She studies it whenever there is anyone here in Catania from England."

He swallowed. Hard. "How... how long have you known?"

Nicoletta shrugged one shoulder. "She told me a long time ago. A day or so after the first ball you attended," she replied.

Donald swallowed again, his heart once again pounding in his chest. "Your father... did the conte know back then as well?"

She shook her head. "I don't think Armenia would have told him." She shrugged again. "But it doesn't matter. Not to me."

Donald took a deep breath, raking his fingers through his sandy blond hair. He wondered if the situation might have been different had he admitted his status as an illegitimate son when he had first met the conte.

Or had the conte already arranged the betrothal before Donald had even arrived in Catania? And if he had, why had he encouraged Donald's involvement with Nicoletta?

Deciding it no longer mattered, Donald stepped out of her hold and dipped his head. "Be well, Nikky. If you'll allow it, I will write to you," he said as his throat thickened and breathing became difficult.

"Oh, please do," she replied, her words interrupted by a sob. "I shall write back. Ellsworth Park near Bampton, Oxfordshire, England," she recited. "I promise."

He couldn't help the painful chuckle that burbled up before he placed a kiss on her cheek and one on the back of her hand before he bowed and took his leave of House D'Avalos.

With a heavy heart and a nearly empty purse, he was on a ship bound for England later that night.

CHAPTER 12
A SHIP'S CAPTAIN
PROVIDES HOPE

A week later, on board The Fairweather, Port of Tangier, Morocco

Donald thought never to share his tale of woe with anyone but his father. The captain of *The Fairweather* pried it out of him, though, when the ship passed through the Strait of Gibraltar and docked in Tangier to take on cargo.

"You're going ashore, are you not?" Captain St. John asked Donald after most of his crew had set off from the sailing vessel. Warned they would need to be back on board by the time the cook served supper, the sailors had hastened their departure.

Leaning against the ship's railing, Donald regarded the captain with a dubious expression. "Is it safe?"

The captain guffawed. "You've just spent two years traveling all over Greece and the Kingdom of the Two Sicilies and you're asking me that?" he chided. Sobering, he said, "Safe enough if you keep your purse well hidden. Don't engage in gambling. Go on. It will give you an opportunity to get your land legs back."

"What about the language?"

"Know any Spanish or Portuguese?"

Donald gave a start. "Some," he admitted.

"French?"

Scoffing as if the captain had offended him, he said, "Of course."

"Then you'll do fine," St. John said. "Come. I'll point the way to the Medina. There's a souk—"

"Souk?"

"Shops. A marketplace. In the event you haven't bought your mother anything whilst on your trip."

His eyes widening at being reminded he would soon be seeing his mother, Donald rushed to the ramp. "Any suggestion on what I should get for her?" he asked, ignoring the captain's laughter.

"You can't go wrong with fine fabric," St. John said. "You'll find some exceptional wool and cottons. Silks. Thread. Jewelry, too."

The two set out up a narrow lane, the climb reminding Donald he hadn't walked much in the past week. His melancholy had him spending most of the days in his cabin writing notes about Catania while trying hard to forget the reason he had stayed as long as he had.

Nicoletta.

With every thought of her, he was reminded she would soon be married to the Marchese Montblanc.

If she wasn't already.

"See that gate?" St. John asked as he pointed to an arched opening in a wall. They were standing in an open square where a few costermongers were selling their wares. "Go through there. Careful in the alleys. Stay to the main streets, and if you think you're lost, just look for the water." He pointed north, where the Atlantic was close to meeting the Mediterranean.

"The view is spectacular from up here," Donald breathed.

"Be back at the ship by five o'clock."

"I will," Donald replied. "Aren't you coming?"

St. John gave him a quelling glance and hurried off the way they had come, leaving Donald displaying a reddened face. He should have guessed the captain would have a woman in Tangier. He probably had one in Valencia, too, for they had stopped there two days ago with the excuse of taking on cargo.

Donald set off, passing through the gate and into a world as foreign as the others he had visited during his Grand Tour. Doing his best not to be distracted by iron workers, butchers, and the stalls featuring brightly colored fruits, vegetables, olives, and dates, he soon found a crowded shop with roll upon roll of fabrics, the spools nearly as tall as he was. Off to one side, a woman worked a huge loom, passing a shuttle between parallel threads so quickly, the wooden device was almost invisible. Entranced, he would have stood watching the display for several minutes but for the tap on his sleeve.

He turned to discover a kaftan-garbed man regarding

him with curiosity. When he spoke, he did so in a language Donald didn't understand.

He shook his head, just then noticing a particular bright spool of fabric. The pink was a deep shade, and the sheen suggested it was silk. Even if his mother rarely attended a ball, she would look stunning in such a color. Pointing to it, he asked, "How much?"

"Anglais?"

Donald nodded and then sighed. He had forgotten to ask Captain St. John about currency. "I have a variety of coins," he said, reaching for his purse.

"You have come from England?"

"Going back to England, actually," he replied, surprised at hearing the man's command of English. From his mode of dress and the fez he wore on his head, he was most certainly a Moroccan.

"To London?"

Donald hesitated to reply. St. John had insisted he stay on board *The Fairweather* until they reached Wapping rather than get off at Southampton. The trip to Oxfordshire was certainly shorter from London. "Yes," he finally said.

"You go soon?"

"Tonight," Donald said. "On *The Fairweather.*"

The man's weathered face lit up in delight. "With Captain St. John?"

Donald couldn't hide his surprise. "Yes. Do you... do you have a message for him?"

"I have fabric that must go to London," he said. He gripped Donald's sleeve and pulled him toward the opposite corner of the shop. "These," he said, waving to four bolts of colorful silk that stood separate from the rest of his wares. "Already paid for, but no one to take them."

Thinking it rather odd someone would buy something but not arrange for its delivery, Donald asked, "Who are they for?"

The shopkeeper leaned over and lifted a tag that had been stitched to one corner of the fabric. His eyes rounded at seeing the words written in bold, block letters.

Ladyship A. Carlington
Marchioness of Morganfield
Park Lane
Mayfair, London, England

Donald chuckled. "That should say, 'The Most Honorable the Marchioness of Morganfield,'" he commented, pointing to the first line of the address. "And then 'Adeline Carlington'."

"You know this woman?" the man asked, his eyes round in wonder.

"I know *of* her," he replied. He had actually met the marchioness once, when he attended her garden party along with his grandparents and his parents during one of their rare visits to London. "My aunt is best friends with her daughter." Nicoletta was the marchioness' niece, but he wasn't about to mention her.

"You take this to her, and I give you this," the man said, pointing to the pink silk.

Scoffing, Donald wondered if the man was joking. "You would give me an entire bolt of silk just for delivering those four bolts to Lady Morganfield?"

The man nodded. "Is a good deal."

"How...? How did you even receive the order from her ladyship?" Donald asked.

"It is a gift."

"What?"

Shrugging, the shopkeeper said, "A lady was here..." He held up two fingers. "Weeks ago. Bought it and said to send it to her, but..." He held out his hands. "I have her money but no means."

Donald regarded the spools of fabric and experimentally lifted one. "They're heavy," he remarked.

"I will have my man carry them to your ship," he offered, waving an arm for a young boy to join him. He said something in Arabic and the boy ran off. "Are you in need of anything else?"

Glancing around, Donald asked about thread.

When the man returned to his side, he held a fabric bag. Inside was a spool of pink thread and yards and yards of gold soutache braiding. "For decoration," the shopkeeper said.

Donald offered the man some coins, mostly liras, but the man declined. "You do me a great service."

Thanking the shopkeeper, Donald turned to discover an old man standing at the front of the shop with a small donkey. The boy was already helping to load the bolts of fabric onto the sides of the beast, attaching them to the saddle. They had been wrapped in Dutch cloth for protection.

He was chuckling as they made their way out of the Medina and back to the port. He shrugged when Captain St. John watched the boy help to carry the bolts onto the ship and stow them in his cabin.

"Currying favor with your mother, I see," St. John said as the boy and the man with the donkey headed back toward town.

"Only one of those bolts is for my mother."

"Oh?" His look of confusion no doubt matched the one Donald had displayed when the shopkeeper had made his offer.

"The rest are for Lady Morganfield. I agreed to deliver them on her behalf," Donald explained.

"In exchange for...?"

Donald held open the bag he carried. "And the bolt of pink silk," he said, arching a brow.

The captain chuckled. "So now you're a courier," he commented.

"Was it a fair trade?"

Shrugging, St. John said, "More than fair, I should think, considering how much I would have charged him to put those in my hold."

Donald sniffed when he detected an unusual odor in the air. "Is that dinner?" he asked, his stomach growling.

"Indeed. Cook likes it here. Buys spices and such. We'll be enjoying one of his favorite meals before long,"

St. John said. He nodded in his passenger's direction. "Your mood is certainly improved."

Donald inhaled softly. "I have been a bit of a wet blanket," he admitted.

"You can tell me about it over dinner," St. John said, as several crew members returned to the ship. Some bore parcels while others came aboard wearing new tunics or leather shoes. "We're about to set out for Portugal."

After a particularly flavorful Moroccan meal of lamb, couscous, and vegetables accompanied by several pints of ale, Donald explained why his mood had been so blue since their departure from Catania.

The captain sat back in his chair and regarded his passenger with a rueful grin. "I'd bet a guinea your girl will give birth to an heir far sooner than she should," he said, crossing his muscled arms over his chest.

"What do you mean?" Donald asked, confusion evident on his face.

Chuckling softly, John St. John leaned forward and rested his elbows on the edge of the table. "You said you were sure her father must have known you two were lovers," he reminded him in a quiet voice. "He *wanted* you to be."

Donald stared at the older man for several moments before realization dawned. "You... you think he wanted her... with... with child?" He scoffed. "Before she married the marchese?"

St. John nodded. "Exactly. If the marchese is truly as

old as you're claiming he is, he probably can't do what he needs to do to get a child on her. D'Avalos knew you could, so…" He let the sentence trail off as he shrugged a beefy shoulder.

Donald stared at the captain for a long time before he asked, "What if she's not, though? With child, I mean?"

Shrugging again, St. John asked, "Did she ever have her monthly courses while you were with her?"

Sure his face was bright red, Donald shook his head. "Not that I… I know of," he stammered.

"Did you use a French letter when you were doing the deed?"

Donald swallowed. "No."

"Were you often intimate with her?"

His face still flaming with his embarrassment, Donald nodded. "Every other day or so," he finally admitted, not adding that it had been every day whilst they had been in Taormina.

St. John let out a guffaw. "Oh, to be a young buck again," he murmured, chuckling some more. He took a long draught from his mug of ale and set it on the worn wooden tabletop. "Congratulations, Slater. If all goes well, you could very well be a father in seven or eight months."

Donald stared at the captain for some time, finally blinking when the words penetrated his alcohol-addled brain. "The babe won't be recognized as mine, though," he said sadly.

"It sounds as if the marchese isn't long for this earth,

though," Captain St. John reminded him. "What's his name?"

"Uh, Ricardo Malgeri, Marchese—"

"*Montblanc?*" the captain interrupted in shock. He scoffed. "He's rich as Croesus," he claimed. "If her ladyship does indeed give birth to an heir, the boy will have a title and a good deal of wealth. Properties. Even a castle, I think," he went on. "Not a bad way to start life, especially for one from Catania. As for how he lives it after the marchese dies..." He shrugged once more. "That could be up to you."

Donald remembered what he had told Nicoletta.

Ten years. He would wait for her ten years.

"From your mouth to God's ears," Donald said, finally grinning at the thought of becoming a father.

His mood was considerably better for the rest of the trip to England—as long as he didn't think of Nicoletta sharing a bed with the Marchese Montblanc.

CHAPTER 13
MISERY BEGETS
A CONFESSION

*M*eanwhile, in the Prince of Biscari gardens, Catania

Staring at the clouds surrounding the peak of Mount Aetna, Nicoletta barely noticed how the afternoon breeze had chilled the air or how it had loosened a lock of her hair from its pins to leave it falling over one shoulder. She wasn't even aware of how long she had stood at the top of the Prince of Biscari gardens until the scuff of a boot had her giving a start. She whirled around and immediately dropped into a deep curtsy, her skirts gathering to form a silk puddle over her slippers.

"Lord Montblanc. My apologies," she murmured, her gaze directed on the pavement at her feet. "I did not know you were there."

A black leather-gloved finger came into view. Startled, she watched as the marchese reached out and barely touched her chin, urging her to lift her face.

When she did so, she found the elderly man regarding her with an expression of longing.

"I did not mean to disturb you, *mia bella*," he said, moving closer so he could offer his arm. "Lady Armenia said I would find you here."

Nicoletta hesitated but finally placed a gloved hand on his arm. "Was I supposed to meet you—?"

"No," he said, shaking his head. His thick wavy hair, once black, was entirely gray and blew about in the wind. For some reason, he appeared younger than he had during the night at the ball when their betrothal had been announced. The planes of his face weren't as sharp, his brows not as foreboding. Perhaps the light of day and fresh air helped in that regard. "But I do wish for your company. There are words I must speak to you. Explanations which need to be made," he stammered.

Regarding him with furrowed brows, Nicoletta finally gave him a nod and pointed to a bench in a nearby clearing. She did her best to stifle a sob as they made their way to the wrought iron seat, its design meant to accommodate two people if they sat close.

Having cried herself to sleep for the past several nights, her thoughts always on Donald and how forlorn he had appeared that last rainy day before he departed House D'Avalos, she knew the marchese would have noticed her puffy eyes and reddened nose.

She had given up hope Donald had changed his mind. Stayed in Catania to remain close to her despite the change in her circumstance. But word from the man in whose lodgings he had stayed and of those who worked at the dock confirmed he had boarded a sailing ship and had departed for England.

Montblanc waited for her to be seated before he carefully settled next to her. His cane, a length of carved ebony topped with a silver lion's head, rested over his lap, held in place with one gloved hand. His other he used to grip one of her hands, holding it so it rested atop his thigh.

She half-expected he would smell of disuse, of the odor so frequently associated with those who were old and infirm. Instead, she was surprised when she detected a hint of citrus and spice wafting past her nostrils. Although his skin appeared translucent where it was exposed, the dark veins beneath visible in the afternoon sun, he did not appear as old as she had first thought. From the shape of his cheekbones and nose, she knew he had at one time been a rather handsome man.

"I know you despair at what has happened," he said quietly.

Nicoletta inhaled softly and turned to look up at him. Although she had seen him about Catania on a number of occasions, it had always been from afar or during an entertainment. She couldn't recall ever being so close to him. Even when they had danced a waltz at his ball the week before, he had held her at arm's length.

"I do," she agreed, deciding she could admit why there were dark circles beneath her eyes and why she did not display her usual easy smile. "You probably think me foolish—"

"I do not," he interrupted.

She gasped. "You don't?"

He turned to regard her with a grimace. "I did not wish for it to be like this, *mia bella*, especially since I know how much it hurts to think you have lost someone you love. To have to give them up for..." Here he stopped and scoffed. "For the greater good."

Nicoletta furrowed a dark brow. "What... what are you saying?"

Inhaling deeply, which was accompanied by the faint sound of a wheeze, Montblanc dipped his head. "I once loved your mother with all of my heart," he said, his hand tightening on hers. "When she died giving birth to you, I cursed God and the heavens. I offered him all of my worldly goods and my fortune should she be allowed to come back to life. But, alas, it was not to be."

Her eyes rounding at hearing his confession, Nicoletta was quick to say, "It's a wonder my father still lives. You must have cursed him even more." She was sure he would have blamed D'Avalos for getting another child on her mother. Her older brother's birth had been hard on the comtessa, but she had survived and lived another five years before Nicoletta's fateful birth.

"Oh, I did. I still do," he admitted. "Every day."

Her gaze caught his, and she flinched at seeing the guilt in his eyes. She narrowed her own when he didn't look away. "And yet you are friends with him," she accused.

He shook his head. "Conte D'Avalos and I are mere acquaintances. Mostly from circumstance. Nothing more," he replied.

Nicoletta thought back to the day she had met Donald in these very gardens. How her father and the marchese had walked side by side through the labyrinth, their conversation kept so quiet, she couldn't hear a word they said as she followed behind. From their manner, she had thought them old friends. "Our marriage will change that, though, will it not?"

He nodded his agreement. "If it must."

Nicoletta furrowed her brows in confusion. "My lord—"

"Father," he interrupted, before letting out his breath in a *whoosh*.

Giving a start, she stared at him. "What?"

"*I* am your father. Your natural father," he said in a hoarse whisper, his gaze darting about as if he feared they would be overheard.

Nicoletta blinked several times, her mouth dropping open to put voice to a sound of protest. He raised a finger to press it against her lips and shook his head.

"Your mother and I were lovers. Long before she married D'Avalos and again after she had given him his heir. When she grew round with my child, I was... I was thrilled. We were so happy." He struggled to clear his throat as his eyes grew glassy.

Staring at him as if he had grown horns, Nicoletta held her breath before letting it out in a scoff. "How... how can you expect me to marry you if what you say is true?" she finally blurted. She had a thought to rise from the bench and race down the labyrinth to the street below. Run until she could no longer run. Given his age, he would not make it far in his pursuit of her.

As to where she would go...

"Because you carry a babe. My grandchild. My heir," he replied.

Nicoletta scoffed as she shook her head, the meaning of his words finally becoming clear. "What if... what if it's a girl?" she countered.

He lifted a bony shoulder in response. "She would still be my grandchild. I would give her... everything," he said. "You as well, of course."

"I cannot be your wife if I am truly your daughter," she argued.

"You cannot, it's true," he acknowledged. "On paper, and for the purposes of lineage and inheritance, you must be, though. Everyone must believe we are man and wife."

She glanced down at where his hand engulfed hers. Despite her initial revulsion at hearing his words, she began to understand why he had done what he had. "How?"

He gave her a wan smile. "We will live together in the castle. Come to town for the entertainments. Behave as if we are married," he explained. "Which, if you think about it, is much like the way a father and his daughter appear when they are together in public." He leaned down and kissed the side of her head as a means of demonstration. "I shall not take you to my bed, of course. You shall have your own rooms. Your own salon," he went on. "We shall dine together and speak of the child as if I am the father."

Nicoletta dipped her head at hearing the last, relief flooding her. The thought of sharing a bed with a man old enough to be her grandfather had been part of the reason she had spent the past few nights in a state of despair. "What of the servants? Won't they suspect the ruse?" she asked. Everyone knew servants shared the gossip from the households in which they worked. If only one housemaid mentioned her suspicion to a friend in town, word could spread to other households and end up reaching the ears of aristocrats eager for the latest *on-dit*.

"I intend to display my affection for you," he said, his words quiet. "Frequently. I have been unable to do so for nearly twenty years, so I have some making up to do in that regard."

Inhaling softly, she stared at him with uncertainty. "Affection?" she repeated softly.

He nodded. "I cannot tell you how many times I wished for you to know the truth. How many times I nearly sought you out," he said, a wistful expression youthening his features. "So that day here in the gardens, when I spotted you with Signore Slater, I realized how it could all work out. For the both of us," he explained. "For the two of you, eventually."

Nicoletta couldn't help the blush that colored her face. Having learned from her aunt, she had always been a consummate flirt. Something had been different that day when Donald Slater appeared, though. As if her heart knew something she didn't. "You knew that I would fall in love with him?" she questioned.

He chucked softly. "You looked exactly like your mother did the moment she met me the very first time," he said, his eyes once again glassy with tears. "My heart was no longer my own. Signore Slater's.... his was lost to you that day. I am sure of it."

Nicoletta stared at the older man for several seconds before she suddenly turned on the bench and wrapped her arms around his shoulders, her hands gripping the fine wool of his coat as she clung to him.

He kissed the top of her head as he held her. "I will give you everything you want, *mia bella*. Anything you need. You are my daughter, after all," he said, a wan grin appearing when she finally pulled away to regard him with tear-filled eyes. "I only ask that you remain with me until such time as I die."

Nicoletta winced at hearing the finality in his words. "And my child?"

"Shall have everything they need. Including a father, should you and Signore Slater decide to marry."

Gasping, she stared at the eyes she now realized matched her own. "You *wanted* him to get a child on me," she breathed.

"It was a necessity, yes," he agreed. "Better him then..." He waved his hand through the air as if to indicate any of the other aristocrats that might have shown her favor.

She glanced away for a moment. "Why him? Did

you arrange for him to be the one?" she asked in dismay. "Does he even know?"

He shook his head. "I did nothing but witness your first meeting with him," he claimed, "and although I rather doubt Signore Slater is even aware of his role in all of this, I will admit I could not have chosen better if I had."

"Even though he's a bastard?" she challenged.

"*Acknowledged* bastard," he countered, surprising her with what he knew. "I was actually thrilled to learn of his lineage. Did you know his great-grandfather was an admiral in the British Navy? That his father was a commander?" Montblanc paused when he noted her expression of surprise. "He comes from a family who understands the importance of service to Crown and country. They are not merely spoiled aristocrats, and I am hoping we will raise your son to be more like them than like... me," he stammered.

"Or D'Avalos," she murmured, her gaze on her mind's eye.

He gave her a wan grin. "So you understand?"

She nodded. "You know I'm going to tell Mr. Slater," she threatened. She had already written a short missive to him, telling him of her despair in discovering he had left Sicily. If he kept his promise, he would write back to her upon his arrival in Oxfordshire.

"I am counting on it," Montblanc responded. When she displayed another look of confusion, he added, "It is my hope he will one day return for you and take you to wife. Be a father to his child. Give you another, perhaps," he went on, his face brightening as he spoke the words. "I know there is a possibility my grandchild... *grandchildren* will end up in England, but they will have possession of all my lands on Aetna, and the villa here in town, and the castle," he went on. "I know it does not seem like it now, my sweet, beautiful daughter, but I do want you to be happy."

Nicoletta settled back against the bench and stared at the marchese for several seconds before finally nodding. "All right. If that is how it is to be, then I shall play along in your ruse." Her eyes suddenly rounded. "Am I allowed to tell my aunt?"

He shook his head. "Not yet, please," he murmured. "We cannot take the risk of exposure," he explained.

"And what of my father... D'Avalos?" she said, giving her head a shake when she realized she felt a good deal of relief at learning he wasn't really her father.

"The man you know as your father must remain so," Montblanc insisted. "I shall favor him with promises of a vineyard when I die. His greed will prevent him from guessing the true reason for my taking you to wife."

Nicoletta nodded her understanding and was about to stand when she paused. "When will we marry?"

He furrowed his gray brows. "It must be soon. The first day of spring?"

She nodded. "Armenia will help with the arrangements and invitations."

"Where would you like to go on our wedding trip?" he asked.

Nicoletta briefly thought of mentioning England but

thought better of it. "Roma," she finally replied. "We should go to Roma."

He nodded as he displayed a huge grin. "I have a villa there, as it turns out," he said. "One I believe you are already familiar with."

Her eyes widening with understanding, she scoffed. "Aunt Armenia was not happy with fath… with D'Avalos when he told her he had sold it to you," she murmured.

"Then after I die, you can give it to her," he replied. "It is unentailed, so I will be sure it is yours to do with as you please."

She blinked several times, shocked at hearing his cavalier comment. "She'll be forever grateful, as will I."

"Then… it is settled? You'll do this with me?" he asked in a hoarse whisper.

Nicoletta glanced towards Mount Aetna. "Ten years," she stated.

Montblanc blinked. "Ten years?" he repeated.

"I will play the role of your wife for ten years," she said. "Signore Slater has promised me he will wait for me for ten years. After that…" She shook her head.

The marchese chuckled softly. "Oh, *mia bella*, I rather doubt I will be alive for half of that," he said on a sigh.

Her eyes rounding when she realized he was speaking of his own mortality, Nicoletta finally nodded. "All right, then. What shall I call you? When we are in public?"

He considered the query a moment. "Montblanc when we are about town. Ricardo when we are in private," he said, wincing at this last. "I would prefer padre, but we dare not risk it."

Nicoletta nodded her understanding. "Perhaps you would be willing to escort me home... Ricardo? It will give you an opportunity to shower me with affection in public," she added, giving him a teasing grin.

He guffawed. "It would be my honor, my lady."

The two stood from the bench and Montblanc offered his arm. Glancing up at him with a brilliant smile, Nicoletta placed her hand on it and the two wound their way down the garden labyrinth to the streets below.

From all appearances, they made a very happy couple.

CHAPTER 14
A RETURN TO ENGLAND

our days later, London docks, Wapping, England

With a mix of excitement and dread, Donald arranged for a porter to load his luggage, a single trunk, and the bolts of fabric into a hackney. After he gave the driver his destination, the equipage set off for his grandfather's house in Park Lane. Given his abrupt departure from Sicily, Donald hadn't sent word ahead of his return to England.

Neither William Slater, Marquess of Devonville, nor his second marchioness, Cherice, were in residence at Devonville House when the hackney pulled up in front of the mansion. Located near the northeast corner of Hyde Park, it was one of the few residences along Park Lane that faced east, which meant its back gardens were practically in the park.

Expecting Hatfield to open the door—the ancient butler had been Devonville House's butler since before his aunt Hannah had moved out—Donald was surprised when a butler he did not recognize appeared and regarded him with an expression of curiosity.

"Is it Hatfield's day off?" Donald asked.

The servant stepped aside. "Mr. Hatfield has been pensioned, sir. I am Rosensburg. At your service."

"Oh," Donald replied, realizing it shouldn't be a surprise the old butler was no longer working. "Donald Slater," he said by way of introduction. "The marquess is my grandfather. I've uh... I've just returned—"

"From your Grand Tour," Rosenburg finished for him. "You were expected some time ago," he added, motioning for two footmen to bring in the luggage.

"I've been aboard a ship for the past fortnight, so I couldn't send word ahead, of course," he replied.

"The marquess and marchioness will be relieved to learn of your arrival when they return from Lady Morganfield's garden party."

"That's *today*?" Donald asked in surprise. Although he had only ever attended the popular early spring event one other time in his life, he remembered it fondly. He had been too young to flirt with any of the young ladies, but he had enjoyed watching the young bucks in attendance make fools of themselves.

"Should I have his lordship's phaeton brought 'round?" the butler asked. "I'm quite sure Lady Morganfield wouldn't mind an additional young man amongst the guests."

Remembering he had four bolts of fabric as well as a message from her sister and brother to deliver to Lady

Morganfield, Donald nodded. "That would be capital. I should change clothes, though," he said.

"I'll show you to your room. You may discover a top coat and waistcoat in the dressing room you left behind the last time you were in residence," Rosenburg offered. "They have both been brushed."

"I appreciate that. Has much changed in men's fashion in the past two years?" Donald asked, not having thought of making an appointment with a tailor whilst he was in London.

"The hems of top coats have dropped another inch or so, but I rather doubt anyone will notice, sir."

Donald chuckled. "Good to know. I'm sure I'll learn more at the garden party."

After taking the time to wash his face and change his clothes, Donald searched his valise for the envelope Lady Armenia had given him.

He regarded the feminine script and winced. Reminders of Nicoletta would plague him for a long time, he considered. If Captain St. John was right in his assessment of the situation, then he should expect to hear word from Nicoletta of her marriage and pregnancy within a few weeks. She had promised to write if he did so.

At first, Donald had decided he wouldn't, but after his conversation with the captain, his thoughts of Nicoletta had been far more charitable. As for who he might tell of his relationship with the aristocrat's daughter and future marchioness, he had already decided he would keep the details secret from his family.

Well, except for his father. He had to tell someone. Besides, he would be the one man who would understand.

With the letter for Lady Morganfield tucked into his waistcoat pocket, he was seated atop his grandfather's sporty yellow phaeton and heading south in Park Lane a half-hour later.

Four bolts of colorful silk fabric, wrapped in a Dutch cloth, were secured to the seat next to him.

CHAPTER 15
ATTENDING A
GARDEN PARTY

A half-hour later

Making his way through the French doors leading into the Morganfield gardens, Donald paused to gain his bearings and grinned when he realized nothing had changed since the last time he was there. The hedgerows were probably taller, which meant there were no doubt a number of young couples hidden behind them and engaging in all sorts of illicit activities. Other than that, the tulips were in bloom as were a bevy of young ladies clustered in groups of three or four, their bell-skirted gowns in varying shades of white, cream, pink, and pale blue. No young children dashed about as they had in the past, which meant Lady Morganfield's invitations had changed to preclude anyone younger than fifteen or so.

He surveyed the green wrought iron tables until he located the one at which Cherice, Marchioness of Devonville, was holding court. Across from her was the hostess of the event and his real reason for making the trip to Carlington House—Adeline, Marchioness of Morganfield.

Meanwhile, his grandfather was engaged in what appeared to be a serious discussion with David Carlington, Marquess of Morganfield, at the back of the gardens. He winced at seeing how gray both aristocrats had become since he had last seen them. Given Parliament would be convening that week, they were probably discussing politics.

A footman appeared at his elbow with a tray bearing glasses of champagne. Giving the servant a nod, he helped himself to one and made his way to stand behind Cherice. He winked at the startled Lady Morganfield before leaning down to kiss Cherice on the cheek. "How do, Grandmother?" he whispered as she gasped and turned to regard him with shock.

"Donald William Stephen Higgins Slater!" she said by way of a scold. She didn't even try to rise from her chair, but regarded him with a look of surprise coupled with delight.

"Oh, I am in trouble now," he said, a huge grin lighting his face as he nodded to the other ladies seated around the table.

"When *did* you get back to London?" she asked, pulling on his hand until he took the empty chair next to hers.

He pulled out his chronometer. "About two hours ago," he replied with a mischievous grin. He turned his attention on Adeline. "I do hope you don't mind an uninvited guest, my lady. I came bearing a gift of exotic fabrics for you."

The marchioness' expression took on a look of confusion. "Fabrics?" she repeated. "Whatever are you talking about?"

"A merchant in Tangier asked me if I might deliver them, and..." He lifted a shoulder. "Someone bought them as a gift for you. Your butler is having them brought into the house right now."

One of the matrons at the table leaned forward. "Silk? From China?" she guessed, obviously in awe. "Do you suppose it was Morganfield?" she asked, referring to Adeline's husband.

Adeline lifted her chin, a prim grin appearing to lighten her olive-toned complexion. "It's a mystery to me, but I assure you, I shall discover the truth before this day is over," she claimed.

"I have a message for you as well," Donald said, reaching into his waistcoat pocket to pull out the missive. "Lady Armenia and the Conte D'Avalos send their regards," he added, holding out the note to the startled marchioness.

Adeline regarded the missive as if it might explode. "You met my sister? And my brother?" she asked in awe, finally taking the note from him.

"I was a guest at House D'Avalos many times for the two months I was in Catania," he said. "They were quite welcoming." He managed to say the last without displaying a grimace. He knew it would be a long time before the bitterness he felt toward the conte would fade.

Adeline set the note next to her plate. "Then you must have met my niece, Nicoletta," she said, a dark brow arching suggestively.

Donald struggled to keep from wincing. The mention of her had his heart clenching so hard, he thought he would die. "I did indeed. She's a beautiful young lady. Unfortunately for me, she is betrothed to the Marchese Montblanc."

Adeline's eyes rounded. "That old fart?" she murmured. "Or... or did he finally have a son and die?"

The other ladies at the table tittered while Donald did his best to display an impassive expression. "He did not, my lady, which is why the conte has promised his daughter to him. They may already be wed by now." The words had his chest constricting even more. After two weeks aboard *The Fairweather*, he had thought his fondness for Nicoletta might fade.

Apparently not.

"I suppose I shouldn't have expected an invitation to the wedding," Adeline murmured. "Enrico knows how long it would take for me to make the travel arrangements, and I simply could not make a trip to... to Catania, did you say?"

"Yes, my lady. On Sicily."

Her eyes rounded slightly before she dipped her head.

"What is it, Adeline?" Cherice asked, concern evident in her voice.

The older matron lifted a shoulder. "My brother is usually in Roma this time of year. He rarely spends time at the villa in Catania," she said, turning her attention back to Donald. "Did you have a good tour?"

"I did, my lady," he acknowledged. "I took lots of notes, and completed a number of drawings. The Greek and Roman ruins were fascinating."

"I do hope you remembered to bring gifts for your mother," Cherice said, arching a brow.

"I have a bolt of silk for her, and I have a gift for you as well," he replied. Before he had taken his leave of the souk in Tangier, he had purchased a looking glass surrounded with a metal frame featuring decorative fretwork. He grinned when Cherice feigned surprise before he glanced around. "Forgive me," he said, "but might I be excused to tour the gardens?"

"Of course," Adeline replied, waving one hand in a shoo'ing motion. "You'll find a number of beautiful young ladies, but do be careful not to engage any of them in anything other than conversation," she warned. "I'd rather not have my garden party mentioned in this week's *The Tattler* for anything other than the guests in attendance," she added, referring to London's premiere gossip news-sheet.

"I wouldn't dare," he promised, bowing once he had stood from the table. "My ladies," he added, before turning to survey the grounds.

When he had taken several steps away from the table, he glanced back, not surprised to see Adeline popping the seal from the missive he had delivered.

Not having given a thought to its contents, he now wondered if he had been the bearer of bad news. It was obvious from her comment about Rome that his discovery of her brother, sister, and niece in Catania was unexpected.

He knew why—Nicoletta had said the villa in Rome had been sold. Something about the conte's efforts to consolidate.

Perhaps D'Avalos had been forced to sell.

Donald remembered the poor condition of the exterior of House D'Avalos. The lack of enough servants to staff such a large villa.

The elegant rot.

No wonder D'Avalos had agreed to marry off his daughter to the Marchese Montblanc. He probably couldn't afford her any longer.

Had the conte's comments about allowing his daughter to buy anything she wanted been all for show? The ball a last-ditch effort to gain a suitor for her? One who might forgo a dowry?

"For a moment, I thought I was seeing a ghost."

Donald gave a start, his attention going to the couple who was suddenly standing in front of him.

"Aunt Hannah. Uncle Henry?" he said in surprise.

"When did you return?" Hannah, Countess of Gisborn, asked as she stepped up and pulled him into an embrace. "I barely recognized you. You've grown taller."

"I arrived in England about two hours ago," he replied, shaking hands with his uncle. "What are *you* doing here in Mayfair?"

"Parliament starts tomorrow, and I thought to actually take my seat this year," Henry, Earl of Gisborn, replied. "You look as if you've spent a good deal of time in the sun."

"I have," Donald admitted. "So glad I was able to bring it with me," he added, waving to the golden orb that was providing warmth as well as sunshine to the afternoon's party. He glanced around. "Where is Grace?" His only female cousin would be about eight years old, he realized.

"We've left the boys and Grace in the care of your parents," Hannah said. She wound her arm through his elbow so she was between the two gentlemen and indicated they should head further into the gardens.

"What about the farm?" he asked.

"Your father is still the foreman," Henry said, referring to Will Slater. "I don't know what I'm going to do when he inherits and moves here to the capital," he added. "Although your grandfather looks rather hale and hearty, I have to face the fact that at some point, your father is going to be the Marquess of Devonville."

"Although I've grown up knowing it, I can't imagine him in the position," Donald murmured. "He's the least aristocratic man I know." Having been a captain and then a commander of a naval ship in his younger years, Will Slater had adapted to life on land upon his resignation from the British Navy. Donald knew he sometimes missed the water, which explained his occasional forays to the banks of the River Isis, where he kept a rowboat.

"We finished planting, so there's not much more I could do until the harvest," Henry commented.

"Everyone's in good health?" Donald asked.

"They are," Hannah replied. "What will you do now that you're back in England? Will you go home?"

Donald nodded. "I thought to. I'm not sure what else I would do, other than write of my tour."

"Build an orangery for me," Hannah said, tittering when Henry groaned and rolled his eyes.

"You still don't have one?" Donald asked, giving his uncle a look of surprise.

"I haven't had the time. Perhaps you could oversee construction while I'm here in the capital?"

"You're serious?"

"I am. It seems every harvest, Hannah's citrus trees are in harm's way when we have to use the greenhouses," he explained. "So I've arranged for a conservatory to be built on the northwest corner of Gisborn Hall."

"Which means I can start some lime trees in the greenhouses," Hannah teased.

"Sounds perfect," Donald remarked. "Anything else I can do?"

Henry exchanged a quick glance with Hannah. "Run my stables?"

From the manner in which his uncle made the query, Donald wondered if he was joking. "Run the stables?" he repeated.

"Handle the breeding. Oversee the grooms. You were always so good with the beasts," Henry commented. "That is, if you're not looking to take a position somewhere else?"

"I could run the stables," Donald replied. He had

always had a knack for breaking the two-year-olds and for keeping the draft horses in good shape for the planting and the harvest.

"So... you weren't looking to seek employment?" Hannah asked. "You would probably excel in a clerk's position, but I cannot imagine you working indoors."

"You are right, Aunt. I do not believe I could abide being inside all day." He considered what he intended to do regarding his notes and drawings from his trip. Assembling them into a book was a project he could do during the afternoons and evenings. "When do I start?"

Henry chuckled. "As soon as you're back home." When Hannah cleared her throat and gave him a pointed glance, he added, "Oh, and if you'd like, the dowager cottage is available. You can move in whenever you'd like. Comes with the position."

Donald's eyes rounded. "My own home?" he asked in awe. "But... what about Nathaniel?" he asked, referring to Henry's oldest son. "Isn't he living there?" A recent graduate of Oxford, the young man had taken up residence in the dowager cottage the year before Donald had departed for his Grand Tour, intent on completing a thesis. Like Donald, he was illegitimate, his mother a former mistress of Henry's.

"Nathaniel married a girl in Oxford last year," Hannah said. "He lives there now. Oversees a college library."

"Nathaniel? Married?" Donald asked in disbelief.

"Surprised us, too," Hannah said. "But she's a lovely girl from a very good family—"

"Father is a professor at one of the colleges—"

"—and she's expecting their first child later this year," Hannah finished with a grin of delight.

Donald chuckled softly. He had always known Nathaniel would choose a life outside of the aristocracy. His mother had raised him to expect to work for his living even if his father intended to provide him an allowance.

"You're really all right with me moving into the cottage?" he asked as they stood before a colorful array of tulips.

"At least until Hannah needs it," Henry replied, which had his countess giving him a quelling glance.

"You have yourself a deal, Uncle," Donald said.

For the rest of the afternoon, he felt far lighter than he had in weeks. Even if he had to wait for Nicoletta for ten years, at least he'd be doing something he enjoyed in the meantime.

*M*eanwhile, back at the matron's table

Claiming she needed to speak with the cook, Adeline, Countess of Morganfield, made her excuses and hurried into Carlington House. Standing next to the French doors for the afternoon light they provided, she unfolded her sister's missive and read the feminine Latin script.

My dear Adeline,

I do hope you and Morganfield are well and enjoying an early spring. I expect you are preparing for your garden party and another Season in London.

The bearer of this missive has been a most welcome guest of late. It pains me that Mr. Slater must take his leave. You see, I was sure he and Nikky might marry—she accepted his offer whilst we were on holiday in Taormina—even if he is not scheduled to inherit a position of note. However, our brother has once again been plotting behind our backs.

He has made arrangements for Nikky to wed Montblanc. As the marchese is a rather ancient man, I doubt it will be a long marriage. Our niece will be set for life, though, given his fortune.

In order to provide a dowry, Enrico has sold the villa in Roma with the excuse he wishes to "consolidate" the D'Avalos holdings. I have not asked who bought it, but it would not surprise me if that property has been added to Montblanc's holdings.

We are down to the villa in Catania and some farmlands at the base of Aetna. At least we are welcome here. Although there are not many of us in town, I am allowed to host one ball a year, although not on the scale of those I once hosted in Roma.

Please do not feel as if we have left you out when it comes to the guest list for the wedding. I expect it shall be a small affair—perhaps only the four of us and some other aristocrats on the first day of spring.

I look forward to your next letter. Do give my

*regards to your husband and to Elizabeth, and I give
you permission to share this news with her.*

Your loving sister,

Armenia

*Post scriptum: Our brother's guilt had him placing
an order for some fine fabrics for your birthday, but I
know not from where or how he intends for them to
reach you. Knowing him, he did not pay enough for
their delivery. If I sound spiteful, know that it is
because I am. A.*

Tears blurring her ability to read the last line of the letter, Adeline sniffled and quickly pulled a hanky from her pocket.

The house she had grown up in now belonged to someone else.

She glanced out the French doors, her gaze taking in the sight of Donald Slater with his aunt and uncle.

She had wondered at his guarded manner whilst at the table, and now she understood why. Most young men who returned from their Grand Tours seemed happy to be home. Donald merely seemed resigned to it.

His heart was obviously somewhere else.

With someone else.

Wiping her cheeks, Adeline realized she would soon be missed if she didn't return to her place at the matron's table. She quickly refolded the missive and stuffed it into her pocket. Straightening her back and pasting a pleasant expression on her face, she rejoined her friends.

"What news from your sister?" Cherice asked once

another glass of champagne had been set in front of her. She had guessed correctly Adeline's real reason for going into the house.

"My niece is getting married," Adeline replied, feigning happiness. She swallowed a sob. "Today, in fact," she added, remembering it was the first day of spring.

The ladies around the table coo'd their delight and turned their conversation to the likely matches in that year's Marriage Mart.

Donald Slater's name was not mentioned as a possible groom.

CHAPTER 16
A HOMECOMING

week later

Although he would have been fine with riding the Royal Mail coach to Bampton in Oxfordshire, Donald was secretly glad his grandfather insisted he be driven home in the Devonville traveling coach.

The springs were fairly new, which helped make the trek more comfortable, as did the macadam covering the surface of the road. Despite the recent rains, the trip was smooth.

When the coach slowed, Donald looked up from one of his notebooks and glanced out to discover they were pulling into the Trout Inn. Located on the River Isis, the coaching inn promised a change of horses and a good meal—the last before his arrival on Gisborn lands and his boyhood home of Ellsworth Park.

He pulled his purse from his waistcoat pocket, relieved to find he had more than enough coins to buy an ale and some food. Earlier, he had discovered there were even some five-pound notes stuffed into the leather pouch.

Cherice had no doubt refilled it prior to his departure from Devonville House. Or perhaps his grandfather had.

The week spent in their company had been a balm for his aching heart as well as a boon to his stomach. Although he had inherited his father's height and broad shoulders, he had grown far too lean whilst on his Grand Tour.

Stepping down from the equipage, he surveyed the grounds, not surprised to discover nothing much had changed in the two years since he had last been there. Located only a few miles from Gisborn Hall and Ellsworth Park, the nearby bridge over the river was the closest river crossing to the farms.

His gaze still on the trees lining the slow-moving water, Donald didn't notice a man approaching him from the inn.

"For a moment, I feared you were my father," Will Slater said, his steps growing more hurried the closer he drew to his son. He pointed to the coach bearing the crest of the Marquess of Devonville.

"Father?" Donald said in surprise.

Will Slater engulfed him with his larger arms, pulling him into a boisterous hug and nearly lifting him from his feet. "We've been worried sick about you."

"Father," Donald managed to say when he was finally standing of his own accord. "You look well."

"That's because I am. You, on the other hand, look as

if you could use a meal or two." He waved toward the inn and then paused to speak with the driver of the coach.

"Good to see you, Parker," he said when the servant acknowledged him with a bow. "My horse is around back. If you could see to tethering it to the coach, I'll ride the rest of the way with you."

"Very good, my lord," Parker acknowledged with a nod.

"Oh, and get something to eat. We may be a while," Will added, waving to the inn. He handed several coins to the driver and turned back to his son. "Unless you're in a hurry to get home?"

Donald shook his head. "I fear my stomach will disown me if I don't eat something," he said, matching his father's strides as they headed in the direction of the inn.

"What news from London?" Will asked when they finally made their way toward the coaching inn's front door. "Other than what Cherice might have included in the letter that arrived yesterday?" he added. Although he liked his father's second wife, he didn't know her well, the two having wed while he was still a commander in the navy. "She mentioned seeing Henry and Hannah at the garden party and that you were there."

Explaining the arrangement he had made with his uncle regarding the orangery and the horses, Donald watched for his father's reaction, expecting he might put voice to a protest. When he did not, he added, "You're not surprised."

Will shrugged. "Henry and I have been talking about it for some time. With Nathaniel having flown the coop—"

"I can't believe he's married," Donald commented.

"—and since he claims his other sons are too young, you're the logical choice to move into the cottage," Will finished.

"I appreciate the vote of support," Donald said as they entered the public room.

They received a hearty welcome from the man at the tap. "Back again so soon?"

Will indicated Donald. "Look who's returned from his Grand Tour."

Ales were poured and a board of meats and cheeses was set before them as they took a seat at a wooden trestle.

"I half-expected you to arrive with an Italian girl on your arm," Will said when the server was finished and had stepped away.

Donald gave a start. "I wish I could have brought her." When he noticed his father's arched brow, he added, "She's been promised to another. Probably already wed to him."

Will straightened in his chair and crossed his arms over his broad chest. "Him who?"

Sighing, Donald said, "The Marchese Montblanc."

Rolling his eyes, Will leaned forward and lowered his

voice. "Although she's never met her, your Aunt Hannah thinks the girl you wrote about is related to one of her friends from finishing school. A cousin of Lady Bostwick's, she said."

Donald nodded. "Lady Nicoletta D'Avalos is the niece of Lady Morganfield," he confirmed. "I delivered a note on her aunt Lady Armenia's behalf to the marchioness when I attended her garden party last week."

A low whistle sounded from his father. "So... are you relieved or—?"

"Dismayed. Angry. I still feel as if I've been punched in the gut," Donald ground out, before stuffing a hunk of cheese into his mouth.

Will showed a grimace. "So... you *were* in love with her."

"Still am," Donald managed before he ate some ham. He swallowed and glanced around the room before leaning over the edge of the table. "I believe I have been... poorly used."

Furrowing his brows, Will said, "You think she was leading you on?"

"Not her. She would marry me right now if she could," Donald claimed. When he noticed his father's expression of confusion, he added, "Her father encouraged our courtship. Made sure we spent a good deal of time together. *Alone.*" Wincing, he finally added, "I think because he wanted to be sure I got a child on her. The marchese is old. Maybe too old to... to father a babe."

Will stared at his son, his face unreadable in the dim light of the public room. "Did you?"

Donald shrugged. "I… I honestly don't know."

"Did you lie with her?"

"I did," he admitted. "Several times. Many times," he corrected sheepishly, before his father could ask.

Dropping his head into his hands, Will took a deep breath, as if he was doing everything he could to keep from scolding his son.

"I understand now what it was like for you and Mother," Donald said softly.

"But I left your mother having given a promise of marriage when I returned, and I had no knowledge I'd left her with child," Will argued.

"I didn't even suspect I had until the captain of *The Fairweather* mentioned it was a possibility," Donald admitted.

"*The Fairweather*?" Will repeated, his brows rising in surprise as he lifted his head.

"The ship I took from Rome to London," he explained.

"You spoke with St. John." Will once again straightened in his chair.

"You know him?" Donald asked, his eyes widening in surprise.

Will scoffed. "St. John's been running that barnacle bed since before I was captaining the *Greenwich*," he claimed. "Leave it to him to be the one to suggest you might have left a bastard behind."

"He won't be a bastard, though," Donald said. "Or

she," he added in a whisper. He hadn't even given a thought to the sex of the baby. "If it's a boy, he'll be heir to a marchesato."

"And if Montblanc is truly old…"

"He is positively ancient, Father. Older than Hatfield, I think," Donald claimed.

Will angled his head to one side. "So, not long for this earth," he whispered.

"I told her I would wait for her as long as ten years. If he dies before then, I'll go collect her or—"

"*We* will go collect her," his father said firmly. "And the child." When he noted Donald's look of shock, he added, "If you think I'm going to let you go back to Sicily by yourself—"

"I would come back to England, Father," Donald assured him.

Finally nodding, Will seemed to settle before he said, "You cannot tell your mother about this. In fact, you cannot tell anyone." His eyes rounded. "You didn't tell Cherice, I hope," he added. His stepmother would surely share the news in every Mayfair parlor she visited, although she would manage to make it sound more positive than it was.

"I know better than that, Father," Donald replied. Although it would have been easy to claim he had fallen in love with an Italian woman, he knew his grandmother would have done everything in her power to find him an English bride. Despite her friendship with Lady Morganfield, Cherice would not easily welcome a

European into the family, even given Donald's inability to inherit a title.

Right now, an English bride was the very last thing he wanted. And he had made sure his grandfather and Cherice knew it before he had left London with the comment, "My Grand Tour has taught me I should not be in search of a wife until I am near thirty years of age."

"You mentioned the orangery," Will stated.

Donald gave a start, surprised by the change of topic. "Aunt Hannah said she's been asking for one for years."

"It's almost finished," Will said with a smirk.

"Already?"

His father shrugged. "I might have employed a few of the locals to help," he admitted. "Henry left me with some blunt, and I thought to spread it around a bit."

"Is there anything left for me to do?"

Will gave him a smirk. "The roof." His expression turned into a full grin as he watched his son's grimace show. "And then we'll have to move all the orange and lemon trees from the greenhouses into it."

"So Aunt Hannah can start growing lime trees in the greenhouses," Donald remarked.

"Lime trees?" his father repeated. He scoffed. "Does Henry know?"

Donald smirked. "Oh, he knows. He was standing right next to her when she mentioned it."

The two were practically laughing when they took their leave of the Trout Inn. On the road to Bampton, they intercepted the Royal Mail coach, where the driver handed off a number of missives addressed to the residents of Ellsworth Park and Gisborn Hall.

Donald's amusement abated when his father handed him a note written in a feminine script. The multiple markings on the outside showed it had passed through several hands on its way to England, although the wax seal was still intact.

"That from her?" Will asked, his attention on another missive.

Donald popped the wax seal and unfolded the letter, his gaze going to the bottom. "It is," he said in a hoarse whisper.

Although the words were written in a form of Italian that was mostly Latin, Donald struggled to make sense of what Nicoletta had written. When he finished reading it a second time, heartened to discover it included an address he could use to write to her, he lifted his head and stared at his father.

"What is it?" he asked from the other side of the coach.

"My child is a Montblanc," he stated.

"So... she is with child?"

"Mine, yes," Donald acknowledged, his heart pounding in his chest.

Will frowned. "Well, he—or she—will be considered a Montblanc due to the fact she'll be married to him," he reasoned.

Donald shook his head. "She's not. She won't be. Because she already is," he blurted in his excitement.

Confused, Will set aside the letter he had been

holding and stared at his son. "Already is... what?" he asked.

"A Montblanc," Donald replied. "Nikky is Montblanc's daughter. A secret daughter, apparently. Their marriage is merely a ruse. A means for the marchese to have a true blood heir."

Will stared at his son for several seconds before he scoffed. "Did *she* know she was his daughter?" he asked. "Before all this?"

Donald shook his head. "She didn't. And no one else knows. Her mother died giving birth to her." His eyes suddenly rounded. "No one *can* know," he stated suddenly.

Acknowledging the words with a nod, Will glanced out the window of the coach to see they were turning into the drive in front of Ellsworth Park. "Then we won't speak of it again," he said. "At least, not until we've learned the marchese has died," he added.

Grinning in delight, Donald began chuckling. "She's going to be my wife," he said happily, waving the letter. He suddenly sobered when he saw his father's expression. "What?"

"You have to keep this from your mother," he warned. "She finds out you have a son or daughter out there in the world... a potential wife..." He let the sentence trial off as he shook his head.

Donald nodded his understanding. "I won't say a word."

· · ·

*L*ater that night

Moved into the dowager cottage and settled in front of a small desk lit with a candle lamp, Donald opened a bottle of ink and penned a long letter to Nicoletta. Although he acknowledged her good news with congratulations, he made sure to be vague as to her relationship with the marchese in the event someone read the letter before it reached her.

He did mention the ten years, though, and how he looked forward to their reunion then, if not before. He also provided his address at the dowager cottage, deciding it best her letters be delivered there instead of at Ellsworth Park.

He didn't wish to risk his mother learning about Nicoletta.

PART II
HOME

CHAPTER 17
A RAINY MORNING
IN OXFORDSHIRE

Six years later, August, 1839 near Bampton, Oxfordshire

As rain fell in sheets in the early morning hours of what should have been the last day of the harvest, Barbara Higgins Slater, Countess of Bellingham, stared out the window of her small salon and winced when she finally spotted her husband. Will Slater, Earl of Bellingham, had spent the predawn hours—when it hadn't been raining—helping his brother-in-law bring in the wheat. Their work in the fields adjacent to the River Isis now complete, Will was soaked to the skin. His white shirt was plastered to his muscled chest and large arms, and water sluiced from his hair and face.

Watching him as he made his way from the Gisborn estate across the farmland behind their manor house, Barbara felt an unexpected frisson deep in her belly. How it was the former naval commander could still have such a profound effect on her even after twenty years of marriage baffled her. But then, she had been attracted to him since the moment she had met him at her come-out ball in London.

Back then, he had already secured a commission in the British Navy. His grandfather had been an admiral in the King's Navy, his uncle a commander, and despite his status as heir to the Devonville marquessate, Will had begged his father he be allowed to serve in the navy.

Water appealed to the Slaters. Will's younger brother, Stephen, had enlisted in the navy, joining about the same time as Will. A bastard son of William Slater, Marquess of Devonville, Stephen had been assigned to the same ship as Will—the *HMS Greenwich*—for their final few years of service in the Mediterranean.

When another frisson interrupted her reverie, Barbara gave a start. Will was already making his way through the gardens and was nearly to the back door. At any moment, he would enter the kitchens, soaked to the skin, and Mrs. Maybury, the cook, would no doubt raise a fuss over him dripping water on the floor.

Despite his title and the ease in which he could fire Mrs. Maybury for her treatment of him, Will allowed her to scold him. With his own mother dead for over three decades, he didn't mind that Mrs. Maybury treated him like the son she never had.

Barbara rushed from the salon and into the nearest bathing chamber. Grabbing several bath linens, she made her way down the Aubusson-carpeted stairs and through the manor house to the kitchens.

Mrs. Maybury looked up in alarm from a bowl in

which she had been frantically stirring. "My lady?" she queried, obviously surprised at seeing the mistress of the house up and about so early in the morning. The sun was barely lighting the eastern sky, although given the rain, it would likely remain hidden all day. "I won't have breakfast ready for at least another hour, ma'am."

"Oh, don't mind me," Barbara replied. "And you might wish to turn your attentions elsewhere," she warned, knowing what she intended to do once Will entered the kitchens.

Not only provide him with the means to dry off but to kiss him senseless.

She only hoped he might be of a mind to accept such displays of affection.

"Yes, my lady," Mrs. Maybury replied, a knowing grin touching her lips as she moved her bowl to another counter and continued her aggressive stirring.

The back door burst open, and Will, breathless, entered and slammed it shut, his move helped by the gusty wind accompanying his arrival.

Barbara was before him in an instant, covering his head with a linen and wiping his face with another.

Chuckling, Will used one hand to rub the linen over his head and through his dripping hair and the other hand to grasp her hip. He dipped his head, and when the bath linen she was using to dry his face dropped away, he leaned down and kissed her thoroughly.

"What are you doing up so early?" he asked when she could no longer stand on her tiptoes.

"Waiting for you," she replied, breathless.

Will's attention briefly darted to the cook. "Is everything all right?" he asked, his brows furrowing with worry.

"Quite. But it would be much better if we rid you of these wet clothes," she whispered. "Otherwise, you'll catch your death."

He grinned, understanding her unspoken invitation. "I'm starving," he replied, arching one of his dark blonde brows. A piece of toast was thrust into his hand, courtesy of Mrs. Maybury, and he turned his attention on the cook. "Much obliged," he said as he took a bite. He placed his free hand on Barbara's elbow and led her from the kitchens.

When they were halfway up the stairs, he glanced over at her. "How long have you been awake?"

She shrugged. "Since you left the bed, I suppose."

"I didn't mean to wake you," he said, his voice sounding his apology.

"I didn't mind, although I did miss the warmth you provided."

"Is anything wrong?" He paused on the stairs.

She shook her head. "No, but I find I am in need of you," she whispered, her face reddening with her admission.

Will allowed a wry grin. "Your bedchamber or mine?" he countered.

"I don't care if it's the *library*," she whispered hoarsely.

Blinking, Will resumed the climb to the second floor, his steps much quicker. By the time they hit the landing, he was moving at a near run, chuckling as they crashed through the master suite door and into the dark bedchamber.

Before he undressed, he pulled Barbara against the front of his body and kissed her hard.

She pulled away with a sound of protest. "You're soaking wet," she complained.

"You must be as well," he teased, one of his brows waggling.

"You won't find out until you get this damned gown off of me," she replied in a huff.

Noting she wore a drab day gown, Will grabbed the edges at the top of the back with his fists and pulled them apart.

Barbara gasped as buttons scattered about on the carpet below and yards of fabric suddenly passed before her eyes. "Will!" she scolded. "My lady's maid will have a fit."

"So be it," he replied, his expression of determination turning into a grin. Even before the gown had completely fallen to the floor, he had the ties to her petticoats undone and her corset loosened.

Attempting to help with the divestiture of his clothing, Barbara undid the tie at the top of his shirt and the buttons that secured his trousers. "Don't bother with the stockings," she murmured.

"Yours or mine?"

She tittered. "Does it matter?"

He kissed her forehead. "Are you sure everything is all right?" His shirt, still wet, sent a spray of water droplets in all directions as it passed over his head and landed in a literal puddle on the Turkish carpet below. He leaned down to pull his boots from his feet.

Pulling her corset over her head, Barbara regarded him with a look of impatience. "I think so," she replied. "Although your son has mentioned a matter to which I'm not sure how to respond."

Will paused in pushing down his trousers and smalls. "Which son?"

Barbara winced. "We don't have to discuss it *now*," she whined.

Chuckling, Will lifted her onto the bed and followed her down until he was hovering over her. "During breakfast then," he murmured. Although he'd been soaked with sweat in his haste to complete the final pass of harvesting, the rain from the thunderstorm had since washed it away. His skin was left damp with the scent of rain mixed with man. He licked a few crumbs of toast from his lips as he stared at her.

"Why did you stop?" she asked, her knees bent and spread wide.

Will's eyes darkened as a mischievous grin appeared on his lips. "How long until breakfast?"

"About an hour."

Barbara let out an exclamation of surprise when he was no longer over her but sliding down her body until his head was between her thighs. "Oh!" she breathed, knowing full well what he intended to do.

Although she had never visited the capital city of the

Kingdom of the Two Sicilies, she knew how to read Latin and she knew about the Roman arts.

She inhaled sharply when Will's tongue laved over her womanhood. Gasped again when his lips took possession. Cried out when he suckled her. And nearly screamed when his tongue once again passed over the swollen nub several times. "Will!" she admonished him, struggling despite his hold on her hips.

She heard him chuckle as he moved up her body, his lips leaving a trail of kisses on her belly and under her breasts. He entered her in one hard thrust, his groan of satisfaction filling the bedchamber.

Still reeling from what he had done to her with his tongue, Barbara gripped his sides with her hands and held on as he drove into her over and over.

His release had his body seizing, his head thrown back as his muscled arms strained to hold him up. He remained suspended over her for what seemed like several minutes before his body gave up its tenseness.

When he finally collapsed atop her, Barbara was ready. She guided his head into the space between her shoulder and neck as she lowered her feet to the bed.

"I love you," he whispered before his body went limp.

Barbara allowed a wan grin, not bothering to say anything in response.

She knew he wouldn't hear it.

CHAPTER 18
A FARMER'S WORK
IS NEVER DONE

*M*eanwhile, next door, Gisborn Hall, near Bampton, Oxfordshire

As her lady's maid brushed her hair, Hannah Slater Forster, Countess of Gisborn, watched out her bedchamber window for signs of her husband and their three youngest sons. At times, the rain pelting the glass made it impossible to see the farm fields to the west and the Ellsworth Park manor home that fronted them. It was nearly as hard to tell if the gray gloom had lightened since Lily had appeared. According to the Old Chelsea clock on the mantel, it should have been early dawn.

"I canna' believe his lordship is out in that awful weather," Lily remarked as she gathered Hannah's pale blonde hair into a ribbon tie before twisting it into a bun.

"They're *all* out there," Hannah replied, her brow furrowing with worry.

"Bill brought the horses in a few minutes ago," the

lady's maid said, referring to her husband. "Said Donald would see to it they was brushed later today. Everyone is soaked to the skin now, but they got the wheat under cover 'afore this latest rain started."

"That's a relief," Hannah murmured. She winced when a hairpin scraped her scalp. "Did you notice if Grace was up yet?" she asked, referring to her only daughter. At thirteen years of age, Grace behaved more like a tomboy than her fairy princess appearance would suggest. Having four brothers, three of them older than her, was her excuse.

Lily scoffed. "Lady Grace is out there with the boys," she replied, stabbing another pin into Hannah's bun.

Hannah swiveled around on her dressing table chair. "No," she said in protest.

"She goes where George goes these days," Lily claimed, referring to her mistress' youngest son.

"Oh, I hope she grows out of it, and soon," Hannah whispered. "No one in London would believe I am the mother of a hoyden."

Chuckling, Lily finished securing the last pin in place. "I'm done, my lady. If you'd like, I'll see to a stack of bath linens for when the boys return to the house."

"Please do. I'll be down in a minute."

Hannah watched the reflection of her lady's maid hurry out the bedchamber door before she stood and made her way through the dressing room and into the master bedchamber. She rushed to the room's south windows, pulling back the dark velvet drapes.

Stretched out below and to the south were two large

greenhouses. Despite the rain, their translucent glass ceilings made it possible to see their contents.

This time of the year, the middle of both buildings would normally be taken up with trestles covered with pots of tomatoes and flats of herbs and vegetables. The perimeters were lined with young orange and lemon trees.

The older citrus trees were secure in the orangery on the northwest end of Gisborn Hall, the building completed shortly after her oldest nephew, Donald, had returned from his Grand Tour.

A grimace crossed Hannah's face as she watched the trestles being moved to the sides. Uncovered carts laden with part of the wheat harvest were pushed in to take their place. She angled her head toward the west to see several more carts, all covered with tarps, lined up along the side of one of the greenhouses. Several tenant farmers as well as Henry and the boys were pulling another covered wagon into place, all of the laborers soaked to the skin from the rain.

In the middle of it all was Grace, evident because her braided blonde hair was uncovered while all the males wore hats.

When several men—all of them Gisborn tenant farmers—shook hands with her Henry, Hannah knew their work was done. She watched as they headed off for their nearby cottages or for Bampton and the remaining figures gathered outside the kitchen door.

She hoped Mrs. Ainsley had breakfast ready.

Heading down the carpeted stairs to the ground floor

of Gisborn Hall, Hannah managed to appear in the kitchens as the last of her family made it through the door, their arrival bringing with it a gust of warm, wet air and an irate scolding from the cook.

"Apologies, Mrs. Ainsley," Randy said. He removed his sodden hat and offered it to Lily, who gave him a bath linen in exchange. "Much obliged." He rubbed the linen over his face and neck before removing his coat and boots.

Meanwhile, the others did the same, their claims of hunger and thirst resulting in Mrs. Ainsley's loud, "Breakfast will be on the table in a quarter-hour. Best get into some dry clothes before then."

Hannah smirked as the boys and Grace scrambled through the kitchens and up the stairs to their bedchambers.

"Two minutes ago, and you would have thought them ready for their beds," Henry said as he leaned down and kissed Hannah on her forehead. "You're up early."

"I could not sleep knowing you were out there in this awful weather," she whispered.

"Couldn't be helped," he replied as he lifted one of her hands to his lips. "But I must admit, I am relieved to have it done. This harvest has been a source of worry for several weeks." A drop of water fell from his dark hair, and he winced when it streaked down Hannah's gown.

"It's only water," Hannah whispered. "Can you remain indoors for the rest of the day?" she asked as they made their way up the stairs.

Henry was about to answer in the affirmative when he aimed a suspicious glance in her direction. "You have something in mind for me to do?"

She scoffed. "Sleep, I would hope. You've barely been to your bed this entire week."

"Oh, is that all?" he answered, sounding ever so relieved.

"Well, I would be happy to join you in your bed," she offered, one of her blonde brows arching suggestively.

He paused on the landing and leaned over to kiss her on the temple. "I can sleep when I'm dead," he muttered.

She grinned as they resumed their trek up the stairs. "There is another matter we should discuss now that the harvest is complete."

"Oh?" There was the sound of suspicion in his response.

They entered his bedchamber, and Hannah went to work undoing his waistcoat buttons. The wet wool made it difficult to slip the jets through the holes, and Henry made no move to help but continued to dry his hair with the linen.

"Well?" he prompted as she pushed the garment from his shoulders, forcing him to give up his hold on the damp towel.

"Randy is quite excited about some Greek temple in Athens and wishes to go on a Grand Tour," Hannah said, moving to untie his cravat. "And I think he should go. As should Tom." She unwound the cotton strip from around his neck, the sodden fabric nearly dripping with rainwater.

"I agree," Henry replied, secretly glad Tom had brought up the matter whilst they were cutting wheat the day before. He found it amusing Randy had discussed the issue with Hannah, but then he knew she favored her oldest and his heir while Tom had always come to him when he had questions or concerns.

Hannah stilled her movements, the wet cravat hanging from one of her hands as she stared at him. "You do?"

A chuckle rumbled forth, and Henry said, "You, my lady, are about to become very damp."

Letting out a squeak of surprise when he pulled her into his arms, Hannah couldn't help but giggle as he lifted her until her feet no longer touched the floor. Given the layers of petticoats she wore, she only felt moisture from his shirt on her bodice, but she knew his breeches were probably soaking the skirts of the gown. "Henry," she scolded. "You say that as if I'm not already." Her brow once again arched suggestively.

Henry's eyes darkened, "Damn, but you're warm," he whispered, sliding his hands up her back to reach her buttons. He quickly undid a few as her toes touched down onto the floor.

Her hands gripping his shoulders, Hannah kissed him on the lips. "I'm happy to share my warmth," she teased.

A moment later, she giggled as she was practically tossed onto his bed, her skirts and petticoats flipped up onto her torso as Henry divested himself of his soaked shirt and breeches. He was over her an instant later, his bare skin cool against her warm thighs, his engorged cock seeking her entrance.

Hannah's chest lifted from the bed when he thrust into her, her inhalation of breath sounding louder than his moan of pleasure as her knees lifted to press against his thighs. He had one of her sleeves pulled down from her shoulder, and his mouth covered the top of the exposed breast to muffle his groans.

"No corset?" he asked, pausing in his quest to pull the rest of her bodice down.

"I was hoping this might happen," she whispered.

"You minx," he accused, his grin wide as he moved to suckle a pert nipple.

"Well, it's been a long time, and you smell divine when you're all soaking wet," she murmured.

"I do?" he countered in disbelief. "I thought I smelled like Muffin McDuff," he added, referring to their Alpenmastiff.

Her grin widened. "You smell like a summer rain and lemons."

Not about to argue—his cock was demanding his attention—Henry pulled out of her and thrust into her again, and from there, they moved in unison, the upward lift of her hips meeting his thrusts until he was on the edge of his release.

He knew what to do to bring her to her ecstasy if his cock didn't do it for him, and he was about to slide a hand between their bodies to see to it, but he felt her clench hard on him, felt the waves of her pleasure pull on his manhood, and he was lost to his own orgasm.

Holding himself over her, his arms straight and his hands pressed on either side of her shoulders, he held his breath until he was forced to take another.

The yards of fabric separating his chest from hers provided a pillow for his body when he lowered his head to rest above one of her shoulders. When his body gave way all at once—he had no energy left to roll off of her —he simply collapsed atop her.

The sudden warmth of the counterpane landing over his bare back was the last thing he remembered before he passed out.

a half hour later, Gisborn House breakfast parlor

"Where's Father?" Grace asked when her mother entered the breakfast parlor.

"Where are the boys?" Hannah countered, surprised Randy, Tom, and George weren't already at the table. Even though the two oldest were young men now, it was hard for Hannah to think of them as anything but her boys.

"George fell asleep, but Randy and Tom are coming down. They decided to take shower baths since they were already wet."

Knowing their shared valet would see to it they were properly attired, Hannah regarded Grace's clothes with a frown. "Are those your brother's breeches?" she asked in horror.

Grace winced. "George's, yes," she replied. "But they're too short for him, so he gave them to me."

"Young lady—"

"I know. I will, Mother. But please, may I wear them until after breakfast? Then I'll go straight to my room and change," Grace argued.

"You'll go straight to your bed and get some sleep," Hannah countered, acknowledging the delivery of her breakfast by a footman. "I'll need coffee," she said to him.

"Yes, my lady," Bertram replied, giving a slight bow before he disappeared.

"Did you even go to bed last night?" Hannah asked, resuming her conversation with Grace.

Her daughter seemed to give the query some thought before she said, "Not really. I was still awake when I heard Mr. Cavanaugh's arrival."

Thomas Cavanaugh, one of the older Gisborn tenant farmers, had arrived well after dinner with word that rain was headed their way. With most of the wheat cut but none of it brought in, he had offered the help of his sons with the last of the harvest.

A footman was dispatched to Ellsworth Park with the bad news, and by midnight, nearly a dozen men— and Grace—had all the draft horses hitched to carts and torches lit throughout the wheat fields. Six hours later and only minutes before clouds, pregnant with rain, delivered their storm, the last of the wheat had been collected in the carts and covered.

As a farmer's wife, Hannah knew all too well what a

bad harvest could do to an earldom. The effects it would have on those who relied on the crops for food and their livings. She also knew Henry seemed to live a charmed life when it came to his fields, for he always seemed to know the best time to plant, when to employ his irrigation system, and when to harvest. Other aristocrats relied on their foremen or tenant farmers to see to their lands, with varying degrees of success.

"Are Randy and Tom going to Greece?" Grace asked, interrupting Hannah's reverie.

Blinking, Hannah dared a glance toward the door, sure she could hear the older sons making their way down the stairs. "If your father agrees, then yes, they'll be going on their Grand Tours," she replied.

"And George?" The query was tinged with a hint of worry, as if Grace didn't agree with the idea.

"No. He's far too young for a Grand Tour," Hannah replied. "He still needs to learn Greek, and it wouldn't hurt him to learn some Italian, too."

Grace appeared relieved at hearing this news, and she returned her attention to her breakfast.

"You and George have become rather good friends," Hannah remarked, a second before her oldest sons filed into the breakfast parlor followed by their father.

Henry bussed her on the cheek. "You could have woken me," he whispered.

She allowed a prim grin. "I thought I had." She winked as she watched him straighten, sure his face reddened with embarrassment.

Bertram went about delivering plates of food while

Mrs. Ainsley poured coffee, and once the servants left the family to their meal, Henry cleared his throat.

Randy and Tom turned their gazes on him. "Yes, Father?" they asked in unison.

"I had a conversation with your uncle whilst we were working. Seems your cousin, David, will be going on his Grand Tour in a month or so."

Randy looked to Hannah while Tom kept his attention on his father. "Can I go with him, Father?"

Henry ate a forkful of eggs before he answered. "You'll *both* be going with him."

The two young men guffawed in delight.

"You'll require an escort, of course."

Given Henry's serious demeanor, the grins disappeared. "Escort?" they repeated.

Exchanging a glance of amusement with his wife, Henry resumed eating his breakfast. Until he had further word from his brother-in-law, Will Slater, he dared not offer up a name. "A cicerone," he stated. "A guide. We'll talk about it later today. After you get some sleep."

The two young men exchanged quick glances before Randy said, "Thank you, Father."

"Yes, thank you," Tom chimed in. "You won't regret it."

Henry furrowed a brow. "A year from now, when there aren't enough men to help with the harvest, I just might," he argued.

Both Randy and Tom dipped their heads but knew better than to respond.

CHAPTER 19
A SERIOUS DISCUSSION

eanwhile, in the master bedchamber in Ellsworth Park

"What did our son want?"

Dozing for a moment, her mind on how good it felt to have her husband's prone body keeping her warm in the morning chill, Barbara slowly opened her eyes.

Will had awakened with a start, apparently surprised to discover he was still atop his wife. His gaze immediately went to the clock on the mantel. "Apologies. I didn't mean to sleep for so long. Or to crush you as I did so," he murmured.

"I didn't mind," Barbara replied with a lazy grin. "Besides, weren't you up all night?" she asked as she watched him rise to his hands and knees. "You must be exhausted."

Will's dark blonde hair, now mostly dry, was mussed and had him looking rather rakish. The rest of him, still naked—except for his stockings—made him appear anything but a gentleman. In London, he would have been mistaken for a pugilist given his muscled arms and the width of his shoulders.

"Not quite," he replied before kissing both her nipples. He rolled off the bed. "We had all the cutting done yesterday, but only half of the hay baled and none of the wheat. When the clouds rolled in, Mr. Cavanaugh noticed and warned Henry. They thought it best we get everything under cover. Keep it dry."

Not for the first time, Barbara wondered how Will could speak so coherently first thing in the morning about such mundane topics as wheat and the harvest. "You baled in the middle of the night?" she asked in awe, imagining how many torches it must have taken to light up the fields so the tenant farmers could see. Given the cloud cover, the moon wouldn't have provided much light, and it had probably rained at some point during the night.

He chuckled. "Not exactly. We piled it onto a few carts and covered them with tarps," he replied. "Some of it went into the greenhouses..." He paused when he heard her hiss. "...and we made sure the plants inside weren't crushed."

"Hannah will have Henry's hide if her lime trees have been damaged," Barbara warned, referring to Will's only sister. Hannah had been married to the Earl of Gisborn for nearly thirty years, and despite having been raised in London, she had settled into the life of a country aristocrat's wife without so much as a peep of protest. Her former acquaintances in London would be shocked to learn that Hannah was essentially a farmer's wife.

Barbara blinked. Anyone in London who might still remember *her* would have a hard time believing that she, too, was now more comfortable living in the country than in the capital.

A few years older than her sister-in-law, Barbara had lived in Oxfordshire all of her adult life, although not by choice. At least, not at first. Her father, the Earl of Greenley, had thrown her out of his London home, Pendleton House, when he discovered she was pregnant with Will's child.

Although she had secured a promise of marriage from Will prior to his departure from England—his naval duties kept him away for eight years—it didn't matter. Her father's incessant gambling and drunken episodes had him behaving erratically.

Thanks to Andrew S. Barton, Esq., the earldom's man of business, Barbara was provided an unentailed property the solicitor had arranged on her behalf. About four miles from the Gisborn properties near the village of Broadwell, the rundown cottage had been her home for seven years before Will found her and their son, Donald, half-starved and in desperate straits.

The memory of how she had grown to despise Will Slater during those seven years flashed through her mind, and she winced. He'd had no way of knowing his letters never reached her. No way of knowing where she was or what had happened to her.

When he did appear, relieved to find her and

stunned to discover he was a father, Will had set to work making a life for them in Oxfordshire. Aided by Henry —the earl had offered him a position as a foreman—they had moved into Ellsworth Park, a country manor house located on part of the Gisborn lands. A few years of renovation later, and Barbara knew she would live at Ellsworth Park for the rest of her life.

Or until Will inherited the Devonville marquessate.

She rather hoped his father would outlive all of them and they would never be forced to move to the capital.

Barbara gave a start when one of Will's hands passed in front of her face.

"Allow me to put you back to bed," he said as he moved to lift her.

"I'm not the least bit tired," she protested, stepping away. "Unlike for you, I find lovemaking rather invigorating," she added with an impish grin. Remembering what had sent her into her reverie, she added, "You didn't damage anything in the greenhouses, I hope?"

Built on fallow land near Gisborn Hall in 1815, along with a modern irrigation system, the two greenhouses had been Henry's idea. They had been the reason the Gisborn earldom had survived the Year of No Summer. Despite the awful weather, the greenhouses had provided the means to grow fruits and vegetables as well as citrus trees for the nearby village of Bampton.

"Not to worry. I made sure there was plenty of room for the carts before we wheeled them in," Will replied as he disappeared into the dressing room. His voice muffled, he asked, "Now, what does our son want? And which son are we talking about?"

Securing her petticoats, Barbara decided it was best to answer rather than wait until breakfast. The sooner she brought it up, the sooner they could adapt to the idea of not having the boys about for a year or two. The resulting discussion would no doubt go on all day.

Besides, there had been the letter she had found in the study, one she knew Will couldn't read given the language in which it was written. If her interpretation of its contents was correct, then much of Donald's behavior of the past six years could be readily explained.

"David would like to go on a Grand Tour," she stated, referring to their second son and Will's legitimate heir. Nearly one-and-twenty years of age, David had completed his studies at Oxford at the end of the last term.

Will chuckled. "He and his cousins must have been talking," he said, referring to Henry's two middle sons, Randy and Tom. "Tom mentioned he had brought up the topic with Hannah when we were loading hay into the greenhouses."

Barbara held up her dress, about to pull it back on when she remembered all the buttons were torn off. She tossed it onto a chair and joined Will in the dressing room, inhaling softly at seeing her husband dressed in only a pair of pantaloons. "Are you going to try and talk him out of it?"

Will pulled on a shirt and began tucking the hem into his pantaloons. "No. I think he should go. I think they should all go." He paused in his task, his gaze watching for her reaction.

Grinning, Barbara rushed up to him and wrapped her arms around his shoulders. "Thank the gods," she murmured, reaching up to kiss him on the cheek.

Shocked by her response, Will stared at her a moment before he allowed a brilliant smile. "I would have thought you'd want David to remain in England," he commented.

Barbara gave a shrug. "Other than helping Henry with the farm, there's nothing for him here," she replied. "At least, not now. If he doesn't go to Greece or the Kingdom of the Two Sicilies, he'll insist on moving to London, where he'll vex your stepmother and have every young miss pining for him after his first ball," she explained as she plucked a fresh corset from a drawer and pulled it on.

Will paused in buttoning up his waistcoat to tie her corset strings. "Why do you say that?"

Rolling her eyes, Barbara disappeared into a sprigged muslin day gown, rather enjoying how Will watched when she raised her arms. "Because he looks like you did when you were that age, and I was one of those young misses who pined for you after *my* first ball," she said when her head poked through the top of the gown.

"Remind me why it is we employ a lady's maid for you," he said, a grin lighting his face as she took the white silk cravat from his hands and began pleating it.

"To do my hair, of course." She wrapped the silk around the back of his neck and then wound it around twice on each side before tying the ends into a perfect knot. "Remind me why it is we employ a valet for you."

"To shave me, of course," he replied, a dimple appearing in the base of his left cheek.

Barbara's eyes widened when she realized he had been intending to hold off putting on the cravat until after he'd been shaved. "Here, I'll undo—"

"Not necessary. I can go a day without a shave," he said before he kissed her on the forehead.

A shiver shot through Barbara just then. She was no doubt reminded of how his whiskers had scraped her thighs only the hour before when he had practiced what he claimed was a Roman art. Although she didn't know whether or not to believe him—she had thought whatever he did more a skill than an art—Barbara had been left wondering if all Roman men knew that particular skill.

Did her sons know of it? Had they employed it on any women? Had Donald done so with the woman in the letter she'd read?

Will's hand passed in front of her face and she gave a start. "Has David been with a woman, do you suppose?" she asked suddenly. "In... in that way?"

Will blinked. "Are you asking if he's bedded a woman?"

She nodded.

"He's been at Oxford for three years," he stated, as if that would be answer enough.

Staring at him, Barbara continued to wait for a response.

"Well, I don't know for certain," Will hedged, "but I rather imagine he's had a tumble or two."

"And Donald?" She winced even before the query was out of her mouth. Their oldest at nearly nine-and-twenty years of age, Donald was illegitimate. She had given birth to him seven years before Will had returned from serving as a master and commander in the British Navy. He had lived with them at Ellsworth Park until he left for his Grand Tour.

Upon his return at the age of three-and-twenty, he took up residence in the Gisborn dowager house, a charming stone cottage located on the corner of the Gisborn lands closest to Bampton. He saw to the Gisborn horses, spending part of his days in the stables and the rest in his cottage writing of his travels in Greece and the Kingdom of the Two Sicilies.

He was also unmarried, a situation Barbara had hoped he would rectify when he returned from his Grand Tour.

That had been six years ago.

In the meantime, he hadn't courted anyone, nor had he been to London to attend the usual entertainments.

Perhaps the reason was the woman who had written the letter.

Will sighed. "I have reason to believe he had an *affaire* when he was on his Grand Tour," he murmured. "Probably thought it was harmless fun until he returned and discovered he had feelings for the girl."

Her eyes widening in alarm, Barbara asked, "Where was this?" as she turned her back to him, intending for him to do up her buttons. "Greece? The Kingdom of the Two Sicilies?" Her gaze darted to the side. "Egypt?"

Instead of answering her or moving to secure the buttons, Will pushed aside her long hair. He dipped his head and kissed her on the nape of her neck, which had frissons skittering down her back.

"If you continue what you're doing, our breakfast will be cold," she warned even as she inhaled softly. "Do you know if he writes to her?"

Will's kisses had migrated to the top of her shoulder. "He who?" he whispered, one of his hands grasping her upper arm.

Giggling, Barbara pulled away slightly. "That tickles," she complained, her grin belying her words. "And I was referring to your son, Donald."

Will dropped his forehead to the top of her head. "Promise me we can continue this later today. Or tonight," he murmured.

Barbara turned around in his arms. "I promise," she replied, lifting her eyes to meet his. Before she could say anything else, Will's lips touched hers, and she was lost in his gentle kiss. When he finally ended it, she had forgotten whatever it was she had asked him.

Hunger did that sometimes.

CHAPTER 20

A DECISION IS ANNOUNCED OVER BREAKFAST

Meanwhile, in the Ellsworth House breakfast parlor

Having arrived in the breakfast parlor before anyone else, David Slater, youngest son of Will and Barbara, and heir to the Bellingham earldom and eventually the Devonville marquessate, took a seat in the breakfast parlor and helped himself to the copy of *The London Times* that had been placed next to his father's place setting.

A footman saw to his coffee and placed a plate filled with that morning's fare in front of him before disappearing into the kitchens.

David had nearly finished reading the newspaper and eaten most of his eggs and bacon when his older brother, Donald, appeared on the threshold. Despite the difference in their ages, their resemblance to one another was apparent. Sandy blonde hair, blue eyes, and square jawlines along with similar builds had their identities occasionally mistaken for the other.

"How do?" David said as he straightened in his chair. He set aside the paper, attempting to make it appear as if it hadn't been opened since its placement on the table.

"I'm starving," Donald replied, taking the chair opposite his brother's. "Been in the stables since before dawn."

David nodded. "At least it's the last time we'll have to do that for a while," he replied as the footman once again brought coffee and food to the table. "Are the horses all right?"

Donald nodded. "They are. Thought Frank was lame —he seemed to be limping last night—but he's fine," he commented, referring to one of the draft horses that had been used to pull the carts of wheat into the greenhouses.

"They're not used to working in the middle of the night," David said.

"You say that as if *we* are." There was barely a hint of humor in the older brother's comment.

"So it's a good thing the harvest is done," their father said as he entered the room behind their mother, obviously overhearing Donald's comment.

"Good morning to you both," Barbara said, her arrival signaling the footman to deliver more food and coffee.

"Good morning, Mother," her sons said in unison. Both young men stood and waited until she had taken her seat before they returned to their chairs.

"David, I spoke with your father, and yes, you can join Randy and Tom on their Grand Tour," Barbara stated, knowing her words would be both welcomed and a surprise.

His fork dropping to his plate, David stared at his mother in shock. "I can?"

"There's only the matter of a cicerone," she added, turning her gaze on Donald. "Would either of you be adverse to you taking on the role of tour guide? I know you kept journals from your Grand Tour. You're the family expert on the subject since your father didn't exactly do one in the usual manner."

Will Slater's eight years in the British Navy had him visiting several of the countries usually included in a Grand Tour, but he had rarely traveled beyond their port cities.

Donald's eyes widened. "You're serious?"

David guffawed. "You're not joking?"

Chuckling, Will thanked the footman who saw to his breakfast and coffee. "My sweet, you certainly know how to bring joy to a man's morning," he said with a wink.

A blush coloring her already rosy cheeks, Barbara was about to scold him for his comment when Donald repeated his query.

"You're serious? You're saying *I* can go back to the Kingdom of the Two Sicilies?"

Barbara exchanged a quick glance with her husband before she asked, "Are you sure you want to take on the responsibility of your brother *and* two cousins for the next year or so? You'll have to return them in one piece given there are heirs involved."

She always hated referring to her younger son as the heir. It wasn't fair to Donald. Will was the father of both young men. But the laws of inheritance were clear. She and Will hadn't been married at the time of Donald's birth, so he couldn't be Will's heir.

"I understand, Mother," Donald assured her. He had long ago accepted his place in the family as well as in Society. If his father wasn't the heir to a marquessate, most wouldn't even know he was illegitimate. "The timing could not be more perfect. I have finished my book on the topic of the Grand Tour—"

"Book?" Will interrupted.

Donald turned his attention on his father. "Yes, sir. I've been transcribing my travel journals. It's what I do when I'm not seeing to the horses," he explained. "I have compiled what I believe to be a young man's comprehensive guide for traveling in Greece and Italy."

For a moment, Will Slater simply stared at his oldest son. "And here I thought you were entertaining young women in your cottage," he teased.

A red flush crept up over Donald's face, and he dipped his head. "No, sir. Other than Mrs. Oxblood, there have been no women in the dowager cottage," he claimed, referring to the Ellsworth Park housekeeper.

Will quickly sobered. Given what he remembered from their conversation upon Donald's return from his

Grand Tour, he had often wondered if his oldest would ever marry. Donald never talked about the young lady he had left behind in Catania, nor had he courted any of the young ladies who lived around Bampton. He had never put voice to the idea of living in London during a Season so he could meet and marry a young lady there.

In the capital, Donald would have had the opportunity to attend any number of entertainments—balls, *soirées*, *musicales*, card parties, and the theatre—as well as dinner parties. Cherice, Marchioness of Devonville and his grandmother, would no doubt see to it he was introduced to every young lady in search of a husband—at least those who wouldn't mind being wed to a bastard.

"Are you in search of a publisher?" Will asked, deciding it best he return the conversation back to the travel guide.

"Three were interested, but I have accepted an offer from Chapman and Hall."

Barbara and Will exchanged expressions of awe. "Congratulations," she said. "Aren't they the ones who publish the monthly magazines and journals? They print Mr. Dickens' fiction, do they not?"

"They do," Donald affirmed. "But they're also creating a library of travel books," he explained. "My proposal arrived at a good time, I suppose."

"My brother the author," David said with a huge grin.

"Nothing is in print yet," Donald warned. "In fact, if I'm to return to the Kingdom of the Two Sicilies, then perhaps I should hold off and update my manuscript with any new information I might discover."

"Can they wait that long, though?" Will asked, reminding his oldest son that he would be away from England for at least a year and probably more like two years.

"I will write them today of my news," Donald replied. "Even if they don't approve of an extension, I can always send them what I have now and provide a new edition when I return."

"Careful, or you'll find yourself offered positions to act as a cicerone for other young aristocrats," his father warned.

Donald guffawed. "You say that as if it would be a bad thing."

David gasped. "It would be for the Gisborn stables," he countered. "Who's going to take care of the horses in your absence?"

"We can find a new groom when it becomes necessary," Barbara said, secretly glad for her oldest son. His writing might provide him an income in addition to his allowance. Make him more likely to take a wife.

"We will have to when these two are gone," Will countered. "Good thing there are some young men in Bampton looking for positions. The Cavanaughs have a couple boys who are about the right age."

Donald chuckled. "I've not even left England, and you're already looking to hire my replacement," he complained, although he grinned as he made the comment.

"You can have it back when you return," his father said, "but something tells me you'll be making a living as a travel writer."

Unaware of his mother's gaze on him, Donald tucked into his breakfast, his mind on a certain woman in Catania.

CHAPTER 21
SISTERS-IN-LAW CONFER

n hour later, Gisborn Hall

Ensconced in the parlor of Gisborn Hall, Hannah hummed softly as she embroidered her daughter's initial on the corner of a hanky. With the other family members having gone to their beds and the servants to the kitchens for their breakfast, the household had grown quiet. The only sounds came from an occasional crackle or pop from the wood in the fireplace and the soft snores of the Alpenmastiff, Muff MacDuff, at her feet.

The sound of footsteps on the stairs had her glancing towards the door, but she was still surprised when Parkerhouse, the butler, appeared.

Muff raised himself from her feet, his manner suggesting he was expecting a problem and might have to bark a warning.

"My lady, Lady Bellingham is paying a call. Shall I tell her you are in residence and escort her up?"

Hannah inhaled softly. "Yes, but send her up while you see to bringing tea," she replied, heartened there was someone else awake on such a cool and rainy day. Barbara was probably the only other person in the immediate vicinity who had managed to get any sleep the night before.

"I feared you would be abed with everyone else," Barbara said when she hurried into the room.

Muff wagged his tail but knew to stay where he was.

Hannah stood and pulled her sister-in-law into an embrace. "I had given it some thought," she replied, motioning for Barbara to take the chair next to hers. "But I quite like the house when it's this quiet. Oh, and I've ordered tea," she added.

"I wasn't going to prevail upon your hospitality, but after that quick jaunt in the rain... I will have a cup." Barbara gave the dog a quick scratch behind one ear.

"What brings you over here?" Hannah asked, settling back into her chair. Assured nothing was amiss, Muff retook his place, apparently satisfied with the little attention he had received.

"I need to speak with someone, or I think I'll go mad."

Hannah's eyes rounded. "What's happened? Did Will not agree to the idea of the boys going on their Grand Tour?"

Barbara blinked. "Actually, he agreed wholeheartedly. I was surprised. And Donald is quite happy to act as cicerone for them," she added, her gaze going to her mind's eye for a moment.

"So… what has happened to have you braving the rain to see me?" Hannah asked, displaying a teasing grin.

Barbara pulled a missive from her pocket. "This was delivered to the house about a fortnight ago. Will opened it, but…" She handed it to Hannah. "He, uh…"

Hannah took the wrinkled paper as if it might explode and regarded the feminine script for a moment. "Cannot read… Latin, is it? Or…?" She angled her head to one side before giving it a shake. "I'm afraid I never learned to read more than a few words, either." She studied the outside of the envelope, immediately noticing the smudge that rendered the first name unreadable. She handed it back to Barbara. "Who is it from?"

"Nikky."

Hannah stared at Barbara for a moment. "The name isn't familiar to me," she said. Her blonde brows suddenly crinkled. "Although… Elizabeth, uh, Viscountess Bostwick, has mentioned a younger cousin by that name," she said, referring to one of her friends in Mayfair. "Nicoletta is the full name, I believe," she said. "Can *you* read the writing?"

"I can, and I did," Barbara admitted. "The letter was intended for Donald, but it was delivered to Ellsworth Park by mistake. I think…" She stopped speaking when Parkerhouse appeared with the tea tray. He set it on the low table in front of them, bowed, and left as quickly as he appeared.

"You think…" Hannah prompted.

"I think my son left something behind in Catania. *Someone*, I mean," she replied.

In the middle of pouring a cup of tea, Hannah paused and stared at Barbara. "A... a lover, do you suppose?" she asked, a playful grin lifting her lips as she waggled her eyebrows. "Named Nikky?"

"I do. And a babe as well."

Hannah set the teapot down onto the salver and stared at Barbara as if she had been burned. "Donald hasn't been to Sicily since... since his Grand Tour," she said. She handed over the cup of tea as she displayed an expression of puzzlement. "What's it been? Five... six years ago?"

"Six, so the boy must be five years old now?" Barbara guessed.

Hannah waved a hand. "Wait. We're talking about my nephew Donald here," she said, as if protesting Barbara's assertion he had fathered a child.

"We are," Barbara agreed.

Hannah scoffed. "He is a model of responsibility," she argued, ready to defend her oldest nephew against any and all accusations. "He would not have left a girl behind if he knew she was with child. And once he learned of it..." She stopped and pointed to the letter. "Is this the first he would have heard from... from this Nikky?"

Barbara shook her head. "It's quite evident they have been corresponding for some time. I have reason to believe Nikky is married to an aristocrat. Someone with the given name Ricardo," she said, opening the letter. "He's quite ill. Apparently quite old as well."

Hannah took a sip of tea before asking, "Will you read it to me?"

Setting aside her teacup, Barbara took a breath before reciting the words, pausing occasionally to interpret the foreign words.

My dearest Donald,

Your latest letter arrived this morning, and I am glad of it as it brings good news of your correspondence with the publishers in London. It seems you are to be a published author. I hope (and expect) your words about Catania might bring more travelers to our shores.

Upon hearing Hannah's soft gasp, Barbara paused. "He told us over breakfast this morning that he's written a travel guide for young men. A publisher in London has agreed to print it."

Dipping her head, Hannah said, "I wondered when he was going to tell you."

Barbara's eyes widened. "How... how long have *you* known of it?" she asked in dismay.

"Only a few days, but..." She waved to the letter. "He obviously shared it with *her* some time ago."

Arching a brow, Barbara immediately understood Hannah's point. "Learning this has me wondering what else he hasn't told me," she whispered.

"Well, I feel as if we're eavesdropping," Hannah

countered. "The opening line says, 'My dearest Donald', so we know to whom the letter was written."

"Should I stop reading then?" Barbara asked, ready to refold the missive.

"You'll do no such thing. Read the rest right now," Hannah demanded.

Dipping her head in an effort to hide her humor, Barbara took a moment to find where she had stopped.

Much has happened since I last wrote, and none of it good. But I have already worried you needlessly. Antony is quite fine. He has learned all his letters and he knows how to read some words. I have seen to it he knows some English, and he practices with Armenia and Father when given the opportunity. He is also now breeched, I believe is what you call it, since he grew out of all of his gowns last month.

Ricardo was quite glad for it, for he thought the boy would be mistaken for a girl given his long dark hair (which I have since cut shorter so now it is curly). Antony now appears to be a very proper young gentleman with good manners and the ability to bow without falling onto his head.

Barbara paused as Hannah lifted a hand to cover her mouth. Giggles escaped them both. "Tom was always losing his balance when he was that age," Hannah murmured.

"David used to topple over. Practically somersaulted the first time he bowed for you," Barbara said as a tear threatened to escape the corner of her eye.

"I remember. He was so serious. Trying so hard to impress me, and I was near to bursting with laughter."

"Which had me in a terrible state," Barbara countered, her grin belying the tears that fell. She sniffled before she continued to read.

We hosted my aunt Armenia and several other aristocrats for a dinner last week. They pretend all is well, but although they do not care for the Bourbons who rule this part of the world, they are not of a mind to put up a fight. Wars are expensive, and none are willing to fund an army.

Two days after the dinner, Montblanc fell ill. He struggles to breathe, and with the heat, he remains here in the castle on Mount Aetna when he would usually prefer to be in town or Taormina for the summer. I would as well, for it is lonely up here.

"Montblanc," Hannah murmured. "I'll have to ask Henry if he might have a book about the European peerage in the library."

"I think his given name is Ricardo," Barbara said, holding up a finger. She resumed reading aloud.

The physician comes every day to administer some foul smelling medicine. There are times I wonder if he is trying to hasten Ricardo's departure from this earth. Perhaps he thinks it would be a blessing, but I know I would miss his kind words and steady presence, as would Antony. He has always been a loving father.

I think of you often—every few days, Antony does something that reminds me of you. I read to him every day, for I want him to know about the world. When we are back in the villa in town, I shall have the portrait artist return to do another miniature of him. He grows so quickly!

I pray you have a good harvest and can write to me soon of it. I want to know you are in good stead.

With all my love (and Antony's),
Nikky

Barbara glanced up, surprised to see Hannah staring at the fire. "So… do you believe me now?" she asked in a quiet voice.

Hannah inhaled softly. "I do," she murmured. "Which has me wondering what *you're* going to do." She tore her gaze from the flames and stared at Barbara.

"I don't know what to do," she replied. "What would *you* do if you learned your oldest boy had fathered a child and kept it a secret?"

Fairly certain Nathaniel knew better—Henry had been rather firm with all three of his sons when it came to matters of the opposite sex—Hannah had never given a thought to what she would do in a similar circumstance.

Until that moment.

"I would meet with him in private. Calmly. Over tea

and biscuits. Tell him what I had discovered and allow him time to explain himself."

Barbara blinked. "You could be that reasonable?"

Hannah scoffed again. "I could try," she replied, lifting her head defiantly, her expression suggesting she wasn't entirely convinced. "Especially knowing he'll be returning to Sicily at some point in the next year," she added, arching a brow to emphasize her point. She suddenly stood, which had Muff rising in alarm, and hurried to one of the parlor windows. "He's in the cottage now," she stated upon spotting a light in one of the stone building's windows. "With everyone abed, now would be the perfect time to take him a tin of biscuits, make tea, and confront him with what you know. Deliver his letter, too," she suggested.

Barbara inhaled softy. "All right," she whispered.

Returning to stand in front of her chair, Hannah regarded her sister-in-law for a long moment before she said, "Be sure you apologize."

Her eyes rounding, Barbara scoffed. "Whatever for?"

"For reading his private correspondence," she replied, arching a blonde brow even as her lips quirked. "He'll forgive you once you tell him how much you want to meet your grandchild."

Barbara stared at Hannah for several seconds. "Grandchild," she whispered, her breath catching. "I have to do it right now," she agreed. "Or I'll lose my nerve."

"Do let me know how it goes," Hannah said,

wincing. "And don't for a single moment think I'm going to be able to keep this a secret from Henry."

Wincing, Barbara set aside her teacup and stood. "And he'll turn around and discuss it with Will," she said, knowing the two men talked about everything that happened on the Gisborn estate.

Stuffing the letter into the pocket in her gown, Barbara said, "So I'd best tell him first."

"*After* you speak with Donald," Hannah stated.

"Yes. After," she agreed. "Oh, and you should all come for dinner at Ellsworth Park this evening," she added. "So we can discuss the particulars of our boys' Grand Tours."

Hannah nodded. "I'll be sure everyone is up and ready to be there at six o'clock," she promised.

A moment later, Barbara had taken her leave of the parlor and of Gisborn Hall, hoping the Ellsworth Park cook had a tin of biscuits and some tea.

She might have to borrow the decanter of brandy from the study, too.

CHAPTER 22
A MOTHER LEARNS MORE

eanwhile, at the Gisborn dowager cottage

Having completed his work in the stables for the morning, Donald hurried back to his cottage, nearly running in his haste to pen a letter.

Of all the conversations the Slater family could have over breakfast on such a cold and rainy day, he could hardly believe the one they'd had that morning.

He was going to return to Sicily. And he had his family's blessing. Well, he was going with a few charges that might make his travels more difficult—and certainly less private—but he could hardly let that keep him from the letter he needed to write.

Had he asked the week before, when news had first arrived from Catania in the form of a bittersweet letter, he might have had to argue his case. Now... now he had to sort some particulars. Sort the timing.

Pulling a sheet of stationery from the few pieces that remained from his last order, he wrote his usual salutation and stopped, the pen poised so a drop of ink formed and was about to fall. Wincing, Donald pulled the pen aside and set it in its holder. Unfolding the letter he had received the week before, he reread it in its entirety, the Latin words smeared so it was difficult to decipher.

My dearest Donald,

I pray this letter finds you and your family in good health. Ricardo succumbed to the illness I described in my last letter, his poor health made worse with his age. I feel guilt that I wished for God to take him, but he was so sick, and he could hardly breathe—it seemed merciful.

I hated that our Antony had to see him like that, poor boy. My brother's family has taken him so he might spend time with his cousins until after the affairs have been settled. D'Avalos is helping in that regard, although his advanced age has slowed him.

Worry not for me or our future as Ricardo has left me my dowry and more—the villa here in Catania and the vineyards and castle on Aetna, the D'Avalos villa in Roma, which I intend for Armenia to inhabit, as well as a coach-and-four, a traveling coach, a pair of matched greys, three riding horses (they would benefit from your care), and the furnishings.

Ricardo had no one else to make a claim to the estate, poor man, his brother having died many years ago. I have come to believe D'Avalos agreed with

Ricardo's scheme to marry me so he would end up with the vineyards—he cares nothing for the villa.

I will wear black for the next half-year as is customary here. Beyond that, I have no plans, but perhaps I could bring Antony to England to meet you then? That you still send me letters after six years has me hoping you wish to see me as much as I wish to see you.

If I have this wrong, please write to tell me so. Otherwise, I remain yours always,
Nikky

Donald inhaled softly, his heart clenching upon reading the last line. Nicoletta, Marchesa Montblanc, might have wished death for her aged "husband" as a means of mercy, but Donald had far more selfish reasons for wanting her natural father dead.

About to begin his letter with a message of condolence—he had to consider the rest of what he might say after his earlier conversation with his father—Donald jerked at hearing a knock at his door. A drop of ink plopped onto the pristine stationery, and he cursed.

"Come!" he called out, pushing his chair back so he could turn and discover who was paying a call.

"I don't wish to interrupt your writing, but I really must speak with you," his mother said as she made her way to his desk.

Donald blinked. "Mother?" She was dressed much as she had been at breakfast, although she also wore a redingote, carried an umbrella, and had something tucked under one arm. He watched as her gaze swept over his desk. Fairly sure she didn't read Latin, he made no move to hide Nicoletta's letter.

"I've brought biscuits. I'll make tea, if you don't mind," she said as she moved to the small kitchen at the back of the cottage.

"I don't mind at all," Donald replied, moving to join her. "There's already hot water in the kettle. What's happened?"

Barbara busied herself with preparing teacups and saucers, her motions quick and efficient. "It's about the Grand Tour," she stated.

Donald leaned against the door frame. "Have you and Father changed your minds? About us going?"

Shaking her head, Barbara poured the water into a teapot. "Not at all." She pulled a folded note from her pocket and held it out to him. "In fact, I invited the Forsters to join us for dinner so we can discuss it then," she said, referring to Henry, Hannah, and their children. "I am hoping we haven't waited too long."

Hesitating before taking the note from her, Donald finally did. He gave a start at seeing the handwriting on the envelope. "When did you receive this?"

Barbara rolled her eyes as she handed him a teacup. "It was delivered a fortnight ago. Your father... he had no idea who it was from because I think he's forgotten whatever Latin he might have learned at school. With the harvest and all, he quite forgot about it, and then I found it on his desk last night. He doesn't know I took it."

Donald studied the address on the front of the missive. Although most of it was legible, the first name was not, the ink having smeared at some point en route from Sicily. The last name, Slater, was clear. "Just a mis-delivery is all," he said, nonchalantly. "No harm."

Her shoulders dropping, Barbara regarded him with worry. "I read it."

His eyes widening, Donald glanced down at the missive and then turned it over. The wax seal had been broken, but then she had mentioned his father had attempted to read it. "I wasn't aware you could read Latin," he murmured.

Barbara scoffed. "I'm an earl's daughter," she stated, obviously miffed by his comment. "And apparently a very ignorant mother."

His head jerked up to regard her with shock. "Mother," he replied quietly.

"When did you meet her?"

About to say something else, Donald hesitated and shrugged. "Uh, January 1833. My first full day in Catania," he stated. "And you needn't be concerned about ignorance. I simply chose not to tell anyone."

Barbara displayed a look of hurt. "But why?" she asked in dismay. "She obviously meant something to you. She was very special to you," she argued. She glanced about the small kitchen, as if in search of something. "Do you have any brandy?"

Donald disappeared for a moment and returned with a decanter. He poured a small amount in her teacup and then did the same with his own.

"She *did* mean something special to you, didn't she?" his mother pressed.

"She did, yes. She *does*," he countered.

"Is *she* why you haven't courted anyone here in England?"

Donald sighed and dipped his head. He could deny it, but his mother had no doubt gained a clear idea of what Nicoletta meant to him.

And what he meant to her.

"Yes."

"You had an *affaire* with her?"

"Mother!"

"Please, tell me the truth, Donald. She's a married woman—"

"Widowed," he interrupted. "Sort of. And she wasn't married when I knew her."

"Widowed?" Her eyes rounded, but she wasn't to be deterred from making her point. "But she was betrothed. When you had your *affaire*?" Barbara guessed.

"Not exactly. Not how you think." He shook his head. "It's all a bit complicated, but I didn't learn she was to marry the marchese until we had spent nearly two months... courting," he murmured. "I asked for her hand in marriage. I gave her a betrothal ring," he added.

"She didn't *tell* you?" The disbelief was evident in Barbara's voice.

"She didn't *know*, Mother. Her father, or rather the man she had always thought was her father, had made the arrangements with a very old acquaintance of his— another aristocrat who lacked an heir—and she was as surprised as I was when D'Avalos informed me Nicoletta would be marrying in March of that year." He paused a moment. "Montblanc is her natural father."

Slumping against the counter, Barbara gripped her cup in both hands and took a sip of her tea, the fight going out of her all at once. "And the boy? Antony?"

Donald resisted the urge to curse. "He is my son," he admitted. A *whoosh* of air left his lungs, as if he'd been holding his breath for a very long time. "I was going to marry her, Mother. I was going to send a letter to Father telling him I intended to stay in Catania. Take a position as a clerk to earn my living—"

"Donald."

"—but the betrothal to the Marchese Montblanc was announced at a lavish ball at his villa in Catania, and I left to come home. He got his true heir—he was Nikky's natural father, you see—"

"What?" she interrupted, nearly spilling her tea.

"—And the fake marriage allowed him to keep his daughter and his grandson close. He gave them everything, and now *my son* is the Marchese Montblanc."

Barbara blinked several times. "Oh," was all she could manage.

Donald chuckled softly. "Antony has Nikky's dark hair and eyes and…." He allowed the sentence to trail off, obviously happy to speak of his son. After a moment, he disappeared to the front room and returned holding a small item in his hand. He offered it to her. "This was painted last year," he said. "He was about four years old at the time."

Barbara gingerly took the oval miniature from him, her eyes widening as she studied the image. "He's obviously your son," she murmured. "Except for the dark hair, he looks exactly like you did when you were that age."

Donald grinned "I'm glad to hear it. I was going to show it to Father. To ask him about it, but I remembered he didn't know I existed when I was four years old."

Clutching the miniature to her chest, Barbara didn't say anything in response, her eyes brightening with tears.

They stood in companionable silence for a time, both drinking their brandy-spiked tea. Donald took the opportunity to read the letter she had brought, gasping softly when the topic of Montblanc's illness was raised.

Had he received the missive when he should have—a fortnight ago—he would have begun plans then to make the trip to Sicily.

"Does the aristocracy even mean anything there any longer?" Barbara asked quietly.

"Not especially," Donald replied, glancing up from the letter. "They are still under the Bourbons, so I think they are tolerated, but not much more."

"But they have property. Villas. Land. Vineyards."

"Property, yes, most of which has been owned by their families for several centuries," he explained. "Some longer."

"Besides her own family, is there anything keeping... Nicoletta is her name?"

"Sí," he replied, unaware he spoke Italian. "She has inherited the Montblanc villa and furnishings in

Catania. Antony has all the entailed properties—a castle on Mount Aetna along with a good deal of farmland," he explained, remembering the details he had read only a few minutes before his mother's arrival. "Her dowry was the D'Avalos villa in Rome. Where Lady Morganfield lived until her husband met and married her," he explained. "Nikky will also end up with several carriages and horses and whatnot," he went on with a shrug. "And a vineyard, although she thinks her father wants it."

Barbara's brows lifted at hearing the list of properties. "So... she is not destitute?"

He chuckled. "Hardly." He watched as her brows crinkled. "What is it?"

"Did you say Lady *Morganfield*?" Barbara asked, surprise evident in her voice.

"Yes. Nicoletta is Lady Morganfield's niece," he explained, realizing he should have mentioned her relationship to the marchioness first.

Barbara scoffed. "You might have started with that," she scolded. Hannah had mentioned Lady Bostwick's cousin Nikky. Since Elizabeth Carlington Bennett-Jones was the only daughter of Lady Morganfield, it was now obvious this Nikky was the same girl.

Donald couldn't help but chuckle. "Apologies."

She once again glanced at the miniature. "Are you going to go and get her? And him?"

Donald blinked. He hadn't thought that far ahead. He had only just learned that morning that Nicoletta's father had died. That she was a widow in the eyes of those in Catania. "She has to mourn for a time," he said, remembering what she had written. "After that, I intend to do what I must."

"Well, don't wait an entire *year*," his mother said on a huff. "You let her know *right now* what your intentions are."

"Mother," he said, taking a half-step back at hearing her rebuke.

"This boy is *yours*. You marry her, and you bring them both here," she demanded, holding out the miniature. "This boy is my grandson."

Donald blinked. "Yes, ma'am." He glanced around the cottage, wincing when he remembered the finery displayed in the Montblanc villa in Catania. The velvet drapes, the perfectly matched wallpaper, the gilt chandeliers, and the painted ceilings of the grand ballroom located on the top floor of a villa unlike the others which displayed the elegant rot he had come to associate with most of Catania upon his exit from the city.

Montblanc's villa had been maintained in a manner befitting a marchese. Perfectly presentable. Professionally painted by skilled artisans. Immaculate in its cleanliness.

He could only imagine how magnificent the castle on the east slopes of Mount Aetna was in comparison.

"Where do you suggest I put her?" Donald asked. "She's used to living in the equivalent of a palace," he remarked dryly.

Barbara opened her mouth to respond but found she didn't have an immediate answer. "We'll solve that after you tell your father."

"What?"

"Before you and David and your cousins leave for Europe, you're going to tell your father."

Donald inhaled to reply, but decided it better he not say what first came to mind.

His mother would not be happy to learn his father already knew about Nicoletta and Antony.

"If you insist," he finally replied. "I'll tell Father everything."

The air seemed to go out of his mother all at once, and for a moment, he thought she might cry. Instead, her lower lip trembled before she captured it with an eyetooth. "Did you know you left her with child? When you took your leave of Catania?"

He sighed, remembering that day at the Trout Inn when he'd had to explain the situation to his father. "No. But I sorted that I might have..." He sighed. "I knew it was a possibility by the time I reached England," he finished lamely.

She gave him a quelling glance. "If only your father had done the same," she murmured quietly.

Knowing better than to respond—Donald had learned long ago the past could not be changed—he lifted the kettle from the stove and refilled her teacup and his own. "You'll make an excellent grandmother," he commented.

Inhaling softly, Barbara regarded him with tear-filled eyes. "Only if you bring Antony home," she whispered.

"I will bring him to England at some point, Mother. I promise you."

Even if it's only for a visit, he didn't add, for now that Nicoletta had been living in Montblanc's villa and castle for the past six years, it was doubtful she would agree to live in a five-room cottage in Oxfordshire for the rest of her life.

But perhaps she would. He wouldn't know until she'd had a chance to see the place.

CHAPTER 23
A GRANDFATHER
IS INFORMED

Later that night

Dinner had been finished for some time before Barbara, Hannah, and Grace finally left the table to take their tea in the parlor. The conversation that evening had been more animated than usual given nearly everyone had spent most of the day sleeping, and the young men were growing excited about their upcoming trip.

"I do hope you're not too disappointed about having to look after us," Randy said, directing his query to his cousin, Donald.

A footman delivered their glasses of port, which gave Donald a moment to consider how to respond. "I won't be if you behave yourselves," he replied, grinning. Despite what he had learned from his mother—and the letter she had delivered—he was feeling lighter than he had in years. Although he knew better than to wish for someone's death, he couldn't help the excitement he felt at the thought of finally taking Nicoletta to wife. The excitement he felt about finally seeing his son. About being a father.

If only he had a grander house in which they could live.

"Tell me, cousin. Will my knowing Ancient Greek be of any help when we're actually in Greece?" Tom asked.

"It will," Donald assured him. "In some places. And your Latin will help in others."

"Which means you'll need to start reacquainting yourselves with the language," Henry remarked, leaning forward to regard his two sons at the table with a meaningful expression. "Perhaps as early as tonight."

"Yes, Father," they both replied in unison.

"We should be going," Henry said to Will. "We have to transport the wheat to the mill tomorrow."

"Understood," Will responded, rising to escort his brother-in-law and nephews to the hall. Henry hurried up to the parlor to escort Hannah and Grace to the vestibule, Barbara joining them to say her farewells.

Once the butler had seen to providing the Forster family with their coats, umbrellas, and a lantern, Barbara kissed her sons on the cheek and headed up the stairs.

Will and David bid them farewell and remained in the vestibule until they were out of sight.

They were about to return to the dining room, but they turned to discover Donald blocking their way. "What is it?" Will asked, sensing something was wrong.

"Mother can read Latin," Donald stated.

Leaning against the arched frame of the vestibule,

David regarded his older brother with a crinkled brow. "She's a countess," he said with a shrug.

From his father's initial reaction of puzzlement, Donald realized he needed to elaborate. "She read the letter that was mis-delivered to you."

Will blinked and straightened. "Was that letter from... from Catania?" he asked, his gaze briefly darting to his younger son.

"Indeed," Donald replied. "Mother knows... everything."

His eyes focused on Donald, Will's expression darkened. "I appreciate the warning," he said.

"Except... she doesn't know that *you* know," Donald added sheepishly.

Straightening, Will crossed his arms and sighed, all the air leaving his body. He regarded his son with a combination of resignation and contempt. "Damn," he muttered. He lifted his head in the direction of the dining room. "Let's continue this conversation in private," he said in a quiet voice.

"Why do I feel as if I've missed something important?" David asked, crossing his arms over his chest so he looked like a younger version of his father.

Donald rolled his eyes. "The woman I intended to marry six years ago lives in Catania," he stated as they took their seats at the table.

"Marry?" David's eyes rounded.

"But unbeknownst to me—or her—she was already betrothed to a marchese—"

"Ouch," David said in a quiet voice, gripping his port glass in one hand before draining it in one gulp.

"—but he's dead now, and I intend to finally marry her," Donald continued.

David blinked. "Good thing you're about to take us on a Grand Tour," he said, his gaze going to his father. "But who's going to act as our cicerone after Catania?"

Will cleared his throat. "I've a mind to offer myself as a guide," he said, his attention on his mind's eye. "About time I took your mother on a wedding trip."

A scoff sounded from his heir. "So much for time away from parents," David said under his breath.

"You would go?" Donald asked in surprise, ignoring his brother's complaint. "I know Aunt Hannah would feel better about sending Randy and Tom away if she knew you were with them."

"Only if I can offer Henry a suitable replacement for *me*," Will countered, his attention still on his glass of port. "I wonder if Thomas Cavanaugh would be willing to take my place as foreman for a year," he mused, not expecting either one of his sons to answer.

"He is the logical choice," Donald remarked. "We can promote Billy to oversee the stables in my stead," he suggested, referring to the husband of Hannah's lady's maid. "Cavanaugh's oldest son can see to the horses," he added. "He's good with the draft horses, and he and Billy get along well," he added.

"His youngest son can take my place," David offered, his gaze darting back and forth between his brother and father. "Not that anyone has to, since I'm the worst farmer in the family."

Both Donald and Will turned their attention on him. "True," they replied in unison.

"Hey," he said in protest.

"I'll let Henry know in the morning," Will stated. "Let's plan to leave for London in a week. Travel before the winter sets in."

"Athens and Rome will be more tolerable in the winter months," Donald said with excitement. "In the summer, you can make your way to the regions north of the Kingdom of the Two Sicilies," he added. "While I see to relocating Lady Montblanc and the Marchese Montblanc to England."

David's brows furrowed in confusion while Will regarded his son with a frown. "Or perhaps *you* should consider relocating to Catania."

Donald stared at his father for a long moment before he leaned against the back of his chair. He hadn't considered living on Sicily since he had first fallen in love with Nicoletta. Given his son's new status as the Marchese Montblanc, he realized his father was right.

Perhaps he did need to move to Catania.

"I'll write another letter to Nikky. Tell her of our plans," Donald murmured, a grin finally returning to light up his face.

Although he felt a moment of panic when he realized he would be in transit when her responding missive arrived, he quelled the sensation.

If they were truly leaving for London in a week, he might see her in as little as a month's time.

"What about your publisher?" his father asked, interrupting his reverie.

Donald blinked. "I'm nearly finished transcribing my final copy," he replied. "So I can bring the original and their copy with me to London," he said, deciding he would simply turn over what he had completed and not offer the option of an updated version. "I'll deliver the manuscript directly to their offices, and we'll take the other copy with us so we have a guide. I'll bring my original notes as well."

Will chuckled. "You might send a letter apprising them of our plans. Perhaps you'll be paid before we sail off."

"Sail off?" David repeated. "You mean to France, right?"

Shaking his head, his father said, "I'm a naval man, son. I have no intention of going to that part of the world by way of land," he remarked. "We'll go via the Mediterranean. With any luck, we'll end up on a ship with a captain who will allow me a turn at the wheel."

Donald and David exchanged quick glances, the younger allowing a look of confusion. Donald scoffed. "Our father was Commander Slater of *HMS Greenwich*," he stated. "He served in the British Navy for eight years," he added when David merely stared at him.

"Oh," the younger man responded. "I guess I'd quite forgotten," he murmured as the other two laughed.

"Off to bed, you two. We have a lot of work to do in the next week," Will stated.

The brothers nodded, David heading up the stairs while Donald made his way to the vestibule. He was donning his coat when his father joined him.

"I am sorry about mother," Donald said by way of an apology.

Will allowed a shrug. "I'll see to it. With any luck, I can settle her with news of our plans."

With only a week to pack and prepare to be gone for a year, she would have much to occupy her time.

CHAPTER 24

A GRANDMOTHER
CONFRONTS HER HUSBAND

half-hour later

When Will entered his master bedchamber and discovered Barbara sitting on the edge of the bed, he knew the next few minutes would be tense.

Uncomfortable.

Painful.

Instead of saying anything, he sat down next to her and took one of her hands in his. "Donald shared rather interesting news after you left the dining room," he said softly.

"Did he tell you we have a grandson?" she asked.

Will thought back to the post-dinner conversation and realized that at no point during his comments had Donald said anything about the new Marchese Montblanc being his son. "He didn't mention it at the table," he hedged.

Barbara turned to him. "You're not surprised," she stated. She suddenly stood, which had him rising from the bed. "How long have you known?" she asked, whirling to face him.

Will took a deep breath, his gaze darting to her hands. He noted how they clenched into fists, and he knew he was in for a beating if he didn't think fast. "Since the day he returned from his Grand Tour," he admitted, reaching down to grasp her fists in his hands.

"You *knew*?" she replied in disbelief.

"I did. I do," he said quietly. He pulled her into an embrace, determined to keep her from pummeling him with her fists or slapping him across the face. The way she began struggling in his arms had him tightening his hold on her.

"You didn't think to tell *me*?" she countered, doing her best to escape, her pounding fists ineffectual in making contact with his torso.

"I promised I would not," he said in a whisper.

She stilled, her body suddenly feeling limp in his arms. "Why?"

He rubbed her back with one hand. "What could I have done? What could *he* have done? What could *you* have done?" he asked softly. "Nicoletta was already married to another," he added in a whisper. "Although, not really if I'm to understand what truly happened."

Barbara looked up and stared at him for a moment. "You could have sailed to Sicily. Brought our grandson back," she said, although there was no conviction in her voice.

"Steal a babe from its mother?" he countered, arching a brow to reinforce his point. "Antony—our grandson—is now the Marchese Montblanc," Will stated. "In possession of a good deal of property and some wealth, it would seem. And he's probably going to become our son's stepson in the next year," he added, brushing away her tears with his thumb.

"I hate you," she whispered, pounding a fist on his chest.

Will gave a start, her words—and the punch—hurting far more than they should have. "I am sorry, Barbara. I thought our son might have been more forthcoming with you, but now I understand why he did not share this news with you."

"What's *that* supposed to mean?" she asked on a huff.

He arched a brow. "He knew exactly how you would react."

Barbara inhaled sharply. "How did *you* react?" she countered. "When he told you?"

Will inhaled and held the breath for a moment. "I was… surprised, and disappointed, and hurt, and resigned to it," he murmured in a halting voice. "I suppose I thought since he'd been a bastard, he would know better." He winced. "But he is determined to marry Nicoletta, that much I am sure of," he added. "They even have Montblanc's blessing. So… given his son's status and the situation overall —Nicoletta may not wish to move here—I think it's best if Donald goes to Sicily with the intention to remain there." Before Barbara could put voice to a protest, he added, "Which is why I'm going to take you on a wedding trip."

Barbara blinked several times. "A wedding trip?" she repeated in confusion.

Sensing the fight had gone out of her, Will gave up his hold on her hands and moved his to her waist. "I know it's well past time, but this way, you can meet Antony and your future daughter. Perhaps we can be witnesses for their wedding..."

He couldn't continue when she suddenly stood on tiptoes and kissed him, one of her hands moving to the back of his head while the other gripped his shoulder.

"Yes," she said when she finally ended the kiss.

It was Will's turn to blink. "Well," he said before chuckling softly. "I told the boys we would leave in a week."

Her eyes rounded. "A *week*?"

"Is that too soon?"

"I can be ready the day after tomorrow," she countered, which had him barking a laugh.

He pulled her into an embrace. "We have some arrangements to make with Henry first," he said. "And some decisions regarding who we take with us. We're going to be gone for at least a year."

Barbara's eyes rounded. "Can I take Stevens?" she asked, referring to her lady's maid.

"Of course," he replied.

She lifted a finger to his face, where his beard was longer than usual given he hadn't been shaved that morning. "What about your valet?"

He gave her a quelling glance. "I rather imagine he'll

have to come along since he's married to your maid," he teased.

Barbara tittered for the first time since that morning. "I love you," she whispered, wrapping her arms around his waist as she placed her head against his chest.

Heartened it hadn't taken as long to placate her as he expected, Will kissed the top of her head, his arms engulfing her smaller body. "Does that mean you'll let me share your bed tonight?"

He felt her nod and silently sighed his relief.

PART III
A GRAND TOUR BEGINS

CHAPTER 25
A PERSON FROM THE PAST

Eleven days later, the docks at Wapping

"I'm glad we were able to spend time with your father and Cherice," Barbara commented, allowing Will to help her down from the Devonville town coach and onto the wooden planks near where their ship was docked. Behind them, Tom, Randy, David, and Donald stepped out of another coach as porters hurried to unload their trunks from the back. "And that they kept to their social calendar rather than stay home on account of me."

"I appreciate you agreeing to attend the theatre," Will replied, giving a nod to the driver after their valises were out of the coach. Although invitations had been delivered to Devonville House within a day of their arrival for such events as a ball and a *musicale*—news of their arrival in Mayfair had spread quickly—only the young men had elected to attend. Cherice had begged them to, since the number of males was always lacking compared to that of the young ladies.

Although Randy had attended *ton* events in the past—he and Henry and Hannah had gone to London the year prior for the Season—the experience was entirely new for the younger Tom. He had declared an undying love for at least three different girls over the course of three different entertainments.

At least he hadn't decided to forgo his Grand Tour in favor of spending the Little Season in London.

"I had forgotten people don't go to watch the play but to see those in attendance," Barbara countered. "I was happy to sit in the back row and let the boys have the front seats."

Will chuckled. "Of course you were. I found the back row rather diverting given you were seated next to me." He waggled his brows and Barbara's face reddened.

"Will," she scolded, glancing about to be sure the young men weren't within earshot.

"I couldn't help myself, given what we'd been doing when we were supposed to be dressing for the theatre," he argued, his attention no longer on her but on the ship docked directly in front of them. "Well, I'll be damned," he murmured, one of his fists moving to rest on his hip.

Barbara followed his gaze as the boys joined them. "What is it?"

"Not it. Who," Will replied, hurrying to the ramp to meet the captain making his way in their direction.

Donald barked a laugh. "Now there's a man who hasn't changed a bit in six years," he commented.

"You *know* him?" Barbara asked, hooking a gloved hand around his elbow to keep Donald from following his father. "He doesn't appear the least bit reputable," she remarked.

"*That* is Captain John St. John. He brought me back from Rome," Donald said in a quiet voice. "In this very ship. *The Fairweather*."

"Lady Bellingham, may I have the honor of introducing you to Captain St. John?" Will asked as he approached Barbara from the top of the ramp with the ship's captain in tow. "He was captain of this vessel back when I was commanding the *Greenwich*," he explained, a smile lighting his face with mischief.

"My lady," St. John said, reaching for her hand with one of his bejeweled fingers. "I am honored, indeed." He brushed his lips over the back of her hand as Barbara gave him a slight curtsy.

"Captain. It's very good to meet you." She aimed a curious glance in her husband's direction, but before he could say anything else, the captain faced Donald and guffawed.

"Now, I recognize *you*," he said, grabbing Donald's proffered hand and shaking it. He indicated Barbara. "Did she give birth to you when she was five?"

His face bright red, Donald did his best to keep from glancing at his mother, sure she would be shocked by the man's comment. He shook his head. "Uh, my brother, David, and my cousins," he said, indicating the other boys. "The Honorable Randolph, heir to the Gisborn earldom, and Thomas Forster." He stepped aside as greetings were exchanged and porters hauled their trunks on board followed by the servants.

"I have a decent sized cabin for you two," St. John remarked, indicating Barbara and Will. "First one on the right at the bottom of the companionway. And three smaller ones for the boys and your servants on the same side. You'll all have portholes, of course, but you'll have to decide who gets the top bunks."

"I'm sure they can work it out," Will replied as they turned to climb the gangway. He offered Barbara his arm.

"Are the younger ones going on their Grand Tours?" St. John asked in a quiet voice as they approached the companionway.

"Indeed."

"And your oldest son?"

"He's... he's going to be their guide. At least for a time," Will stammered. He was glad Donald had seen to making a copy of the travel guide he had written—text as well as drawings—the pristine pages now in the hands of an editor at Chapman and Hall. The original manuscript was packed in his satchel along with the notes and drawings he had done whilst he was on his tour six years prior. If they had to leave Donald in Catania, Will had decided he would employ the guide and take over as cicerone.

"And you?"

Will gave a start, surprised the captain would ask. "A... uh, long overdue wedding trip," he finally said.

"Ah, *Roma*," St. John said, the word exaggerated as he placed both hands over his heart. "You will love it."

Will grinned, not about to admit he had already visited the city when the *HMS Greenwich* had put into port near there three decades earlier. "When do you plan to depart?"

"Since we have space, Nattersley has us taking on a few crates," St. John said, referring to the owner of the shipping company. "They're being loaded now. Once they're aboard, we'll be off."

"No other passengers?" Will asked.

"Normally, every cabin would be full, but not this trip."

Will furrowed his brows. "Any particular reason?"

St. John shrugged. "The doors to two of the cabins were damaged. Had a bit of a scuffle with the last bunch of passengers, so my cook has moved his stock into them," he explained. "Saves him the trouble of going down to the cargo hold."

"Does that mean our meals will be at the captain's table?" Will asked.

"Of course. Cook will have breakfast ready before we hit the Channel, and dinner is at seven."

"I hope he knows there are four hungry young men," Barbara murmured.

St. John chuckled. "Can't be any worse than my crew, but I'll remind him."

They stopped in front of the opening in the deck where steep stairs led down to the cabins and the cargo hold areas. "Oh, dear," Barbara murmured. "How am I to...?" She stopped mid-sentence as Will quickly descended the steep steps and turned to hold up his hands.

"I've got you," he said.

"Well, I'm not going to jump," she argued. "This part I believe I can... Oh!"

Before she quite knew what was happening, Will had his arms wrapped around her bell skirt at her knees. She was forced to bend and grip his shoulders as he lowered her until her booted feet touched the wood-planked floor.

He straightened, grinning broadly. Upon seeing her look of shock, he said, "We'll work on it."

"I was more concerned about climbing *up*," she said, shaking out her skirts and ignoring the snickers sounding from above.

Behind her, the boys scrambled down the companionway and disappeared into their respective cabins, their excitement infectious as they called out which beds were to be theirs.

Before she could step into the first cabin, Will had one arm around her shoulders and another beneath her knees.

"Whatever are you doing?" she asked as she was suddenly lifted into his arms, forcing her to wrap her hands around his neck lest she end up on her bum.

"It's our wedding trip, remember? I think I should carry you over the threshold." He did so, taking care to be sure they could make it through the small doorway without snagging her redingote on the wooden frame. By the time he set her down in the middle of the small room, she was giggling and he was chuckling.

They both sobered as they glanced around. "Where's the bed?" she asked, finding only a small desk, square table and two chairs. Their trunks had been placed under the porthole window.

"Against the wall," Will said, when he spotted some ropes. "We have to lower it using the ropes," he added, when he noted her look of confusion.

"That's rather ingenious," she murmured.

"Do we have bed linens?" he asked.

"Several sets. I made sure the boys each had their own," she replied, moving to one of the trunks. "Are you thinking to go back to bed before breakfast?"

Will moved to stand behind her and wrapped his arms around her waist. He kissed her on the side of her neck. "Maybe. But not to sleep," he whispered.

"Will," she breathed in disbelief.

"I cannot help it," he said. "I have the horn for you. Ever since we were in the coach. I nearly had you sit atop me," he claimed.

She glanced over at one of the chairs tucked under the table. "Do you think it will hold both of us?"

He chuckled. "We can find out," he said, grinning as he undid the fastening at the top of his pantaloons.

Unbuttoning her redingote, Barbara gasped when she saw how his manhood sprang out. He quickly pulled out the chair and took a seat before reaching for her.

Gathering her skirts so most of the fabric was off to the sides or behind her, she straddled him. Wriggling until she felt his tip at her entrance, she tittered. "I cannot believe we're doing this," she murmured.

"There's water in the ewer," he said. When he noticed her eyebrows furrowing in question, he added, "So we'll be able to clean up without having to leave the cabin."

Her titters turned into a fit of giggles. "Will," she whispered, adding a gasp when he thrust up and entered her.

He leaned forward until his head was pressed against the space above her breasts, his hands under her skirts to grip her hips. "You smell so good," he whispered.

"As do you," she countered, lifting and lowering herself on his rod as quickly as she could manage.

"So glad you don't wear drawers."

"Never," she replied, inhaling sharply when his thumb made contact with her womanhood.

"I cannot hold on any longer," he whispered, quickening his movements.

She tightened her hold on his shoulders. "You needn't," she said, her words combining with her mewl of pleasure. She did her best to mute her cries by taking his lips with hers, her ecstasy forcing her to take a breath at the same moment his groan of satisfaction sounded.

Will leaned back, nearly causing the chair to topple over. "Well, that's certainly one way to bless a new living quarters."

Barbara raked her fingers through his hair, scraping his scalp with her fingernails. "Yes, it is," she whispered, grinning in delight. She glanced around the small cabin. "Do you realize this will be our first home away from home since... since we were married?" When Will didn't respond, she sat back and glanced down to discover his eyes were closed. Scoffing softly, she glanced out the porthole window and inhaled sharply when she realized the scenery was passing by. "We're moving."

Will stirred beneath her. "Have been since we stepped inside the cabin," he murmured.

"How... how could you tell?"

"How could you not?"

Barbara started to answer—she hadn't been aware of any movement—but she grew suspicious. "Were you trying to distract me?"

"Did it work?"

"Will!" she scolded. "I wanted to see us depart from the dock."

He chuckled. "Why?"

She inhaled softly. "This is the first time in my life I will have left England."

Angling his head to one side, Will furrowed a brow. "Apologies. But if it's any consolation, we haven't left England. And we won't for some time. We have to make it to where the Thames meets the North Sea. Then we'll head into the Channel."

"So... we'll be able to see England for a time?"

He nodded, helping her to stand as she held up her skirts. "For a whole day, I imagine."

"Oh. Then you're forgiven," she said, her attention on the sight beyond the porthole.

"Hold still," he said, pulling a handkerchief from his pocket.

Barbara gave a start when he used it to wipe her thighs. "Aren't you a model of chivalry?" she teased.

He chuckled as he put his pantaloons to rights and Barbara shook out her skirts.

The sudden knock on the door had both of them inhaling sharply. Will hurried to open it, finding the four young men on the other side. "What is it?" he asked with worry.

"Breakfast is served," Donald stated. "Your presence has been requested by our captain."

Will chuckled as Barbara joined him. "Then let's not keep him waiting." He turned to her. "Do you think you can handle climbing the companionway?"

She nodded.

"I'll go up first and help pull you up if you need assistance," he offered.

She gave him a quelling glance. "I can do it." She watched as the boys all bounded up the steep stairs and onto the deck above. Gathering her skirts so she had most of the bulk in one arm, she used the railing and made it almost to the top before Will reached down and captured her around the waist. He had her up and on the deck whilst attempting to stifle a laugh when she scolded him.

"You're light as a feather," he said, offering his arm. "You always have been."

She shook out her skirts and hooked her hand into his elbow, well aware a couple of the crew watched with amusement from where they worked on the deck. "I won't be after I eat something. I'm starving," she murmured.

"As am I," he said.

Set for eight, the captain's table was far more formal than Barbara expected. One of the sailors was seeing to pouring coffee while another delivered platters of coddled eggs, bacon, kippers, bread, and ham.

When his passengers had all been seated—Captain St. John insisted Barbara be seated to his right and Will at the opposite end of the table—he announced breakfast was served. "We're not formal here, and there are no footmen to serve you, so you'll need to pass the platters around the table."

"Fine with me," Tom said, anxious to get the first offering.

"I understand you brought my son back from his Grand Tour six years ago," Barbara said when she had helped herself to several foods.

St. John nodded. "He was so tanned from the sun, I mistook him for an Italian when he boarded," he said jovially.

"Do you frequently transport young men on their Grand Tours?"

He shook his head. "Rarely. Most take the land routes. They might board a ship on a river to cover more ground, though."

"Will we go to Sicily first? Or are you headed straight for Rome?" Randy asked. In the haste to leave England, the exact itinerary hadn't been shared with the cousins.

The captain glanced first at Donald and then at Will. "Depends on the wind. Sometimes I go to straight to

Rome, but if the winds favor us, I can make a slight detour and go around Sicily and then head north through the Strait of Messina. The main current there runs south to north," he explained. "Cook always likes to take on supplies at Catania." His gaze went to Donald. "I prefer not to go that way when we leave Rome, so I will simply skip it on my return trip."

"You take on passengers in Rome?" Will asked.

"I believe I'll have a full ship, yes," he replied. "Always a good deal of cargo, too."

"If you go around Sicily, will we be close enough to see the Greek temples at Agrigento?" Tom asked. "From the water?"

"We would, although they are far more impressive if you take a tour of them on land," St. John remarked. "You are going to spend time on the island, I hope? The Isle of Ortegia, Syracusa, Catania, Taormina, Palermo...?"

"They're all on the list," Donald said. For a moment, he had a thought about collecting Nicoletta and Antony and taking them along for the tour of the island. He didn't think she had ever been anywhere but Catania, Taormina, Naples, and Rome. If her family had taken the land route from Catania, they would have ridden in a coach north along the eastern coast to Messina. From there, it was a short ferry ride to the mainland and then coach-and-fours to reach Naples and Rome.

"Should we start in Catania?" Will asked, directing his query to everyone at the table.

Murmurs of agreement sounded, Barbara beating

Donald in putting voice to her vote. He gave the captain a look of embarrassment, and St. John's eyes narrowed slightly.

"Catania, it is," the captain stated, helping himself to another serving of ham. "I'll send word back to Nattersley when we dock at Valencia. The *Bellingham* should be in port when we arrive."

Will gave a start. "The *Bellingham*?" he repeated. Even though the Bellingham earldom was a courtesy title associated with the Devonville marquessate, it was still a surprise to hear the name associated with a sailing vessel.

"It was named long before you had the title," St. John said with a grin. "After some naval officer in the last century, I believe."

"Ah, that would be my grandfather, the admiral," Will stated. "Before he inherited the Devonville marquessate."

St. John chuckled. "Well, you don't want to be getting onto it at Valencia, because it will be headed for London when we set off for Sicily," he warned.

There was a round of chuckles before Will glanced around the table to discover most of the food had been eaten. "Our compliments to your cook," he said. "It appears as if we have finished off breakfast."

"If you'd like, you can take a turn at the wheel. My first mate Rodney should have us into the Channel by now," St. John offered.

Will smiled broadly. "It will be my pleasure."

CHAPTER 26
SAILING TO SICILY

Later that week

Despite a day of rough seas and gray skies, the boys and Barbara managed to avoid feeling seasick. Meanwhile, Will had enjoyed the challenge of navigating *The Fairweather* through the Channel and the Strait of Gibraltar while Captain St. John played cards with the three youngest cousins.

Left to their own devices, Barbara spent time reading a novel and doing needlework while Donald studied his notes and talked with his father while he manned the wheel.

"Will she really have to mourn the marchese for an entire year?" Donald asked, his gaze directed through the captain's spy glass. He was studying the skyline of Tangier, his memories of the port city mixed. Although he had acquired silk for his mother in exchange for delivering bolts of fabric to Lady Morganfield, it was also where he had learned from Captain St. John that he might be a father.

Besides his having to give up a girl for whom he had grown to love, he realized how badly used he had been by her father.

"Depends," Will replied, his attention following Donald's. He took the spy glass from his son and surveyed the horizon. Although a number of ships were traveling through the strait, none seemed as if they might host pirates.

"On what?"

Will handed the tube back to Donald. "Societal expectations. Whether or not she felt affection for him." He arched a brow.

"She grew to love him," Donald murmured. "He was her natural father," he added.

"Then… she'll wear widow weeds for at least six months and then go into half-mourning. That is, if Sicilians are anything like the English in that regard."

A groan sounded from Donald, which had Will chuckling softly. "By the time you see her, more than a month will have passed." He angled his head to one side. "You really believe you still love her? You still wish to marry her?"

His son nodded. "Of course I do. I have since…" His face reddened, which had Will arching his brow again.

"She is no doubt Catholic," Will said, almost making it a question.

Donald nodded. "I know. We can marry in a civil service," he replied. "It need not be an issue."

Will winced, obviously not convinced. "Was she your first?" he asked in a voice barely loud enough to be heard above the sound of the ship slicing through the water.

"First and only," Donald replied.

The words confirmed what Will had suspected ever since Donald had returned from his Grand Tour. "Her son already has a name. A title. Property," he gently warned.

"I know. But I can still be a father to Antony. For the rest of my life."

Will stared at his oldest son for a moment before he finally gave him a curt nod. "From what you've told me, and from what your mother seems to have discovered, it would seem you have nothing to be concerned about when it comes to the marchesa. She obviously still holds you in high regard."

Donald nodded. "We made a pact, Father. I promised I would wait for her for ten years."

"You're not getting any younger."

Grimacing, Donald agreed. "Hopefully we can give Antony some brothers and sisters."

It was Will's turn to grimace, and his son noticed. "What is it?"

Will glanced around, as if to confirm they were still alone on deck. "I always wanted to give your mother a girl, but when David was born…" He allowed the comment to trail off.

His son's brows furrowed. "You mean she can't? Have another baby, I mean?" Donald asked, obviously surprised.

Shaking his head, Will said, "I promised her if we had the opportunity to take in an orphan—from the village or Gisborn's lands—we would do so, but there haven't been any," he explained. "And despite her warnings to Hannah that she would steal Grace from her…" He shrugged as he aimed a teasing grin in his son's direction.

"I can't imagine Grace would be the daughter Mother would want," Donald commented. "She is such a hoyden."

Will guffawed. "Much to my sister's dismay," he agreed. After a moment, he sighed. "She'll grow out of it. You watch. When she's eighteen or so and has her first Season in London, her days of being a tomboy will be well and far behind her."

"From your lips to God's ears," a feminine voice said from behind him.

Will whirled around to discover Barbara approaching from the companionway. A parasol hovered over her head, and one gloved hand was pressed to her midriff. "Sweeting, are you all right?" Will asked in concern.

"I think the seas have finally decided to have their way with me," she said, screwing her face into a wince.

"There's no shame in seasickness," Will said, motioning for Donald to take the wheel. He escorted Barbara to the deck railing.

"I feel much better now that I'm up here," she

claimed. "I think I just needed some fresh air," she added, her gaze on the horizon. Her eyes widened. "Are there always so many ships headed in and out of the Mediterranean?"

"Uh… we're going through the Strait of Gibraltar," he replied. "It's only about eight miles wide, so it's a bit of a bottleneck for ships. Once we're through, the other vessels will spread out a bit," he explained.

"What's that odd noise?"

Will furrowed his brows. "Noise?"

"The… the chattering? It sounds as if… as if we're being scolded."

Will chuckled. "Ah, the monkeys," he stated. "I wasn't even aware of them until you mentioned it."

She gave him a worried glance. "How you didn't hear them makes we wonder if you're losing your hearing."

He kissed her forehead. "I'm listening for other sounds," he countered. "Like the sails flapping or the hull scraping on something." He escorted her closer to the wheel so he could take over from Donald.

"I think you've been at the wheel more than our captain," she accused.

"You say that as if you think I mind," he countered.

Her eyes narrowed. "You love it, don't you? Steering a ship?"

He shrugged. "I didn't realize how much I missed it until yesterday," he admitted. "And I'm a bit surprised at how quickly it's all come back. You needn't worry about me putting in for my own ship, though," he assured her. Two decades on land—overseeing hundreds of acres of farmland and spending time with tenant farmers—had changed him. At some point he would inherit the Devonville marquessate, and although there would be less farmland to manage, there would be mines and three villages to oversee. He was secretly glad his illegitimate brother, Stephen, had taken to the task when their father had offered him the responsibility. When William Slater, Marquess of Devonville, did finally die, Will hoped Stephen would continue what he was doing.

Her gaze on the horizon to the south, Barbara sighed. "I remember hearing tales of this place when I was a girl. My uncle used to speak of Gibraltar and the monkeys. Of Tangier and pirates. Of the souks in Rabat and Marrakech and Fez, although he never said how he ended up so far inland from the ocean," she said.

Will knew immediately which uncle she spoke about. As the second son of an earl, Matthew Higgins had served time in the British Navy long before Will attended the naval academy. "Did you ever wish to go to those places?" he asked. Until she had learned about Antony, she had never seemed anxious to travel.

She grinned. "Truth be told, I think I preferred to hear about them, because I could not believe they would be as exotic as he made them out to be."

"Ah, you thought you would be disappointed should you ever see them for yourself?"

"Something like that," she admitted.

"What about Rome? All the other places we're planning to go?" he asked, his attention going to the top of the companionway. The captain, whose attention was directed toward Tangier, made his way to him.

"Something wrong?" Will asked.

St. John paused to kiss the back of Barbara's hand as he bowed before her. "Your younger nephew has managed to lighten my purse far too much," he complained, taking the wheel from Donald. "I'm quite sure he wasn't cheating."

"That's because he knows better," Barbara said. She tugged on Will's sleeve. "I do believe the captain wishes to take back control of his ship," she added, arching a brow.

St. John chuckled. "Should you wish for a change from gentleman farmer to sailor, I'm sure Nattersley could see his way to hiring you on as part of the crew of one of his ships," he teased.

"Don't tempt me," Will said, chuckling.

"Any trouble?"

Will shook his head. "I had my suspicions about that frigate," he said, pointing to a ship going in the opposite direction.

"She's harmless," St. John commented. "I am glad my route doesn't go to Greece or beyond, though."

"Oh?" About to head to the railing with Barbara on his arm, Will paused.

"The Turks are at it again with Egypt," the captain said. "Trying to get it back. I've heard pirates are taking advantage in the Aegean."

Will considered their plans for future travel beyond

the Kingdom of the Two Sicilies. "Good to know," he said.

When they reached the railing, Barbara glanced up to regard her husband with worry. "What are you thinking?"

He shrugged. "That I am glad we plan to visit Catania first," he replied. "We can make plans for Greece as we learn more. I expect we'll be welcome there, though."

"Why do you say that?"

"We helped them win their war for independence from the Turks," he explained.

She nodded her understanding. "Are you thinking of returning to this life?" she asked, waving a gloved hand to indicate the ship.

"What?" he asked in surprise. When he saw her furrowed brows and look of worry, he shook his head. "No, my sweet. I will admit, I enjoy a turn at the wheel now and again, but... I shan't be captaining a ship again in this life."

Obviously relieved to hear it, Barbara stood on tiptoes and kissed him on the cheek.

He grinned. "So I take it you're not interested in being my first mate?" he teased.

"I thought I already was," she replied, arching a brow.

His responding guffaw could be heard at the other end of the ship.

• • •

*I*n front of the wheelhouse for the entirety of Donald's conversation with his father, Randy crossed his arms and shook his head. He might not have been able to hear everything that was said, but he now had a better understanding of his oldest cousin. Of why Donald eschewed courting. Why he didn't show any interest in the young ladies they had met at the ball they had attended prior to leaving London.

He thought of Donald's promise of ten years made to a woman he had probably only known for a few weeks.

Ten years?

How could anyone make such a vow at the age Donald had been back then? Back when had first visited Catania?

Could I? he wondered, his gaze on the cerulean blue waters straight ahead.

Would he do such a thing as promise a young woman he would wait for her?

Never in his life had he felt affection for a young lady, so he found he couldn't answer the question for himself.

"I hope she's worth it," he murmured, finally pushing away from the wooden structure to make his way to the companionway.

A game of cards with his brother seemed the best way to put thoughts of his cousin out of his mind.

CHAPTER 27
SICILY IN SIGHT

*E*ight days later
After a stop in Valencia to rendezvous with the *Bellingham*, drop off cargo, and allow the ship's cook to restock his stores, Captain St. John piloted *The Fairweather* until they were nearly to Sicily. If he followed his usual route, the ship would go directly to the Port of Civitavecchia northwest of Rome. "What's it to be?" St. John asked of Donald, who had joined him at the wheel when the sun was barely above the eastern horizon. "Straight to Sicily or straight west to Rome?" Although there was still a band of clouds left from the rain that had fallen the night before, as well as a strong tailwind, the sky promised a fine day.

"Can you afford this detour?" Donald asked, his voice barely audible over the sound of the wind. "If we do go to Catania? How late will you be making the port at Civitavecchia?"

St. John chuckled. "With this wind? I'm likely to

arrive earlier than scheduled, even with the detour," he replied, although he made the comment in jest. "We're fortunate there are not other passengers aboard or you might be arguing with them."

"I was reminded Lady Montblanc must mourn the marchese," Donald murmured.

St. John took a deep breath and let it out. "Does she still feel affection for you?"

Donald's eyes widened. "Yes, of course. Her letters—"

"Then we're going to Catania," the captain stated.

"By way of the Strait of Messina?" Donald asked, thinking it might be the fastest route.

"No. Too dangerous. We'll go along the southern side so your brothers and Lady Bellingham can get a view of some of the Greek temples and the Isle of Ortegia from the water. Then we'll head north to Catania."

"*I've* never seen that view," Donald said before he dipped his head. "I appreciate it, Captain. I do hope you won't be in trouble with Mr. Nattersley, though."

"No reason for him to know," St. John said. "I'll still be docking in Rome to drop off some cargo and pick up passengers and more cargo." With the slightest turn of the wheel, the ship shifted and seemed to slice through the water even faster than it had been traveling.

His gaze on the ship's bow, Donald said, "I couldn't help but notice you didn't seem surprised to see me when we boarded a fortnight ago."

The captain shrugged. "Truth be told, I half-expected I was going to see you far sooner than this."

Donald winced. "Believe me, I wanted to return. I wanted to go back to Catania the moment you mentioned the possibility I might be a father."

Making another adjustment on the wheel, St. John finally faced the young man. "Will you take them back? To England?" he asked.

Glancing toward the companionway, as if to confirm they wouldn't be overheard, Donald shook his head. "Her ladyship's husband..." He winced at saying the lie out loud. "He was a marchese. He had lands and properties, and now they belong to... well, to my son," he replied. "Lady Montblanc has been living in a castle on Mount Aetna. I cannot begin to offer her and the marchese anything close to that in England," he explained. "I think it best I remain here with them."

St. John chuckled. "Does Lady Bellingham know that?"

Donald displayed a grimace. "She knows my thoughts on the matter, but I wanted to wait until after I discussed the matter with Nikky."

"Nikky?" St. John repeated, one of his brows rising in surprise.

"Lady Montblanc," Donald said, his face reddening.

"If you stay, what will you do for your living?" the captain asked, his attention going to something on the horizon ahead. "I cannot imagine you happy living a life of leisure as the consort of a widowed marchesa." From the tone of his voice, it sounded as if he was teasing, but there was an undercurrent of concern, too.

Donald's gaze followed St. John's as the captain lifted a spyglass to his eye. Land appeared and dropped from sight with the ship's movement through the rough water. "I intend to continue my writing," he said, squinting in an effort to see whatever it was that had the captain's attention. "What is it?"

St. John gave him the spyglass. "We've made better time than I thought," he murmured, giving the wheel another quarter turn. "We just passed Marettimo," he said, referring to a small island west of Sicily. "And Favignana is directly ahead." He turned the wheel even more, sending them on a more southerly route.

Donald held the tube to his eye and scanned the growing land mass. "Is that Trapani?" he asked in awe, referring to one of the western-most towns on Sicily. A windmill, its vanes spinning with the strong wind, appeared in and out of focus. Inside the building, their movement turned a screw mechanism necessary for harvesting salt from the Mediterranean.

"Marsala, actually. Have you been?" St. John asked in surprise.

"No... but I read about it. I've seen drawings of the windmills," Donald replied, his gaze still directed through the spyglass. With the slight change in the ship's direction, more of the island's land mass came into view to the south, cliffs gradually rising from the sea to begin the one-hundred-and-seventy-mile southern coastline of Sicily.

"At the rate we're going, we'll see Girgenti late this afternoon," St. John said. "Some of the temples at sunset. Should be quite impressive."

"Is it true they look like they're made of gold?" Donald asked, still holding the spyglass to his eye.

"Last I saw them in the late afternoon, they did," St. John said. "Trick of the light, I suppose."

Tom and Randy appeared from below, the two arguing over something the older brother held in one hand. Donald gave the spyglass back to the captain and regarded them with a curious expression. "What's wrong?"

Randy held out a small book. "Tom says this is the travel guide we should be using once we reach…" His gaze had gone to the cliffs. "Whoa. Where are we?"

"Sicily," Donald said, taking the book from Randy. "Where did you get this?" he asked, examining the title page of the guide, *Boswell On the Grand Tour*. From the date included under the author's name, he realized it was about eighty years old, and he chuckled softly.

"At a shop in Valencia. Are you familiar with it?" Randy asked.

"I read it before I went on my Grand Tour," Donald admitted. "Some of it proved very helpful at the time, but now it's quite out of date. There have been a number of discoveries since then."

"That was written long before the temples on Sicily were re-erected by the Duke of Serradifalco," St. John added, indicating the green clothed-covered book.

"You'll find the drawings no longer match what you'll see should you visit the Valley of the Temples."

"Serradifalco? The name is familiar, but who was he?" Randy asked, his gaze on the horizon.

"An archaeologist. Domenico Antonio Lo Faso Piestrasanta," St. John said in a sing-song voice, a grin lighting his face. "I rather enjoy saying his name."

"We learned about him at Oxford," Tom said, his eyes rounding. "Are we going to see his restored temples?"

"Later today, apparently," Donald replied, paging through the brittle pages of the guidebook until he reached the section covering the "Kingdom of the Two Sicilies". He found a page with a drawing and held it open so his cousins could see it. "This is one of the best preserved temples, but the duke restored the pediments, so it's even more complete," he said, referring to the Temple of Concordia.

David joined them, although his attention was on the approaching cliffs. "I thought the water felt rougher," he commented.

St. John grinned. "You take after your father when it comes to the water. Have you thought of a career in the navy when you're finished with your Grand Tour?" He handed the spyglass to the heir.

"Other than an occasional dip in the River Isis, I've barely been around water," David said, attempting to keep the spyglass steady as he aimed it toward the growing shoreline. "So I don't think I'll be following in Father's footsteps."

"Grandfather wasn't in the navy," Donald commented, hoping his brother wasn't thinking to take to the seas upon his return to British shores.

"But great-grandfather was," Tom said. "So… your son will be a navy man," he said as he clapped David on the back of his shoulder.

The others chuckled as David's eyes widened. "I haven't even met my future wife, and you already have my son a Portsmouth man." He shook his head before suddenly grinning. "He could become an admiral like his great-great-grandfather."

His brother and cousins rolled their eyes before Donald punched St. John in the shoulder. "Now look what you've done."

The captain chuckled softly, glad when the young men made their way to the companionway. He turned the wheel over to his first mate and made his way into his cabin, determined to study the map of Sicily's shore.

He wanted to be sure to provide the very best viewing experience for his passengers.

CHAPTER 28
A VIEW FROM THE SEA

*L*ater that afternoon

As crewmen adjusted the main sail and the top mast sail, Captain St. John watched as the Earl and Countess of Bellingham and their sons and nephews lined up along the leeward deck and gazed north.

Only the hour before, the family had hurried to the deck when the Greek temples at Selinunte were spotted by the barrelman. Perched in the crow's nest on the foremast, the sailor seemed to enjoy watching the passing scenery as much as the ship's passengers, and the captain made sure to tease him. "You would think you had never seen a Greek temple before," he called up.

"That's because I haven't, cap'n," the lanky man shouted in glee.

St. John chuckled as he made sure to steer clear of a series of fishing boats heading toward the docks southeast of Agrigento, their nets full from a day at sea. Up the steep hill from there and to the east, the remains of a crumbling city wall and the limestone columns from ancient Greek temples stood out atop a plateau, their Doric columns cast in a golden orange glow from the late afternoon rays of the sun.

"Look at how they're lined up," Tom remarked in awe, his attention on a pair of columns left standing at the Temple of Hercules.

"Originally there were fifteen temples in Akragas," Randy said. "At least, that's what the guidebook claimed."

"How many are left?" Barbara asked, gasping when her attempt at using a pair of opera glasses was finally successful and the Temple of Concordia was briefly in her sites. "This one looks as if it could still be in use."

"Probably is," Donald remarked. "But as a church."

The captain had found another spyglass in his cabin, and Will was expertly using it on another set of ruins before he passed it to David. "Eleven, or eight, depending on how you count them," he said. "Along with some Roman ruins."

"The Normans were here, too," Donald said, finally capturing a spyglass from his cousin. He concentrated his viewing efforts on the very last of the string of ruins. "The Temple of Hera was badly damaged in an earthquake—"

"I thought the Carthaginians took it down," Tom said in protest.

"—and the Carthaginians helped," Donald acknowledged. "But the duke saw to re-erecting at least part of her columns," he explained. "The worst of the damage occurred at the Temple of Zeus. There's so much rubble, it's hard to distinguish what it once was, but a few of the telemons have been reassembled. They were twenty-five feet tall, and that was only half the height of the temple."

"What is a telemon?" Barbara asked in a whisper, her gaze going to her husband.

"A giant figure of Atlas made to act as a column. Held up the temple walls," he replied, keeping his attention on the plateau even as he raised his arms and stood with his elbows bent to imitate how the columns had been posed.

"It must have been quite a sight when... well, when would this have been?" she asked.

"Over two-thousand years ago," Randy said.

"Twenty-three-hundred years ago," Tom stated, rapping his brother's shoulder with the back of his hand.

"We're moving so fast, they'll be out of sight soon," Barbara complained.

Will grinned. "There will be more to see."

"From the water?"

He nodded and pointed farther down the coast, where white cliffs could be seen rising from the water in a series of terraces.

"Are those stairs?" she asked in awe.

"*Scala dei turchi*," the captain said as he joined them at the railing. Rodney had taken the wheel at his behest.

"The stairs of the Turks," she interpreted.

St. John didn't try to hide his surprise. "Indeed. They are rather large, but they are negotiable. You'll see a series of them along this part of the coast."

"Did the Turks really use them to climb onto the island?" she asked, her opera glasses now trained on the formations.

"Actually the Saracen pirates did," Will said. "Back in the sixteenth century. They used to land there and plunder the coastal villages."

"Are there still pirates about?" Barbara asked, her worried gaze going to St. John.

He gave a quick glance in Will's direction before shaking his head. "The Saracens are no more," he assured her.

Although she didn't look completely convinced, Barbara returned her attention to the coastline. "I do appreciate you sailing close enough for us to see all this, especially with the sun setting so quickly."

"It's been my pleasure," the captain replied. "We are fortunate to have had good winds these past few days."

"When will we reach Catania?" she asked.

Will chuckled softly. "Patience, my lady. We haven't even made it to the Isle of Ortegia."

Barbara's lower lip was evidence of a brief pout before he leaned over and kissed her on the forehead. "Probably tomorrow."

She brightened. "I don't think I'll be able to sleep a wink tonight, I am so excited," she murmured.

Will smirked. "I may have to take advantage of that situation," he teased.

Visibly reddening in the late afternoon sun, Barbara grinned and turned her attention back to the shore.

CHAPTER 29
AN ISLE OF WONDERS

*L*ater that night

By the time *The Fairweather* reached the Isle of Ortegia off the coast of Syracusa, dinner had been served and the men were enjoying a glass of port with the captain. Standing at the railing, Barbara watched in awe as Rodney, the first mate, took the ship closer to the small island. Rectangles of light dotted the limestone buildings that seemed to rise straight up from the water, their shapes barely visible in the dim glow of a new moon.

"Is there even a shoreline?" she asked of the older man.

"Around on the other side there's a bit of a beach, I suppose," he replied. "Otherwise, it's pretty well covered with buildings. Has been since after the last big earthquake."

What seemed like several feet above the water, a straight wall gave way to what appeared to be a promenade, torches lighting the stone walkway. A few men leaned against support pillars, occasional puffs of smoke signs they were enjoying a post-dinner cigarillo or smoking a pipe. Strains of lively music could be heard coming from an open window.

"What is that?" she asked, her eyes darting to where torchlight illuminated what she thought might be some sort of tree rising from an abyss.

"Ah, the papyrus still grows in the Fonte Arethusa," he replied, setting the wheel before joining her at the railing. "One of the only places you'll find papyrus growing besides on the banks of the Nile in Egypt." He pointed to the greenery and then dropped his hand lower. "There's a fresh water spring there, you see. An ancient spring."

"Did you say Arethusa?" she asked.

"I did," he agreed.

"She was a nymph of Artemis," Will said, joining them at the railing. "The river god Alpheus—"

"The son of the god Ocean?" she asked, briefly glancing up to see her husband staring at the fluffy greenery.

"Indeed. He fell in love with her. Tried to seduce her every way he could, but she wasn't interested. She grew so annoyed with his attentions, Artemis turned Arethusa into a spring so she could escape from her undersea home of Arcadia. This is where she ended up."

By the time Will finished his telling of the Greek myth, the ship had sailed well past the papyrus and was nearing the castle walls of Maniace.

"It looks positively medieval," Barbara remarked.

"That's because it is," Will said before he allowed a guffaw. "That fortress has been there for six hundred years." He stepped closer to her and wrapped an arm behind her waist, his gaze still on limestone and granite walls. "Which has me wondering how old the Montblanc castle is."

Barbara glanced up at him. "Will it take long to reach it? Donald said it's on Mount Aetna. Isn't that a volcano?"

Will nodded. "It is," he acknowledged. "I suppose we'll find out as soon as tomorrow."

The ship reached the end of the castle's walls and Will noted how Rodney hurried back to the wheel. He chuckled.

"What is it?" Barbara asked.

"I think our speedy trip is about to slow down."

She gave him a worried glance. "Why do you say that?" she asked. Despite the nightfall, there was still a stiff breeze filling *The Fairweather's* sails.

"We're about to take a sharp turn to the north," he replied. Even as he said the words, a number of crewmen had appeared on deck, rushing about to change the direction of the sails.

Barbara's attention was still on the castle, though, as she tried to imagine what sort of home her only grandson was living in.

What if it truly was better than what they could offer in England?

CHAPTER 30
CATANIA, FINALLY

The next day

"Nervous?" Captain St. John asked when he joined Donald at the railing, the harbor of Catania within sight. They had finished breakfast the hour before when a sudden change in the direction of the wind had forced the crew to take down the top mast sail. Another sail had been dropped as Rodney steered *The Fairweather* closer to the harbor. With every reduction in speed, Donald's anxiousness grew more apparent.

"That and... excited, I suppose. I don't even know where to find her," Donald said on a huff.

"Well, she'll either be at the castle or at Montblanc's villa. You do remember where that is, do you not?"

"In Via Dei Crociferi," Donald murmured. "It's hard to miss."

St. John whistled in appreciation as he rolled his eyes, recognizing the name of the street as one of the more impressive in the large city, lined with magnificent villas and churches. "If she's at the castle, it could take you most of the day to get to it. You should be able to find a coach for hire near the dock." He knew the rest of the family was below deck, finishing their last-minute packing. No matter what happened with Donald and Nicoletta, the rest of the group had agreed to disembark at Catania to begin their tour of the island.

"I've a mind to dock here for a day or two until I learn your fate," the captain teased.

"Then Nattersley really will take your ship from you," Will warned with a grin as he stepped up to join them at the railing. Barbara was on his arm, although her attention was on the crew members who were bringing their trunks up from their cabins. Tom, Randy, and David topped the companionway one by one, their gazes immediately going to the skyline. All three carried valises and wore their more formal traveling clothes.

"You have everything packed?" Barbara asked.

"There's nothing left in those cabins but the furniture," Randy assured her.

When the servants appeared with their own valises, Will turned to Captain St. John and held out his right hand. "I know you'll be busy for the next few minutes, so allow me to thank you for all your help on this trip. And for allowing me so much time at the wheel."

"It was my pleasure," St. John replied. "With any luck, I'll be the one taking you back in a year or two," he added.

"We probably will go out of Rome after we do a tour here and in Greece," Will said.

A slight bump had them looking beyond the ship. The crew had already begun throwing ropes to the dock, one of the sailors swinging through the air on a rope before he dropped to the wooden planks below to grab the loose ropes and tie them around posts.

"To be twenty years younger," St. John murmured as he watched his sailors see to securing *The Fairweather* to the dock.

When the gangway fell to the dock and was in place, one of the crew hurried up and said, "We're ready for departure, Capt'n."

St. John inhaled and caught Donald's gaze. "The very best of luck to all of you," he said.

"I'll send word when I have secured a promise of marriage," Donald said.

"I thought you already had that," St. John countered.

"Well… a wedding date, then," Donald amended before he followed his parents, glad to see porters had already appeared to see to their trunks. "You would think they were expecting us," he added, his comment directed to the captain.

St. John shook his head. "Opportunists," he claimed with a grin. "Now, go find your girl," he ordered.

"Aye, Captain," Donald replied.

Once the entire family was off the ship, Donald led the way to where a hackney was parked. In his rusty Italian, he asked about the Cavarallo lodgings in Via Garibaldi and was assured they would be taken there. By the time his parents and his cousins were ensconced in the hackney, a second had pulled up to take him, David, and the Stevens. Donald couldn't help but grin at seeing the property he had called home for nearly two months during his last stay in Catania still looking the same as he remembered it.

When he knocked on the door, he was welcomed as if he was a long lost family member. "Signore Slater has returned," his host cried out, pulling him into an embrace. "I knew you could not stay away," Pietro Cavarallo claimed, slapping him on the shoulder.

Donald chuckled. "Have you rooms for all of us, Signore Cavarallo? We need four rooms for eight people," he added, holding up four fingers to reinforce the number.

"Sí, signore," Cavarallo said, opening his door wider. "Breakfast at nine o'clock and dinner at seven."

Donald chuckled. "*Grazie*," he said before waving in the direction of the two hackneys.

Within minutes, a servant was seeing to trunks as his parents, cousins, and the servants spilled forth and into the villa's courtyard.

Despite his impatience, Donald saw to acting as an interpreter until rooms had been assigned and luggage had been delivered.

"Would you like company?" Will asked when Donald said he was about to hail a hackney to take him to the Montblanc villa. If Nicoletta wasn't there, the servants would certainly be able to provide directions to the castle.

Donald considered the offer. "I suppose Mother will not take no for an answer," he guessed, glancing back to the courtyard door to discover she was already there.

"She won't," Will agreed, a smirk appearing.

"All right. If we have to go the castle—"

"It will be an all day trip, I know," his father finished for him. Will turned and waved for Barbara to join them.

She rushed from the wooden door, her skirts held up so her ankles were on display. Even though they had only been at the Garibaldi residence for less than an hour, Barbara had already changed into a different gown and hat.

Donald lowered his head to hide his humor as his father helped her into the hackney. "The Montblanc villa in Via Dei Crociferi," he said to the driver.

Blinking, the driver nodded. "Sí, signore," he replied. Once Donald was in the hackney, the equipage took off with a start, the wheels bouncing over the worn lava blocks that made up the streets of this part of Catania.

The trip was short, and when Donald exited the hackney, he asked if the driver could wait. "Lady Montblanc might not be in residence," he said by way of explanation.

"Oh, but she is," the driver assured him. "Ever since Lord Montblanc's death, she has been here to receive mourners. Callers," he added.

Donald's heart skipped a beat. He handed the man some lira. "*Grazie*," he said. He urged his mother and father to join him before he faced the villa's carved wooden door and pulled the chain that would signal their presence to a servant.

They didn't have to wait long. An immaculately dressed butler opened the door only minutes later. "*Sì?*" he said, his gaze going from Donald to the couple who stood behind him.

"The Earl and Countess Bellingham and Signore Slater to see Lady Montblanc and the new Lord Montblanc," Donald said.

The butler's eyes narrowed before he opened the door wider. "This way," he said. "Marchesa Montblanc has not received callers all day, though. You may have to return on the morrow," he warned.

"Is she in good stead?" Donald asked, concern evident in his voice. "Is *he* in good stead?" he added, now even more worried.

His manner guarded, the butler seemed to think on his response. "As good as could be expected. His lordship misses his padre."

Donald winced at hearing the comment. "Of course he does," he replied.

They were led into a parlor featuring comfortable furnishings and immaculate paintings and statuary. Donald was about to settle himself on a hardback chair but nervousness had him instead pacing in front of a massive fireplace. Meanwhile, his mother flitted about, admiring the artwork as his father dutifully followed her and grinned at seeing her enthusiasm.

As quiet seemed to engulf the room, the vibrations of

the rushed footsteps of a child could be felt through the carpet followed by a feminine voice sounding a scold.

Donald froze in place and stared at the open door while Barbara and Will stood side by side in front of a settee. Collectively, they held their breaths until a dark-haired boy appeared. He, too, froze, his eyes wide in a face framed with black curly hair. "*Nonno? Nonna?*"

In unison, Donald and his father bowed while his mother dipped a deep curtsy. When they straightened, they discovered the young marchese was no longer alone.

Nicoletta, Marchesa Montblanc, stood behind him.

CHAPTER 31
A TOUR BEGINS

*M*eanwhile

For the brief time Tom was in his room at the Cavarallo villa, he wondered if he would ever feel such affection for a girl as to travel nearly two-thousand miles to see her again. Although he was sure Donald hadn't told him everything, he was beginning to suspect there was more to his cousin's impending reunion with the girl he called Nikky than what he had admitted. Especially after Donald claimed he was going to take the girl to be his wife.

He couldn't imagine things being the same betwixt them after such a long period of time had passed. And now there was a boy to consider. Another man's son.

He shook his head when he remembered his older brother, Nathaniel, had been another woman's son. Yet his mother had accepted him as if he were one of her own. She had never treated him any differently from the way she treated the four children she had carried in her womb.

As the servants saw to collecting clothes to be laundered, he and Randy discussed the possibility of their older cousin never returning to British shores. Overhearing the remark, David joined them, scoffing at the claim. "Of course he'll return. He'll bring her and the boy, probably for a wedding trip."

"Well, until they return from wherever they've gone, we should go exploring," Tom suggested. "I found a map in Donald's notes," he added, holding up the folded sheet his cousin had purchased at a shop during his first visit to Catania.

"We're going for a walk," Randy said to Mr. Stevens. "Be back before dinner."

"Careful you don't get lost," the valet replied.

The three cousins headed down the stairs to the courtyard below. They were about to open the arched wooden door leading to Via Garibaldi when Tom said, "Well, all I can say is this marchesa must be some beauty."

At that very moment, two young ladies passed by the door, their arms interlinked while one carried a parasol in a gloved hand. When they saw the expressions of surprise on the young men's faces, they tittered but hurried on their way.

"Beauty, indeed," Randy remarked, awestruck.

Despite keeping his voice low, it was obvious the girls had overheard him, for their giggles grew louder.

David chuckled. "It sounds as if we're going to have

to worry about you next," he accused as they filed out onto the black pavement and headed in the direction of the Roman theatre.

"Not me," the oldest cousin claimed. "Although I will admit it will be nice to simply look, the girls we see on this tour will be nothing but novelties."

"Novelties, you say?" his brother questioned.

"Yes. The thing about novelties is they soon lose what makes them novel and they simply become the norm," Randy explained. "I fully intend to take an English girl to wife when it's time to start my nursery."

The other two murmured likewise intentions as they made their way through the thin city streets, Tom keeping track on the map as best he could.

CHAPTER 32
MOURNFUL THOUGHTS

*E*arlier *that day, at Villa Montblanc in Via dei Crociferi*

The sense of despair Nicoletta had felt during the three weeks since Montblanc's funeral had finally begun to settle into a sort of numbness. The number of aristocratic callers who stopped by to pay their respects had dwindled to one or two a day. At least they acknowledged her son as the new Marchese Montblanc, promising him their allegiance should a situation arise requiring it.

She couldn't think of what that might be given the status of noble families in the Kingdom of the Two Sicilies. Most of the peers pretended nothing had changed despite the Bourbons having taken control. At least their lands hadn't been confiscated, and what small fortunes they still possessed could be hidden away.

Nicoletta had done everything her true father had advised whilst he suffered the last few weeks of his life.

She had hidden jewels and gold in small chests beneath floorboards, sewn money into the hems of several gowns, and even stuffed coins into the crown of her bed's canopy.

"You have sent word to Signore Slater?" he had asked between labored breaths.

"I have," she acknowledged. "But I only told him you were ill."

She remembered the pained expression he displayed upon hearing her words. "I will be dead before he arrives," he complained. "I wished to see him again."

Surprised at hearing his words, Nicoletta asked why.

"He promised to wait for you—"

"And he has," she assured him.

"I wished to give him my blessing. To marry you," he struggled to get out. "To be a father to his son."

"Shh," she had responded, holding a finger to her lips.

"You needn't mourn me for a year, *mia bella*. Wear black if you must, but let your heart be his."

"Ricardo," she gently scolded. "Of course I shall mourn you."

The closer Ricardo Malgeri came to death, the less guarded he was about keeping their secret. When he called her *figlia*—daughter— in the presence of a servant, the lady's maid had directed a look of sorrow in Nicoletta's direction.

"He knows not what he says," the maid murmured when her mistress visibly winced. "Poor man."

At least she had taken comfort in the knowledge

Ricardo wanted her to marry Donald. Wanted Antony to know his natural father. As to when they would meet, though, she hadn't a guess.

Until that morning when Trimarco, the butler, brought her the morning's post. Atop all the white envelopes bearing words of sympathy and sorrow was a letter from England.

A letter from Donald.

My dearest Nikky,

Please accept my sincerest condolences on the loss of your beloved father. I know what he has meant to you these past six years, and I mourn his loss for our son and for you.

I received your letter this morning, and a few hours later, was given another in which you wrote of Montblanc's illness. Please know that if I had been in possession of it when it should have been delivered, I would have made arrangements to travel immediately.

Given this latest news, I will depart for London in a week and board a ship as soon as passage can be arranged.

Although my father and I have kept you a secret from my family all these years, my mother now knows.

Everything.

Since I cannot expect you to come to England—it would not be fair to you or to Antony—she insists on coming with me. Since my father would not let her go without him, he is going as well.

With two cousins and my younger brother

wanting to embark on their Grand Tours, they are joining us, too.

There is much to discuss once I reach you, but know that my love for you has not waned. I still want you to be my wife and hope that we may be wed when your mourning period is over.

Please give my love to Antony. I look forward to meeting him as much as I look forward to seeing you again.

With all my love,
Don

Tears of relief had begun streaming down her face as she read her lover's words. A glimmer of happiness replaced the numbness. Despite having told Trimarco she would not be accepting callers this day, she rang for her lady's maid and dressed in her very best day gown, its silk bell skirt wide and its waist tucked in tight beneath her bosom. Her hairstyle, far more simple than the elaborate coiffures she had worn when Montblanc was alive, featured a lock of hair resting on one shoulder. No gray strands marred the raven black hair, and although she was noticeably older, her skin didn't display the lines around her eyes or mouth that Armenia complained about these days.

When she regarded her reflection in the cheval mirror, she recalled how concerned she had been about Donald seeing her naked the very first time she had invited him to her bedchamber. How worried she had been that he might think her too fleshy.

Well, she was more so now, although she hadn't eaten as much as Montblanc had encouraged her to do so over the years.

The thought of her father didn't bring tears to her eyes as it would have the day before, but it did have her thinking of Antony.

Anxious for her son's company, she had gone up to the schoolroom to find him with his tutor. He had already learned his numbers and how to write his name on a slate, but he tended to vex the older gentleman with his requests to learn English.

"I will see to your English," she told him in English, giving the tutor an apologetic glance.

"He is distracted today," the tutor complained. "He keeps saying someone is coming to meet him."

She gave her son a smirk. For the past year, Montblanc had been telling him he had another grandfather and a grandmother that he would one day meet. She had sometimes read him the letters from Donald, the boy curious about life in England. "Perhaps I should take him out for some air. The Prince of Biscari gardens?" she suggested, knowing he liked the labyrinth.

Antony's eyes lit up. "Can we?"

"I'll be sure he is ready for lessons on Monday," she promised as the tutor closed his leather satchel. "*Buona giornata.*"

A few minutes after the older gentleman had departed the schoolroom, she and Antony were on their way to his bedchamber to see to a coat when the butler appeared with word they had callers.

"I knew someone was coming," Antony said, interrupting the servant.

"I've put them in the parlor," Trimarco said as Antony took off at a run down the corridor. "Should I deliver tea?"

"Antony!" Nicoletta called out in a scold. "No running in the house." She turned back to the butler. "Tea, *sí*," she said before hurrying after the boy. She soon slowed her own steps in an effort to collect her thoughts and make sure her gown wasn't mussed from her visit to the schoolroom.

She gave a start when she saw how Antony stood in the corridor facing the parlor, noting how his eyes widened and his face displayed surprise.

When she heard him say, "Nonno? Nonna?" she came to a halt behind him and nearly burst into tears.

CHAPTER 33
A REUNION

Donald wasn't sure who moved first or who spoke first, but the next few seconds happened in a blur. He remembered saying, "Antony?" before Nicoletta appeared. He remembered swallowing and nearly tripping over his feet in his attempt to reach her as tears filled her eyes. He had her in his arms, his momentum turning them in a half-circle before her feet once again touched the carpet.

Meanwhile, Antony passed him, his arms held out as he raced to where Barbara had knelt, ready to capture him. She barely had her arms around his shoulders before the boy escaped and lifted his arms to his grandfather. At that point, the boy ended up in the air, squealing in delight as Will tossed him up over and over again.

Despite his desire to kiss Nicoletta, Donald found he couldn't when a chuckle of relief burbled forth. "They're going to spoil him rotten," he whispered, his arms tight around her waist and shoulders. He studied her face then, surprised to see that although she still looked the same, she displayed an air of elegance she hadn't possessed back when they had first met.

She glanced over her shoulder in an effort to see what he meant. "No more so than Ricardo did," she murmured. She turned to face him, staring at him for several seconds before she said, "I received your letter this morning."

"I feared it wouldn't arrive before me," he replied before his eyes rounded. "Have we come at a bad time?"

"The best, actually," she said, one of her hands reaching up to cup his face.

Donald took the hand in his, surprised to see that in addition to a rather ornate ring, the one he had given her with a ruby solitaire was still on the base of her fourth finger. "You still wear it?" he asked in surprise.

"I have never taken it off," she replied.

"So... you're going to marry me?" he asked in a whisper.

At the sound of her son's squeals—Will was holding him upside down—Nicoletta tore her gaze from Donald's. "Oh, where are my manners?"

Extricating herself from his hold, she hurried into the parlor. Barbara curtsied and Will bowed, his move made awkward when he was forced to pull Antony onto his hip.

"Nicoletta, Marchesa Montblanc, may I have the honor of introducing you to my mother, Barbara, Countess of Bellingham, and my father, William, Earl of

Bellingham?" Donald said, joining her at her side. She dipped a curtsy as Antony urged Will to let go so he could join her at her side.

Will stepped forward and took her hand to his lips. "I'm very pleased to finally meet you, my lady," he said. "And you, my lord," he added, directing his gaze on the boy.

"As am I," Barbara said, directing a wink in Antony's direction.

Nicoletta displayed a brilliant smile. "It is I who am glad," she replied, her English stilted.

"I am very pleased to meet you," Antony said in perfect English. "Will you throw me in the air again?"

"It's my turn," Donald said, lifting the boy up over his head before he grimaced. "Oh, you might be too big," he said, grunting with his efforts.

As he made eye contact with the boy, he was struck by how familiar he appeared. The dimple at the base of one cheek matched his own, as did the shape of his brows and eyes. "My son," he whispered, lowering him until he could hold him tight against his body.

"Are you going to be my new father?" Antony asked.

Donald nodded. "I am," he replied, before glancing over to see Nicoletta's bright eyes. "Who told you?"

"Nonno, before he went to the angels." His face screwed into a wince. "I miss my nonno," he added before lowering his head to Donald's shoulder, heaving a huge sigh of sadness.

Tightening his hold on the boy, Donald noted how his father held onto his mother's hand, how the two had moved so close to one another as they watched, their bodies nearly touched. They were no doubt remembering the first time his father had met him, at the ramshackle cottage on the outskirts of Broadwell. He had been seven years of age and so leery of the tall man—leery of anyone who paid a call on him and his mother—he held a gun aimed at his chest.

The gun wasn't loaded, but his father didn't know that at the time.

His father must have been thinking of the same incident, for he suddenly grinned and said, "Well, at least he didn't greet you by aiming a gun at your midsection."

Nicoletta's eyes rounded as she directed a curious gaze at Donald.

"I'll tell you later," he murmured.

The sound of a clearing throat had them turning to discover the butler holding a tea tray. "Ah, Trimarco has brought tea," Nicoletta said. "Please, do be seated. We have much to discuss." She turned her attention on the butler and rattled off a number of instructions. He bowed and assured her all would be ready before he departed.

Will and Barbara exchanged worried glances before she settled onto the settee. Nicoletta joined her as Trimarco set the tray onto the low table in front of the settee, which forced Donald and Will to take adjacent chairs.

"Patience," his father whispered, as if he knew exactly what Donald was thinking.

"Is it that obvious?" he countered, his gaze darting to Antony. The boy had managed to wedge himself between his mother and grandmother, much to Barbara's delight.

"I do hope you do not mind his joining us for tea," Nicoletta said. "I dismissed Antony's tutor before your arrival. Otherwise I would send him back up to the schoolroom," she added as she prepared the cups for tea.

Antony's lower lip protruded in a pout, the comical expression sending Will into a fit of chuckles. "Where have I seen that look before?" he asked rhetorically.

"Father," Donald said in protest.

"Every moment spent with him will be precious," Barbara murmured. "He is my first grandchild."

"I am glad he is here. He's rather handsome in his long breeches," Donald said.

Nicoletta grinned as she held out a cup and saucer to Barbara before offering a plate of biscuits. The ceramic dishes were colorful, their intricate patterns featuring blue and golden yellow stylized flowers. "Ricardo insisted he be breeched before he was even four years of age," she said, referring to when the boy went from wearing gowns to pants. "His dark, wavy hair had him mistaken for a girl on more than one occasion, so I cut it short, but then it was so curly..." She sighed.

"Well, he does not look like a girl now," Barbara assured her.

Nicoletta handed a cup and saucer to Will. "How long will you stay in Catania?"

His gaze darting to Donald, Will said, "We took

lodgings in Via Garibaldi for one week. We can stay longer if—"

"You shall give them up and move in here to the villa. I'll see to it Signore Cavarallo receives compensation," Nicoletta stated, obviously familiar with the lodgings in which they had arranged to stay. She held out the plate of biscuits. "Where did you plan to go after only one week in Catania?"

Barbara and Will exchanged quick glances. "That's terribly kind of you," Barbara stated. "But there are eight of us in our party."

Nicoletta turned her attention to Donald. "The *familia* you mentioned in your letter," she said by way of confirmation.

"Yes, my brother, David. Two cousins. Two servants, and us," he affirmed. "My brother and cousins have come for their Grand Tours," he added.

"Your letter mentioned it, *sì*," she replied, giving him tea. "Still, there are enough guest bedchambers for all of you," she insisted. As if she was used to her word being final, she turned to Donald and said, "Ricardo did not wish for me to mourn him long, so in answer to your question, he insisted we marry as soon as is possible." She added milk to a cup of tea and handed it to Antony. He held the cup between both hands as he drank.

Donald's eyes rounded. "He did?" he asked in disbelief.

She angled her head to one side. "He would have been happy to have you stay in Catania all those years ago," she said. "Even provided you with employment.

He thought you would make a trustworthy…" She struggled to come up with a word. "Accomptant? To record his expenditures in a ledger," she explained.

"I would have been trustworthy, of course," Donald said, "but I do not believe I could have abided being so close to you knowing you were married in the eyes of your staff and all of Catania," he added in a quieter voice.

"It was fortuitous Donald returned to England when he did," Will stated. "There was much for him to do there. He's been in charge of the Gisborn stables. Breeding and training horses."

"He told me in his letters," Nicoletta said, aiming a grin in his direction. "The Montblanc horses would do well with him overseeing the stables should he wish to do so."

Donald's eyes rounded. "I would, my lady," he said.

Nicoletta dipped her head before she turned her attention back to Will. "I understand you are a fair foreman, Lord Bellingham. That you are a hard worker, despite your standing in the English peerage," she said, setting her saucer on the table. "Should you be interested, I may be in need of a new foreman to oversea the Montblanc farmlands on Aetna."

Will held up a hand. "The Earl of Gisborn would not be happy if I left his employ," he said with a huge grin. "Besides, it won't be long before I will inherit the Devonville marquessate." He sobered and asked, "What is it you grow on the slopes of a volcano?"

"Grapes, wheat, vegetables, oranges, and limes," she replied. "The soil is quite rich."

Will scoffed. "Well, I certainly know about everything but the grapes," he admitted. "Do you expect your current foreman to… to quit your employ?"

"Retire, actually," she replied sadly. "I will… pension him, I believe is the word. There is another he has been training to take over, but the man is not as well liked by the workers" she explained. "I do not wish to lose my employees in the event he angers them needlessly."

Will indicated he understood her concern. "That is a risk, but even if I accepted such a position, I wouldn't be able to communicate with the workers," he claimed. "I'm afraid I'm not well versed in your language."

"'Tis a pity," Nicoletta responded. She offered the plate of biscuits to everyone, including Antony, who placed his teacup on the table before he took one. "I instructed Trimarco to have your rooms prepared and dinner for eight ready at seven o'clock. Will that give you enough time to move in to your rooms here?"

Will and Barbara exchanged quick glances. "I should think so," he replied. "Even if our servants have unpacked everything—"

"They're seeing to the laundry right now," Barbara whispered.

"I expect we can be dressed for dinner and back by seven o'clock," Will said. "It's terribly generous of you to offer your house. Your hospitality."

"I have been looking forward to this day for many years, my lord," she replied. "I am grateful you have brought Donald back to me." She glanced down at her son. "As for you, young man, you might be a marchese, but you still require an afternoon nap," she said.

Antony rolled his eyes before he scooted off the settee and turned to take Barbara's hand in his. "I must take my leave, nonna," he said on a sigh. "But I will see you at dinner."

Barbara suppressed the giggle that nearly bubbled forth. "Do have a good nap, my lord, and I look forward to kissing you goodnight later this evening."

Antony displayed a huge grin before he turned to Will. "Good day, my lord. I will see you at dinner."

Will stood and executed a bow. "You as well, my lord," he said, grinning when the young boy bowed in return.

Antony was halfway to the door before he turned around and made his way to stand before Donald. He was about to bow, but couldn't when his father pulled him into an embrace. "Sleep well, young man. I'll see you at dinner."

Grinning, the boy hurried out of the parlor.

"He is so well-behaved," Barbara remarked.

"I do not wish for him to grow up spoiled, like my brother," Nicoletta said, one dark brow arching.

"Does your brother live here?" Barbara asked, her expression conveying her surprise the marchesa had a brother.

"He lives in Naples now. He finally took a wife several years ago, and she has already given him two sons. I did not expect him to marry until he inherited the D'Avalos contea, so I am glad he has his heirs," Nicoletta explained. "He was kind enough to bring his family to Catania for a fortnight after Montblanc died, so Antony could spend time with his younger cousins."

"Was it his first time meeting them?" Barbara asked.

"*Sí*. And they are just as spoiled as my brother," Nicoletta claimed.

Barbara tittered before she glanced over at her husband. "We should be going. There's much to do before we return for dinner."

"You will plan to stay, though?" Nicoletta asked as she rose from the settee.

"Of course," Will assured her. "I expect the boys are out exploring, but they were instructed to return to the lodgings in time for dinner."

The four walked down to the courtyard where a black coach waited. Two matched gray mares were hitched to it, and a driver sat on the box.

"Tomasello will take you back to your lodgings," Nicoletta explained. "He'll explain everything to Signore Cavarallo. I'll send the larger coach for you at six o'clock, if that is satisfactory?"

Will chuckled. "Again, you're being very generous, my lady." He reached down to take her hand to his lips. "But it's much appreciated."

"My lady," Barbara said as she curtsied. She turned and Will helped her into the coach. He paused a moment, his gaze darting to Donald. When he saw his son's slight shake of his head, he said, "We'll see to it your trunk is loaded and brought back."

"Thank you, Father," Donald said, one hand already clasping Nicoletta's much smaller one.

The two stood and watched as the coach threaded its way through the arched courtyard door. When a groom had the wooden doors closed and had disappeared, Donald turned to Nicoletta. "I hardly know where to start," he whispered, bringing one of her hands to his lips.

Nicoletta blinked before she tittered softly. "Then allow me to be your guide," she said, threading her arm through his elbow to lead him back into the house.

CHAPTER 34
A VIEW FROM THE TOP

*M*eanwhile, in the Prince of Biscari Gardens
"Are you quite sure we're allowed to be here?" Tom asked as he, Randy, and David climbed a set of stairs surrounded by short hedges. "This looks like a private garden."

"Signore Cavarallo said we could," Randy stated. "Besides, it's where Donald met Nikky."

"That's Nicoletta, Marchesa Montblanc, to you," David stated, his gaze darting about to take in the scenery. "Mind your ankles. There's a goose over there," he added. Upon taking a few more steps up, he spotted why. A pond featuring a pair of swans and several more geese reflected the midday sun, the brightness forcing him to lift a hand to shade his eyes.

"Well, she'll be Nikky to us if your brother does right by her," Randy commented as he turned and surveyed the area around them. "This is quite the view," he murmured.

"What do you mean, does right by her?" David asked. The last to finish the stairs, he joined his cousins to admire the scenic view of Baroque buildings and the Mediterranean sea.

"I may have overheard something I shouldn't have," Randy said between labored breaths. He turned and waved the others to follow him as he made his way along a footpath leading deeper into the botanical gardens—deeper and higher. The chirps and chatter of birds ceased as they moved along, as if their presence was suspicious.

"Eavesdropping, were you?" Tom asked.

"Not intentionally. Can't help it if they didn't know I was there."

"There where, and who?" David queried, his attention on an especially knobby plane tree.

"On the ship. Uncle Will and Donald. It seems our cousin didn't just leave a girl behind," Randy said, coming to a stop when he had reached the top of the hill. He turned to the north and stared. "Whoa," he murmured.

The other two followed suit, their eyes rounding upon seeing Mount Aetna. Rounding more when they realized the wisp of a cloud above it wasn't a cloud at all but steam emitted from the mouth of the volcano.

"Do you think it's going to erupt?" Tom asked with worry.

"If the locals thought so, they wouldn't still be here," Randy guessed.

"Where would they go?" David countered.

"South, of course," his older cousin reasoned. "Going

north only circumvents the base of the mountain. You'd end up in Taormina—"

"Which is where I hope we plan to go—"

"With Aetna still in sight," Randy finished.

"Are those vineyards?" Tom asked, squinting in an effort to bring the lower slopes of the mountain into focus. He scoffed when he saw David holding a pair of opera glasses to his eyes and took them from him.

"Hey," David protested.

"Vineyards and... looks like wheat fields," Randy guessed. He took the opera glasses from Tom and held them up. "You can see the paths some of the lava took on its way down the slopes," he said in awe.

"Aren't they taking an awful risk farming on a volcano?" David asked.

"The last few eruptions did send some lava flowing down, but not far enough to reach those farm fields," Randy said. "Signore Cavarallo told me about it."

David bent down and picked up a few pieces of what appeared to be black granules. He held them out in his palm. "Looks like this stuff is everywhere," he commented.

"Bits of lava... *lapilli*, it's called in Latin," Tom said confidently.

"Little stones," David interpreted.

"So the streets here are paved with *lapides magni*," Randy teased, referring to the lava blocks that made up all the streets they had been on in Catania. "Let's hope we don't get hit with one of them."

The others murmured in agreement and headed back

down the path to another that crossed it. "You were saying something about my brother?" David prompted.

Randy cleared his throat. "I think you might be an uncle," he said in a quiet voice.

David stopped in his tracks. "An uncle?" he repeated. "That would mean…" He clamped his mouth shut.

"Donald has a child? Here?" Tom asked in disbelief.

Randy nodded his head. "And the marchesa is the mother."

The other two glanced at each other before David scoffed. "Surely he would have said something. It's been… six years since he was here."

"He did say something. To your father," Randy murmured. "Uncle Will seemed to know all about it when they were talking on the ship. I think Aunt Barbara knows, too, which I'm beginning to think is the real reason your parents have come along on this trip."

"They wish to meet their grandchild," Tom said, understanding dawning. "Huh." He glanced up at the greenery above them, happy for the shade from the Mediterranean sun. "Which means they're doing so right now," he reasoned.

"Explains a lot," David said, his gaze on his mind's eye.

"What do you mean?"

He shrugged. "Donald has never courted anyone. Never shown any interest in even the prettiest girls in Bampton," he murmured. "That ball we went to a few weeks ago? He only danced because Mother made him," he added.

"I always thought it was because he's a bastard," Tom commented. "Thinks he's unworthy."

"Thomas," Randy scolded. "He's an acknowledged bastard. Which for a young man is almost as good as legitimate," he claimed.

"He's not so young anymore," David said. "There are times..." He stopped speaking and chuckled softly. "Times I think he acts like an old man. Stays in that cottage, writing all day long."

"Which has resulted in a book," Tom reminded him. "He's going to be published. By the time we return to England, he could be famous," he claimed.

David nodded. "Could be," he agreed. "Well, I don't know about you two, but I think I'd like to know more about this child of his," he added. "We should head back."

The other two shrugged. "We can go to the Roman theatre on the morrow," Randy suggested.

"Agreed," Tom said. "Besides, I'm hungry."

"You're always hungry," Randy complained.

The three made their way down the labyrinthian paths and stairs to the street below, briefly stopping to purchase oranges from a costermonger on their way back to Via Garibaldi and their lodgings.

CHAPTER 35
AN AFTERNOON TO REUNITE

Meanwhile, at the Montblanc villa

As Nicoletta led Donald back into the villa and up the stairs to the second floor, he was struck by how quiet the house seemed. Not once did they see a maid or a footman.

"Where is everyone?" he asked

"Probably napping," she said quietly. "In the middle of the afternoon, when the heat is the greatest, we sometimes sleep."

"Even the servants?"

"Of course. I do not wish for them to despise me," she said. "In House D'Avalos, Father always insisted they work the entire day, and I realized how much the servants detested him because he would not grant them time in the afternoons to rest." She grimaced. "I know how they feel. My thoughts of him have not been charitable these past few years."

"Because he made you marry... or pretend to marry Montblanc?"

She shook her head. "I know I said I did not want to be Montblanc's wife—and I truly wasn't— but I understand why he did what he did," she whispered. "My dislike for D'Avalos is due to his greed. Everything he has done has been driven by his desire for money. For power," she explained. "Montblanc gave me permission to give the D'Avalos villa in Roma to Aunt Armenia, and I have kept this information from D'Avalos. He shall not learn of it until Armenia tells him why she is moving back to Roma—*if* she even tells him," she explained.

"So he will not benefit from Montblanc's death?"

Nicoletta chuckled softly. "He has been given the vineyards he has lusted after for as long as I can remember," she replied.

"Why do you sound amused?" Donald asked, suspicious.

"They produce little in the way of fruit any longer. The vines are old. Some diseased. He will discover this if he lives long enough for the next harvest," she explained.

Donald nodded his understanding and glanced around the unfamiliar corridor in which they walked. "Where are you taking me?" he asked.

"To my apartments," she said, giving him a curious look. "That is..." She paused and stopped to stare up at him.

"What is it?" he asked.

Her head tilted to one side as an expression of

uncertainty crossed her face. "Have you... changed your mind. About...?"

She couldn't finish the sentence when he pulled her into his arms and kissed her. "I haven't changed my mind at all," he whispered, before resuming the kiss.

Nicoletta's hands went to the sides of his face as she hungrily returned his kiss, her quiet moans urging him to continue. After a moment, he pulled away. "Apparently, you haven't either," he whispered, touching his forehead to hers.

She grinned and shook her head. "Come. Make love to me," she murmured, turning to push the handle on a carved wooden door. "We have time before—"

"Lead the way, my lady," he said. Before she had a chance to step through the doorway, he lifted her into his arms.

"Oh!" she cried out before one of her hands covered her mouth. "What are you doing?" she asked in a whisper.

"Carrying you over the threshold. Something I intend to do again when we are properly married." Donald set her down on the edge of the bed and moved to close the door. He struggled to find a locking mechanism before he heard her titter. "How do I lock it?"

"We won't be disturbed in here," she assured him. "Not until I ring for my maid."

"Well, you won't be doing that for at least..." He stopped speaking as he glanced around the ornate room. Besides the Turkish carpet covering the floor, the rich, dark velvets hiding the windows and the bed seemed to swallow up their voices. Silk covered the walls, the moiré pattern shifting with his every movement. The entire ceiling looked as if it had been painted by a master, winged cherubs tumbling about as if on a mission of mischief. The furnishings, varnished to a high sheen and featuring carved edges, were obviously created several centuries in the past. "You sleep in here?" he asked as a grin spread into a smile.

"Quite well, yes," she replied, grinning at seeing his reaction. "My sitting room is in there," she added, pointing to an open door. Beyond was a salon furnished with upholstered settees and chairs, their brighter colors and the the lighter carpet at odds with the bedchamber.

Donald sighed, a look of disappointment crossing his face.

"What is it?" she asked, worry evident in her voice.

He scoffed softly. "I cannot offer you anything like this back in England," he murmured. "I live in a stone cottage on the edge of my uncle's estate. Five rooms, none of which..." He spread his arms to indicate the obvious wealth surrounding him.

Nicoletta stepped off the high bed and into his arms. "We don't have to live in England," she said. "You can live here."

He blinked and then shook his head. "I had hoped I might one day take you there."

"We will go. When Antony is older," she suggested.

He considered her comment. "So... not for a wedding trip, then?"

She lifted a shoulder. "After hearing about your plans to take your cousins on their Grand Tour, I was hoping you might..." She paused and inhaled softly.

"Take you along?" he guessed, his face brightening at the thought. "You wish to travel with my family?"

She lifted a shoulder. "I think your mother might appreciate a female companion."

"We would bring Antony, of course," he said, grinning at the thought of being able to show his son all the wonders of the Greek and Roman ruins they would visit.

"Yes," she agreed. "I could not leave him."

"Nor could I."

"So... we will do it?"

Donald chuckled as he tightened his hold on her. "*Sí*," he replied. "I love you." As he kissed her, he moved to undo the fastenings of her gown even as she unbuttoned his coats. Clothing fell to their feet, layer upon layer, until she was left in a chemise and he wore only his smalls. He gave a start when her hands smoothed up his bare chest and down his arms.

"You are... larger... and harder than you were," she whispered, her fingers probing along the lines of his muscles.

He displayed a grimace. "Remember, I've been performing labor. Working with horses," he said, one of his hands cupping a breast before gently kneading it.

"You should continue doing so," she murmured.

"You are larger as well," he said, an eyebrow arching

in appreciation. A look of uncertainty crossed her face, so he was quick to add, "I do not mind a bit."

She pressed her lips to his chest and kissed her way to one of his nipples.

"That tickles," he said in protest, his grin widening when she flicked her tongue across the nubbin.

He lifted her face with a finger and kissed her on the nose. "May I remove your chemise?"

Uncertainty flickered over her face. "Perhaps when we are under the bed linens."

"Nikky," he said in a pleading voice. He let go his hold on her to capture handfuls of the velvet counterpane to pull it down to the end of the bed. A few pillows scattered in the wake of his moves, but he ignored them and turned to lift her onto the bed. He had his smalls stripped from his body before he climbed onto the bed and hovered over her. "I have thought of this moment nearly every night since I left you," he whispered before taking her lips with his.

She returned the kiss in equal measure, her hands skimming down his sides until one reached his turgid manhood and palmed it.

He broke off the kiss. "You minx," he murmured before he moved down her body, pushing up her chemise so he could kiss her heated belly and breasts.

"I no longer have the body of my youth," she whispered.

"You have the body of a goddess," he murmured between kisses. "Your breasts are still gorgeous," he added, before covering one with his mouth.

She lifted her chest in response, gasping at the feel of his tongue and lips on her nipple as her knees bent to cradle his hips. But he didn't make a move to enter her, instead continuing his crawl down the front of her body.

"As I recall," he whispered between kisses, "You liked it when I did *this*." A moment later, his tongue flicked over her most private place, and Nicoletta jerked beneath his hold.

"*Sì*," she murmured over and over again, as his lips and tongue worried her womanhood until she could barely breathe from the sharp darts of pleasure. When his tongue entered her, she cried out his name as the intensity of the orgasm increased, sending waves of ecstasy with each contraction.

His need too great to hold on, Donald finally lifted himself over her and entered her in two thrusts, his moves coinciding with her pleasure so he was buried deep inside her. He was about to pull out nearly all the way, but her hands had gripped his buttocks to keep him close. He thrust into her over and over, his arms straining to hold him up until his own impending release had him stopping his movements.

Beneath him, Nicoletta held her breath and waited for the moment she knew he would feel his greatest pleasure and gripped him hard with her inner muscles.

His soft chuckle and groan of appreciation filled the quiet bedchamber, and when he could no longer hold himself up, he lowered himself until his head landed in the pillow next to hers. "I have missed you," he whispered between labored breaths, one hand smoothing up her torso to push aside the chemise until her breasts were once again exposed.

Nicoletta turned her head until she could kiss his cheek. "Did you really think of me? That often?" she asked.

Although his eyes were closed, Donald wasn't yet asleep. "Every night. Every morning," he whispered. When a soft snore sounded and he rolled off her, she knew he was asleep.

Nicoletta sat up and pulled the chemise from her torso, the fine fabric having become twisted during their lovemaking. She tossed it to the end of the bed and then grasped the edges of the bed linens to pull them up and over their bodies.

She was about to lie back when she felt a warm hand press against the middle of her back. Glancing behind her, she grinned at seeing Donald was still asleep. She turned and settled against his side, her head nestled in the small of his shoulder as she draped one arm over his stomach.

"I nearly tore it from your body," he whispered.

She gave a start. "My chemise?" she asked, surprised he was even awake enough to speak.

"I didn't want there to be anything betwixt us. I don't want there to be anything... ever... to be..." His words faded before another soft snore sounded.

Sighing, Nicoletta grinned and allowed the sound of his heartbeat to lull her into sleep.

She might have slept until it was time to dress for

dinner, but for the small hand that shook her awake an hour later.

"*Mamma, posso dormire con te e il papà?*"

Momma, can I sleep with you and papa?

Nicoletta didn't have a chance to answer, for Donald chuckled softly and said, "*Sì, figliolo, sali.*"

Yes, son, climb on up.

As Antony struggled to climb onto the bed, Donald reached over and pulled on his nightshirt until he had crested the edge and could crawl the rest of the way to wedge himself between his parents.

"You may regret having allowed him to do this," Nicoletta warned in a voice filled with humor.

"Mayhap," Donald said in a whisper. "Maybe not."

They slept until it was time to dress for dinner.

CHAPTER 36

A FAMILY'S
SECRETS REVEALED

eanwhile, at the lodgings in Via Garibaldi Randy, Tom, and David had reached Via Garibaldi and were making their way to the Villa Cavarallo when a glossy black town coach slowed and stopped in front of the building.

Exchanging glances with one another before they approached the equipage, the three were surprised when a groom opened the door and Will stepped out. He turned and helped Barbara down before greeting them. "Your timing is impeccable," he said. "We have a dinner invitation for this evening."

The driver said something and Will looked to Barbara to interpret.

"He says he has been instructed to wait to take us back to the Villa Montblanc," she explained. She directed a response to the driver before heading through the courtyard door followed by her son and nephews.

"Where?" Randy asked in surprise.

"Villa Montblanc. Lady Montblanc—"

"Nikky?"

Barbara paused and directed a glare at Randy. "Nicoletta," she corrected, arching a brow to emphasize her point.

Randy looked suitably chastised before he said, "Pardon. I meant no offense." He glanced around. "Where's Donald?"

"We left him back at Villa Montblanc," Will replied. "He's... catching up," he added, his face reddening with his words.

"So... it's true, then?" David asked.

"What's true?" Barbara asked as Signore Cavarallo opened the door for them. He was about to follow them up the stairs, but the groom hailed him from the coach, and he excused himself.

Once Cavarallo was out of earshot, David resumed his questions. "Donald and she were... were lovers?"

Barbara gave a start. "Did he tell you that?" she asked.

David shook his head. "Is it true then? That I'm an uncle?"

"Where did you hear *that*?" his father asked.

Both Tom and David turned to stare at Randy.

"I might have... mentioned the possibility... earlier today," Randy stammered. "Something I heard on the ship."

Will inhaled softly. "Let's go to our rooms, and I'll fill you in."

They filed up the stairs and into a parlor next to their

bedchambers. "You were going to learn about this during dinner tonight anyway," Will said by way of a preamble. "So I suppose there's no harm in telling you now. Donald probably should have told you all before we even arrived, but I think he wanted to be sure."

"Sure about what?" David asked.

"Sure that Lady Montblanc still loved him," Barbara said. "And she does," she added, displaying a look of awe as she happily sighed.

"And the boy?" Randy pressed.

Will inhaled softly. "He is Donald's son." The sound of footsteps on the nearby stairs had him moving to close the door to the parlor. "And Montblanc's grandson."

Confused glances were exchanged before Will added, "Lady Montblanc is Montblanc's daughter. Apparently he had an *affaire* with her mother—"

"He had loved her long before she married Conte D'Avalos, you see," Barbara put in.

"—*After* she had given Conte D'Avalos an heir," Will continued. "Montblanc needed an heir, so he married Nicoletta—"

"Ewww," Tom let out, cringing in disgust.

"*Pretend* married his daughter," he corrected, "so that her son would be a true heir to the Montblanc fortune," he explained. "Most importantly, he wanted Nicoletta to marry Donald. He knew Donald was the father of Antony, you see."

"Antony?" David repeated.

"Your nephew."

"He's five year's old and so adorable," Barbara gushed.

"Does Donald still feel affection for Lady Montblanc?" Randy asked, careful to use her title. "Or is he going to marry her out of a sense of obligation?"

"He never stopped loving her," Will stated.

"How long have you known you were a grandfather?" David asked, obviously bothered he knew nothing of the existence of a close relative.

Will dipped his head. "I learned of Lady Montblanc the day Donald returned home from his Grand Tour," he admitted. "It was almost a year before the boy's birth was confirmed in a letter he received from Nikky."

"Nikky?" Randy repeated, as if he was teasing his uncle.

"I'm entitled. She's about to become my only daughter—"

"*Our* daughter," Barbara interrupted.

Will chuckled. "A welcome member of our family," he added. "So… I would ask you all to be on your very best behavior this evening. In fact, she's asked us to stay at Villa Montblanc for as long as we're going to be in Catania, so pack your trunks."

"What about Signore Cavarallo?"

"She said she would see to compensating him for his trouble," Barbara explained. "I think she has a good deal of influence here in town."

"What will Donald do after he marries her?" Tom asked. "Take her to England?"

Will and Barbara exchanged quick glances. "I don't

think that's been decided just yet," she said. "After seeing what little I did of Villa Montblanc, I rather doubt Donald is going to ask her to move to England."

"Nor should he," Will said, his gaze directed out one of the north-facing windows. Mount Aetna was perfectly framed in the wavy glass, white steam hovering over its peak. "His son is a marchese. He's in possession of a sizable fortune. Properties. Lands. He needs to remain here in the Kingdom of the Two Sicilies."

Barbara dipped her head, obviously not pleased to hear his words.

"How long will we stay here in Catania?" Randy asked.

"A week," Will replied. "From here, we'll head down to Syracusa and then to the Valley of the Temples. Make our way around the entire island to Taormina before heading over the Strait of Messina to the mainland."

"Sounds as if we'll be in Sicily for a few months," Tom reasoned.

"That's the plan," Will affirmed. "Any other questions?"

When they shook their heads, Barbara reminded them to pack and dress for dinner.

An hour later, their trunks loaded into the back of a cart and with the five of them stuffed into the Montblanc coach, they headed to Villa Montblanc.

CHAPTER 37
PRIVATE MOMENTS
OF A NEW FAMILY

eanwhile, at Villa Montblanc

"Should we let him sleep?" Donald asked after he kissed Nicoletta awake. The late afternoon rays of the sun were barely bleeding along the edges of the velvet drapes, the scarlet fabric lending a vivid red to their wash on the surrounding walls.

Nicoletta tittered. "If he sleeps too long, he won't easily go to bed when he's supposed to later tonight," she reasoned.

"He looks like an angel."

"He can be. Sometimes," she whispered, sitting up so she could reach down and snag her chemise with a crooked finger. "Sometimes he pretends he is a spoiled aristocrat." When she pulled the chemise over her head, Donald made a sound of disappointment, and she grinned. "Like someone else I know," she added in a tease.

Donald scoffed. "When have *I* ever behaved like a spoiled aristocrat?" he argued.

"The day you left Catania."

Blinking, he sat up and stared at her as she smoothed the garment into place and moved to step off the bed. "What?"

She turned and placed a hand on Antony's shoulder to shake him awake. "Had you stayed only one more day, you would have learned the truth of the matter as I did. You would have been offered a position. A place to live. We could have..." She let the sentence trail off when Antony stirred and rolled over to finally sit up. His sleep-tousled curls were wilder than usual.

"Papa?"

Donald's gaze turned to Antony, his heart clenching at hearing the simple word. "*Figlio*," he replied, grinning despite his momentary offense at hearing Nicoletta's claim. "Time to wake and dress for dinner," he said. "Tonight you'll meet your... *zio*," he added, struggling to remember the word for 'uncle'.

"Zio?" the boy repeated, his attention going to his mother.

"Uncle David," she said. "And your cousins—*cugini* —Randy and Tom."

His eyes rounded. "When?"

"Before dinner. Now you must go find your nurse and get dressed," she said, helping him to crawl off the bed. Once his feet hit the floor, he was off and running toward the door. A moment later, his footfalls could be felt as he hurried down the corridor.

Nicoletta turned her attention back to Donald, sighing when she saw his look of hurt. "What's done is done," she said with a shrug. "We'll speak no more of it."

Donald climbed out of the bed and rushed around it to take her into his arms. "I will regret for the rest of my life, leaving you as I did," he whispered into her hair. "I was young and naive and... heartbroken."

She pulled away to look up at him. "As was I," she murmured.

"I will make it up to you," he said. "Tonight, I'm going to tell my family that we're coming with them. We'll bring Antony, and we'll see all the sights this island has to offer."

She nodded, a wan smile replacing her momentary melancholy. "We leave in a week?" she asked.

He nodded, remembering only the month before the sense of anticipation he had felt upon learning they would be leaving the Gisborn estate to head to London in only a week. The chaos of packing and preparing. "Can we manage, do you suppose?" he asked.

"The servants will help," she said. "And speaking of servants, I must ring for my lady's maid and bathe," she added, stepping out of his hold. Her gaze traveled up and down his naked body. "As for making it up to me, you will stay in my bed every night. Make love to me every night and every morning," she insisted.

Donald blinked twice. "My lady, you do realize that's not a punishment?"

She gave him a teasing grin. "Even if I require it of you more than that?"

He shook his head and chuckled. "Who's the spoiled aristocrat now?" he teased. At seeing her expression briefly change to puzzlement, he added, "I'm going to adore being married to you."

She gave him a shoo'ing motion with a hand. "Go off to your own bedchamber and leave me. We have guests arriving soon."

His eyes rounded. "My own bedchamber?" he repeated. "Where is that?"

She pointed to an adjoining door. "Through there."

Donald gathered up his clothes and did as he was told, his laughter loud when he stood in the center of a huge master bedchamber and surveyed his elegant surroundings. "I'm really going to adore being married to you," he called out.

Back in the mistress' bedchamber, Nicoletta grinned. "I'll remember you said that when we are old and wrinkled."

Chuckling, Donald pulled on his clothes before he headed out the door to discover what had become of his trunk.

CHAPTER 38
AN ANNOUNCEMENT
BEFORE DINNER

wo hours later

The Montblanc coach bearing Lord and Lady Bellingham, David Slater, and Randy and Tom Forster pulled into the courtyard at the Baroque villa during the Golden Hour. Partially hidden by the foothills of Mount Aetna, the sun cast off the last of its warm rays as the sky in the east displayed brilliant pinks and oranges.

"These sunsets in the Mediterranean are so gorgeous," Barbara said as she stepped out of the coach, helped down by her son, David. His attention was on the marble fountain in the center of the courtyard, water splashing from a dolphin's mouth, the creature held by a marble statue of Poseidon. Ceramic pots of oleanders and red frangipani shrubs lined the courtyard's circumference, their pink blooms a stark contrast to the black lava blocks making up the circle drive.

"I remember them well," Will said, offering his arm.

Trimarco, the butler, had already opened the door to the villa, his posture rigid as he stood at attention. Six footmen hurried out to meet the dray cart bearing the trunks and valises.

"Welcome back. I will show you to your rooms," Trimarco said in stilted English, turning to lead them up the stairs. "Dinner will be served at seven o'clock in the dining room on the first floor. Liquor will be served in the parlor at half-past six o'clock should you wish to join her ladyship."

"We'd like that," Barbara said. "Lady Montblanc said you would have accommodations for our servants?"

"*Sí*," he replied, continuing the climb up the circular staircase. "The coach is going back for them now. I will show them to their rooms and provide directions to your apartments."

Not having been in the villa before, the boys followed behind, their gazes darting about in wonder.

"Montblanc must have been rich," Tom murmured as they climbed the marble stairs.

"He was," Will said, his head briefly turned so his quiet response wouldn't be heard by the servant. "Now Antony is."

When they reached a second landing off the circular stairs, Trimarco led them down a long corridor, pausing to indicate three separate guest bedchambers for the boys and finally a door he said was to an apartment for Will and Barbara.

The sound of Randy's low whistle upon entering his room could be heard by the others.

"This is twice the size of my bedchamber at home," Tom said, joining his brother to survey his room.

"You have a painted ceiling, too?" Randy asked.

"I do," Tom said, his gaze going up and around as he admired the molded stucco statuary in the corners. "There are *putti* everywhere," he said, referring to the cherubs painted on the ceiling and displayed in white stucco.

"My room, too," David said, grinning when he joined the other two. "This place must have taken decades to paint."

"Aunt Barbara is probably asking Uncle Will if she can hire an Italian artisan to redo her bedchamber," Tom said on a chuckle.

A pair of footman arrived with the first trunk, and Randy directed them on where to take it. Another pair followed, and still another, until all the luggage had been delivered.

Barbara emerged from the apartment to remind the boys to dress for dinner. "Wear your best," she said, before she spun in a circle as she admired Randy's room. "Although Signore Cavarallo's villa is comfortable, this is..."

"Far better," Donald said, appearing in the open doorway.

"There you are, Cousin," Randy said. "Is your room next door?"

Donald chuckled softly. "Mine is at the other end of the corridor," he replied. "I have a special arrangement with the lady of the house."

"Donald," Barbara scolded. "Don't be crass."

"Well, I do, Mother. We're to be married soon," he argued. He glanced around. "Has anyone seen my trunk?"

"It's in our apartment," Will said, joining them. He had changed into a formal waistcoat but wore no cravat. "Anyone seen Stevens?"

"Here, my lord," his valet called out, his breathing labored from having climbed the stairs. He was followed by his wife, who carried a stack of clean clothes.

"In here," Will said, ducking into his apartment.

Donald followed and helped himself to several pieces of clothing from his trunk. He began changing, his movements hurried.

"I suppose your bedchamber is much like this?" Will asked in a quiet voice as Stevens saw to wrapping a cravat around his neck.

Glancing around as if noticing the room for the first time, Donald nodded. "Except for the color of the velvet and..." His gaze went to the ceiling. "The subjects in the painting, it's much the same." He tucked his shirt into his pantaloons and pulled on a silver embroidered waistcoat.

"Does this house really belong to Antony now?" Will asked.

"It does," Donald affirmed. He chuckled softly, remembering what Nicoletta had said about the boy earlier. "Nikky is quite determined he not become a spoiled aristocrat."

Will arched a brow. "See to it you don't, either."

Settling a tail coat over his shoulders, Donald sobered. "Yes, sir."

*M*eanwhile, on the way to the parlor

"Where's papa?" Antony asked, a finger tugging at his neckcloth.

"Dressing for dinner," Nicoletta replied, pausing before a mirror in the corridor. Although the light from a nearby sconce wasn't very bright, she could make out her reflection in the looking glass. The crepe gown she wore was of the latest style, but the gummed silk fabric still scratched her wrists where it was tightest. The black matched her hair, though, and although she usually appeared pale whilst wearing mourning clothes, her color was still high from her earlier lovemaking with Donald.

"You are more gorgeous every time I see you," Donald said, making his way in her direction. He bowed to Antony and took her hand in his to kiss the back of it. "Might I be allowed to escort your mother to the parlor?" he asked, turning his attention to Antony.

The boy grinned. "I am escorting her," he claimed.

"Ah. Then I shall follow," Donald replied, aiming a look of disappointment in her direction.

"You looking especially... is *dashing* the right word?" she asked.

"Yes, thank you," he replied, falling into step as they made their way to the parlor. From the other end of the corridor, the rest of his family were headed in their direction.

"I am nervous," Nicoletta admitted.

"You needn't be. You've already met my mother and father," he reminded her.

"What of your cousins, though? Your brother?"

"Well, I would tell you to imagine them naked, but I think that is not such a good idea in the event you think they possess a better physique than mine."

Nicoletta burst into a fit of giggles, her amusement still lighting her face when his parents entered. They curtsied and bowed while Antony ran to Will with his arms lifted.

"Antony," his mother scolded.

"Ah, the marchese wishes to fly, does he?" Will teased, lifting the boy into the air.

Donald introduced Randy, Tom, and his brother, the three taking turns bowing and kissing the back of Nicoletta's hand.

"You did not tell me your cousins are so handsome," she chided. "That your brother is, too?"

They laughed at Donald's expense before she encouraged them to sit and enjoy a glass of vermouth. "Or if you prefer, prickly pear liquor," she suggested, as Trimarco saw to distributing glasses of the clear libation. Once everyone had been served, they looked to her for direction. "*Saluti!*" she said, raising her glass a few inches. They all followed suit, Anthony the last to join the chorus.

When the room quieted, Nicoletta asked, "Which of you is to be an earl?"

"That would be me, my lady," Randy said. "My father is the Earl of Gisborn."

"Ah, so you are the oldest?"

"*Sí.*"

"Then I shall ask you. Since your cousin Donald and I are to be married very soon and this is *your* Grand Tour, I wondered if I might be allowed to join you? And bring along my son?"

Obviously surprised by the request, Randy straightened. "Of course, my lady." He glanced at Donald. "It's not really for me to say, though." He turned his attention to Will and Barbara. "I think Uncle Will outranks me."

"Ah, but he and Lady Bellingham are on their wedding trip, are they not?" she asked. "Whereas I would like to go on a Grand Tour."

Randy chuckled. "If you're waiting for an invitation, you have it, my lady. Besides, if what you say is true and you marry soon, this tour will become *your* wedding trip."

She glanced at Donald, who was vigorously nodding, before she displayed a brilliant grin. "You make a good point, Lord Randy."

He acknowledged her comment with a shrug. "As for Lord Montblanc... I think I can speak on behalf of my brother and cousin when I say he can be a member of our Grand Tour," he said. "He's our cousin, after all."

Antony beamed in delight as David and Tom laughed.

"He's going to be so spoiled," Donald chuckled, a moment before dinner was announced.

EPILOGUE

S*even months later, in Catania*

Giving his mother one last hug, Donald stepped back and handed her his handkerchief. Tears had begun streaming down her face even before their trunks were loaded on the ship that would take her, Will, Randy, Tom, and David to Greece. "We'll join you when you are ready to tour the mainland," he said, reminding her of their plans.

"Are you quite sure you cannot come with us?" Barbara asked.

"Mother, I'm about to become a father again. I do not want Nikky to have to endure such arduous travel when she is so close to her confinement," Donald explained.

"Of course not," Barbara agreed, scooping Antony into her arms. "I am going to miss you so much, and, oh dear, you've grown far too heavy to lift, my little lord," she added before setting him down.

"*Ciao, nonna,*" he said, kissing her cheek.

Will embraced his son and then Nicoletta, careful to stay clear of her rounding belly. "We'll see you again soon," he said. "I can hardly wait to meet my next grandchild." Even as he said the words, he reached down and lifted Antony so the boy sailed over his head before he gripped his ankles and held him upside down.

Antony shrieked with joy.

"Darling, do remember, he's a marchese," Barbara scolded.

"Ah, but I rather doubt I'll be able to lift him like this the next time I see him," Will countered. "He'll be far too heavy and tall." He brought his grandson to an upright position and made sure his feet were firmly on the ground before he gave up his hold on him. "Take care of your parents," he said.

"I will," Antony replied. "Take care of my *nonna*."

Chuckling, Will said, "I will."

The cousins and David each shook Donald's hand before they headed up the gangway.

With the ropes already untied and the crew waiting for Will and Barbara to board, they were quick with their final farewells. A few minutes later, and the steam-powered Greek ship *Son of Apollo* left the dock headed east.

Donald, Nicoletta, and Antony waved until the ship was too far away to see anyone on board. Donald lifted his son onto his shoulders before he offered his arm to his wife.

Nicoletta threaded her arm through his, and they

made their way back to where the Montblanc coach had parked.

"There will be two colts joining your stable in the next month," he said. "Probably about the time you're giving birth."

She inhaled softly. "You are sure?"

He nodded. "I bred the mares before we departed. They're both doing fine in their new pasture on Aetna."

"You are still happy with the idea of seeing to the stables? Even now?" she asked. They had spent over six months traveling around Sicily, not only visiting the sites along the coasts but also going inland to discover the Norman-style churches and intricately glazed ceramics in the mountain village of Erice and the Ancient Greek sites in Syracuse.

"I am," he replied. "And I'm going to write another book."

"You are?"

"About traveling in Sicily. I have new drawings and a journal full of notes," he explained. "There's just one place I haven't been to recently, though."

"Oh? I was sure we had seen all of the island."

He chuckled. "Would you be amenable for a visit to the Roman theater?" he asked. "The boys went there without me, and I haven't been since the first time you took me there."

Grinning, she glanced up at Antony, who was enjoying his ride on his father's shoulder. "Seven years ago, was it not?"

"Indeed," he replied, chuckling softly. There were

times when his first trip to Catania seemed as if it had been only seven weeks ago rather than seven years.

"We can walk there from here," she suggested.

"Are you sure you can manage?"

She grinned. "I am with child. Not infirm," she reminded him. "Besides, you can rub my feet when we are home."

He let out a guffaw before he gave instructions to the coach to meet them at the Roman ruins.

The walk was not long, but it was mostly uphill, so by the time they reached the theatre, they were ready for a rest. Given the low clearance at the entry, Donald was forced to remove Antony from his shoulders. The boy walked between them, his hands held in theirs as they made their way through the access passageway and into the open area of the theatre beyond.

Much like the first time they had been there, they had the space to themselves.

"Do you remember what we were doing here?" Donald asked as they settled onto a set of large limestone blocks that had at one time been some of the seats of the theatre.

"I taught you how to kiss me," Nicoletta replied, grinning in delight.

"You were quite insistent I do it a certain way," he commented.

"Because I liked it that way," she reasoned.

"And now?"

She grinned. "I still like it that way," she replied.

"Antony, close your eyes," Donald instructed. "I'm going to kiss your mother senseless," he added, grinning.

The boy scrunched his eyes shut as Donald pulled Nicoletta into his arms and kissed her, angling his head to one side and pulling her as close as he could manage given her protruding belly.

When they finally ended the kiss, Nicoletta tittered when she saw her son still had his eyes closed.

"You can open your eyes now, darling."

Antony slowly opened one eye and then the other, as if to make sure his parents were no longer kissing. "Are you going to do it again?" he asked, grimacing.

They chuckled as they both leaned over to kiss him on the head. "Every day for the rest of our lives," Donald said.

"Every night, too," Nicoletta added, tittering when she saw his pained expression.

"You are a spoiled aristocrat," he accused.

"I am indeed," she admitted.

Deciding it best he not say anything, Donald simply offered his arm and led them out to the coach for the ride back to Villa Montblanc.

AUTHOR'S NOTES

Where did these characters originate?

If you've been a regular reader of my historical romances, you probably recognized Henry and Hannah Forster, Earl and Countess of Gisborn, and William and Cherice Slater, Marquess and Marchioness of Devonville, from THE SEDUCTION OF AN EARL, Will and Barbara Slater, Earl and Countess of Bellingham, from THE CARESS OF A COMMANDER, and David and Adeline Carlington, Marquess and Marchioness of Morganfield, from THE KISS OF A VISCOUNT. If not, you can still discover how they met and married since those novels are available at all major book retailers in e-book, paperback, and audio formats.

Grand Tours

Lasting anywhere from a few months to three or four years, Grand Tours served as an educational rite of passage for young men who had just completed their university studies.

The primary value of the Grand Tour lay in its exposure to the cultural legacy of classical antiquity and the Renaissance, and to the aristocratic and fashionably polite society of the European continent. In addition, it provided the only opportunity to view specific works of art, and possibly the only chance to hear certain music. It was commonly undertaken in the company of a cicerone, a knowledgeable guide or tutor.

Tourists of Italy might aim for famous festivals such as the Carnival in Venice or Holy Week in Rome before they would make their way slowly through Lucca, Florence, Siena and Rome to Naples and then return north by revisiting Rome before heading to Venice through Loreto, Ancona and Ravenna. Meanwhile, young men ventured all over Sicily and then on to Greece, where their travels featured ancient Greek temples and Roman relics.

Prince of Biscari Gardens

Should you ever have the fortunate experience of visiting Catania in Sicily, you won't find these gardens on a map. Instead, you'll find the *Giardino Bellini* or Bellini Gardens. Located between Via Sant'Euplio and Via Salvatore Tomaselli, the main entrance for this gorgeous urban park is located along Via Aetna. It's well worth a visit.

The original section of the Bellini Gardens belonged to the Prince of Biscari and was called the Prince of

Biscari Gardens, but in 1854, the land was either purchased by or given to (reports vary) the Comune di Catania and refurbished in 1864 to make them into a public garden. By 1867, the gardens included an enclosure for monkeys and an aviary, and hosted deer, cows, swans, and geese.

Many ancient and exotic plants make up the botanical portion of the park, which includes a pond, fountains, swan pool, playground, and the Avenue of Illustrious Men. The trees featured include plane trees, magnolias, palms, pines and evergreens. From the highest peak in the gardens (at the top of the Avenue of Illustrious Men), Aetna's landscape is on full display. The park is the oldest in Catania and is named for the white marble bust of Vincenzo Bellini by Tito Angiolini displayed therein.

Prince of Biscari

An antiquarian, polymath, and patron of the arts, Ignazio Paternò-Castello (1722-1786), 5th prince of Biscari, is credited with having excavated and restored many of the monuments in Sicily. In the process, he developed a large collection of Greek and Roman artifacts, some from the Roman theatre and amphitheater in Catania.

Architect Francesco Battaglia refurbished his Palazzo Biscari in Catania. Located next to the palazzo was the Prince of Biscari garden maze, or labyrinth, named for the long, intersecting avenues throughout.

Much of the prince's collection of urns, vases,

statuary and coins is now housed in the Museo Civico Castello Ursino in Catania.

Ignazio Paternò-Castello (1781–1844), 7th prince of Biscari, was the owner of the property during the time of this story.

ABOUT THE AUTHOR

A self-described nerd and lover of science, Linda Rae spent many years as a published technical writer specializing in 3D graphics workstations, software and 3D animation (her movie credits include SHREK and SHREK 2). Mythology, immortality, and ancient Greece have been lifelong interests.

A fan of action-adventure movies, she can frequently be found at the local cinema. Although she no longer has any tropical fish, she does follow the San Jose Sharks. She makes her home in Cody, Wyoming.

For more information:
www.lindaraesande.com
Sign up for Linda Rae's newsletter:
Regency Romance with a Twist
For articles on research and travels, read Linda's Rae blog:
Regency Romance with a Twist